REALM BOOK 1

THE FALL OF TITAN

By H.G. Ahedi

For Dad, always

Dedicated to my nephews

Parampreet & Harshmann

Special Acknowledgements

Shwetha D'Souza

Diana Orton

Melissa Webb

Christina Abdel Shaheed

The only way to discover the limits of the possible is to go beyond them into the impossible.

Arthur C. Clarke

Chapters

CHAPTER 1: THE ORIAS 1

CHAPTER 2: DISTANT COUSINS 20

CHAPTER 3: NEMESIS 43

CHAPTER 4: SECTOR 1001 68

CHAPTER 5: THE UNEXPECTED VISITOR.... 91

CHAPTER 6: DNA NEVER LIES 126

CHAPTER 7: THE ROGUE PLANET 165

CHAPTER 8: JUSTICE IS ARBITRARY......... 195

CHAPTER 9: ALTERNATIVES.................... 222

CHAPTER 10: DISAGREEMENTS............... 243

CHAPTER 11: JUDGMENT DAY 252

CHAPTER 1: THE ORIAS

SATURN

The silence in space was always uncomfortable for Argon Keston. But today, he didn't know if it was the silence or the reason he was out here. For the third time, he checked the environmental controls. The temperature was normal, but he still felt cold. He rubbed his hands together and surveyed the beautiful auroras projected on the viewscreen. He admired the colors dancing around his ship. It was an extraordinary sight, and yet he knew that within seconds of opening the airlock, deadly gases would kill him.

Atlas was one of many squadron ships. The semicircular spacecraft was ten feet wide and fifteen feet long. Her weapons were located at the edges. The pilot's cockpit was in the elongated section, which emerged from the middle. Three other fighter ships just like her hid in the vast rings of Saturn. Monitoring. Waiting.

Argon was a young, slender man who was quiet and gentle with kind green eyes and thick brown hair. He was amiable and innocent-looking and preferred to keep a well-trimmed beard, which made him look a bit more mature.

Today, for the first time, he wore the uniform of the

Imperial Command: a black half-sleeve t-shirt with navy-blue trousers and a high-neck maroon jacket. All his life he wanted to command his ship and fly into the unknown, but today he was getting the first-hand experiences of the dangers of space. Wearing this uniform, he actually felt the burden of being a fighter, a leader, someone responsible.

Argon moved back and forth, waiting for the signal. It had been six hours. Too much time had passed.

It had all begun two months ago on just another day on Titan. Lieutenant Adrian Olson and his team had been conducting a routine survey of the perimeter. Unexpectedly, they'd detected an unusual energy signature, and there it was: an unidentified spacecraft.

Adrian had hailed the ship immediately. But the alien ship had been beyond communication range and had disappeared within minutes. Two weeks had passed, and the unknown visitor had reappeared with two of its friends, this time closer to the perimeter.

Their arrival had sent a wave of excitement through the citizens of Titan. They'd tried to contact the three ships, welcoming them to their home. But the outsiders had remained silent. The ships had drifted close to the perimeter and began scanning. Alarms had gone off, and Titan's patrol ships had been dispatched. The alien ships had quickly disappeared but had left a sense of restlessness in their wake.

Argon wanted to believe they were explorers, but he did not. These aliens frightened him. He felt as if the cockpit of Atlas turned colder. He recalled the meeting on Earth with the Imperial Command. Some believed invasion was inevitable, while others sought more diplomatic methods.

He wondered about their choices. Did they have any? Could today be the beginning of an interstellar war that would change their lives forever? Would they survive? Would he see his family again? No one he knew had experience with war. For generations that had lived in peace, interstellar war was a frightening concept. But leaving Titan or any other colonies undefended was not an option.

Since their first appearance, the crew of Titan had kept looking for signs of the aliens, and the Imperial Fleet remained on standby. Days passed, and things began to settle down. Everyone thought they would never come back. Argon wished it too, but his wish was not granted. Twelve hours ago, Adrian had detected the unusual energy signature again. Like it or not, it had begun.

Admiral Jacob Donavan was in charge of the fleet, and his priority was to take a diplomatic approach. He wanted to communicate with the aliens. Argon's squadron was a backup if things went south. Argon wasn't sure the admiral's plan was going to work. In fact, no one knew if anything was going to work. They had limited ships, resources, and fighters. The admiral had full confidence in the fleet. But Argon didn't think he was qualified for this mission.

Argon had just finished training as a pilot, and before he could think about his future, these aliens had appeared, and he'd been appointed as the squadron leader. He was surprised; he thought Byron Thames, his best friend, would have been a better choice. But the decision wasn't his to make.

A large asteroid drifted in front of his viewscreen. As if they were a family, three small asteroids followed the larger one. The gaseous cloud surrounding the ship dispersed momentarily, and Argon saw the perimeter. A vast security system built by his ancestors to protect Earth and other colonies like Titan. At this distance, it looked like a glowing chain of stars.

He looked to his left and saw a small yet powerful ship belonging to Byron Thames. Not too far away from Byron's ship was another craft. It appeared almost like a ghost, flooded in the gases of the planet's rings. Argon knew Micah Dew was out there, waiting. He was surprised he had remained silent for so long. To his right was the fourth ship. Its pilot, Clio Ranger, was a patient, quiet, intelligent young girl.

Argon's eyes drifted toward the panels. Adrian hadn't contacted them. Maybe it was a good sign. But he knew they were out there.

Suddenly, the silence was broken. "They're here. Be ready. The fleet is approaching the gates," a voice crackled on the radio.

Straightening up in his chair, Argon was about to power up the engines, but he stopped. The admiral had told them to power down their ships. He thought this would help them remain undetected. Personally, Argon thought the aliens wouldn't care. He thought they were here for something, searching for something. Their scans bothered him. One day, he would have his answers, but today, he would settle for defending his home.

TITAN, DECK 1, BRIDGE

"Well?" asked Commander Anastasia Waters. She stood in the middle of Titan's bridge with her legs apart and her arms folded. The perimeter glowed brighter than any stars she could see. Her big black eyes remained glued to the viewscreen. Anastasia was an athletic long-legged woman with thick, wavy hair tied up neatly in a bun. She wore bellbottom trousers, a black body-fit sleeveless top, and a navy-blue turtleneck jacket. She was the commander of Titan, one of the most powerful space stations built by man. But at the moment, she felt powerless. Imperial Command had ordered her to stand back, and not join the fight. She was to wait and watch the fleet engage the enemy and she didn't like it.

Lieutenant Commander Adrian Olson turned. "The energy signature has reappeared. But this time, it's stronger." The second in command of Titan, was a short-statured man with pale-white skin, deep-blue eyes, and auburn hair.

"What do you mean?" asked Anastasia.

"Their ships emit a peculiar energy signature. When the first ship appeared two months ago, the energy signature was detected because we were surveying that section of space. Otherwise, we would never have known the ship even existed."

"And this time?"

"It's the same energy signature, only stronger."

Anastasia nodded.

The bridge was a disc-shaped hall. Two doors opened into elevators that connected it to the ten decks of the space station. The lights dimmed. An alarm went off. Anastasia lowered herself into her chair and crossed her legs. Her eyes remained fixed on the viewscreen. Waiting. Anticipating. Part of her wanted to join the fight; another part told her to obey orders. She felt as if she were fighting herself.

Lieutenant Evan Weeds sat opposite Adrian and was busy monitoring communications and operations. He was a stocky man of average height with a round face, a sharp nose, and thin dark-brown hair.

To Anastasia's right, Titan's tactical officer, Lieutenant Edward Ward, stood with his arms crossed. He watched the movements of the fleet on the screen like a hawk.

Anastasia gently tapped her feet and swirled. The scientists were huddled together near the science station. From experience, Anastasia knew that if Dr. Chris Kent had found something, he would have told her already. He would have told the entire quadrant. "Anything, Doctor?" she asked despite knowing the answer already.

Dr. Kent turned. "Nothing yet."

Anastasia raised her eyebrows, and without a word, she turned back to the viewscreen.

"Commander, the signal is gone, and a cloud has appeared," Adrian announced in an edgy tone.

All of Anastasia's breath left her. The viewscreen glowed. She leaned forward to see a vast cloud of purple and blue raging through space.

"It looks like a storm," muttered someone.

"Lieutenant Weeds, contact the Freedom," Anastasia ordered.

"Yes, Commander."

"Can you see the cloud?" Anastasia asked Admiral Donavan.

"Yes," Jacob's calm voice echoed on Titan's bridge.

"I think we should call for reinforcements."

"Don't worry. We can handle this. Our priority is to make contact."

"We've tried that before and failed," said Anastasia.

"I know," Jacob replied. "But we should try again."

"I insist that we call reinforcements or let Titan . . ."

"No. We cannot defy the orders of the Imperial Command."

"Fine," Anastasia replied reluctantly. "Good luck, Admiral."

"Thank you. You never know. We might make some friends today."

Or our worst enemies, thought Anastasia. The purple storm disappeared, and ten ships appeared beyond the perimeter.

The computer announced, "Spatial anomaly Orias detected. Alert. Alert. Spatial anomaly Orias detected. All officers report to your stations. All officers report to your stations. All civilians return to their quarters or remain in secure locations."

"Orias?" asked Anastasia.

Adrian turned to face her. "Well, we had to call them something. Since I detected them first, I thought I could name them."

"What does Orias mean?" asked Evan.

"In mythology, it means 'noblemen of hell,'" Adrian replied calmly.

The bridge became silent, and all eyes fixed on him. Anastasia was fond of her crew's quirkiness, and often indulged them. Another time, Anastasia would have laughed her heart out, but today was not that day.

"How many times have I told you to stop reading those stupid books?" muttered Evan. His eyes met Anastasia's. She tried not to smile.

"Ahem. I-I thought it would . . . be interesting and funny," explained Adrian.

"It's not," Anastasia told him.

"Commander," said Dr. Kent. "Our initial scans show no humanoids or any signs of life on those ships."

All heads turned toward the doctor, but Anastasia couldn't look away from the viewscreen. "Drones?" she asked as ten Earth ships flew past Titan.

"The alien ships have the same energy signature as the cloud but no engine or life signs that we can detect. But something tells me they're more than just drones."

Anastasia twirled on her chair. "What do you mean?"

"It's a hunch. Since we've never encountered these . . . Orias before, our technology may not be advanced enough to detect them."

"You mean you don't know," said Adrian.

"Not at this point."

Anastasia turned her attention back to the screen.

"Commander, we're ready," said Cyr Storm, Titan's engineer. "The shields are up and at full power. All systems are ready to go. The weapons are fully powered, and we have enough fuel in case we have to head back to Earth."

Cyr's words gave Anastasia some comfort. "Excellent."

"Commander, the fleet is nearing the gates of the perimeter," announced Evan.

"When the fleet is ready, open the gates," Anastasia instructed.

Never had Anastasia thought she would be thankful to have the perimeter to guard their home. It had been built before her time, and she'd always thought it was a pain. All her life, she'd hated taking approval for what she loved to do: explore space. When she'd been captain of Marion, she'd had to go through tedious procedures involving long and detailed paperwork. It was frustrating when bureaucrats tried to control the tiniest aspects of her projects.

A female voice broke the silence on the bridge. "Emmeline to Commander Waters. Emmeline to Commander Waters. Are you there? Commander?" Emmeline was an enthusiastic astrophysicist cadet who worked under Dr. Kent.

Anastasia felt Dr. Kent's eyes on her, but she ignored

him. She pushed the green button on the small screen on the hand rest of her chair. "Yes, Emmeline."

"Commander, has the anomaly disappeared?"

"You mean the cloud?"

"Yes."

"Yes. It's gone. The alien ships are here."

"Warn the admiral not to engage the alien ships if the cloud appears again," said Emmeline. "I repeat: do not engage the alien ships if the clouds return. It's—"

"Lieutenant Weeds, relay the message at once," Anastasia said. "Emmeline, explain?"

"It's a theory. I think the cloud is a gateway. My scans . . ."

"A gateway?" asked Anastasia. "To where?"

"I don't know!"

FREEDOM

Jacob sat silently on the bridge of Freedom. He had received Emmeline's message. *That girl knows her stuff*, he thought. *But she's naïve and needs to learn a lot.*

His chair was in the middle of the small bridge. His crew moved around the bridge effortlessly, preparing for battle. The computer made announcements from time to time. A continuous alarm echoed in the background.

The admiral didn't take his eyes off the viewscreen. He was a hefty man with black eyes and short, curly hair that was beginning to turn gray. A snake tattoo ran down the back of his neck and disappeared into his uniform. As the biggest member of his family, he'd been nicknamed "the giant." He lived by two rules: enforce the law and stay in control.

Freedom, the ship he commanded, was just like him, old and stern. It was a medium-sized craft, roughly fifty meters long and twenty meters wide. Loaded with powerful phasers, torpedoes, and multiphasic shields, it was one of the best ships in the fleet. The craft had withstood the test of time. It had helped discover and study numerous nebulas and explore uncharted planets and solar systems. It had also helped set up new space stations and carry food and medicine. Most of all, Freedom had been successful in finding three new homes just like Earth. Jacob had felt dejected when they'd had to return to Earth report to the Imperial Command and reassess their plans. Then the Orias had appeared, and everything had changed.

For the last decade, Jacob had used Freedom for exploration. The last time he remembered using the phasers was to blast an asteroid. Today, he might use it to begin or end a war.

Freedom was followed by a small group of ships. Jupiter and Marion were fine ships, almost of the same size, but they were more powerful than Freedom. The rest of the ships were smaller and equipped with the latest technology and weapons.

Having nine other Earth ships did not give Jacob any comfort. Most of them had been standing in the space dock two weeks ago, and their commanders had never left the solar system. His attempts to gather more ships with experienced commanders had failed. Prometheus was the nearest ship and his greatest hope, but it was in a part of space affected by an ion storm, which was likely to interfere with communications. Since he'd never heard back, Jacob didn't know if Captain Lockhart had received his messages.

The viewscreen of Freedom displayed the glowing perimeter ahead. In front of them was a magnificent sparkling vertical web of white and blue color. It reminded Jacob of a magical web in a children's story he'd read to his granddaughter. The princess powered the web telepathically, and it had kept her kingdom safe from monsters that lurked in the darkness beyond its borders. Today, the perimeter that separated Jacob from the Orias appeared no different.

With a heavy heart, Jacob said, "Lieutenant Weeds, we're ready. Open the gates."

"Yes, sir," Evan replied.

The bright light in front of them disappeared, and a huge

spiral opening appeared. Jacob turned to Eugene Walker, Freedom's pilot. "Eugene, take us out."

"Yes, sir."

Freedom, along with other Earth ships, passed through the gateway. When they cleared the gates, it closed behind them.

Never had Jacob felt so vulnerable and alone, not even when he had taken Freedom through uncharted space. He stared at the ten alien ships approaching the perimeter. The Orias ships were long and cylindrical. They reminded the admiral of missiles his ancestors had built in the twentieth century, though these were longer, heavier, and had a slightly different design. The cylinders were curved into spikes at the ends.

"Open a channel," Jacob told the communications officer.

"Channel open, sir."

"This is Admiral Jacob Donavan of Freedom. We represent the Imperial Command, which governs this section of space. We are a peaceful race eager to open communications."

A minute passed in silence.

"Perhaps you can start by identifying yourself," Jacob added.

The alien ships kept moving forward.

"Alien vessel, I advise do not enter this region of space without authorization."

The outsiders remained silent.

Jacob glanced at his tactical officer. Taking a long breath he said, "If you do not respond, and attempt to cross our boarders we will retaliate."

The bridge was silent again.

He repeated the message once more and waited. He glanced at his communications officer, who shook his head. "Convert the message in all languages and dialects in the digital library and broadcast it on all channels," Jacob instructed.

The officer nodded.

The bridge was so quiet that for the first time, Jacob could hear the beeping of the communications console.

"Sir, I've scanned the ships. I can detect no power signatures or weapons. As far as I can tell, there's no one on those ships," said the tactical officer, Lieutenant Tessa Clark.

"Oh, they're there . . ." Jacob stopped mid-sentence. The Orias ships glowed red, and their spikes burned like fire. "What the . . .?"

A bright flash emitted from the lead Orias ship and hit one of Earth's ships, blowing it to pieces. Jacob grabbed his seat as the bridge shook. A couple of gasps echoed on the bridge, and the alarm blared.

"Fire!"

Freedom steered toward two Orias ships and launched torpedoes. A huge ball of fire filled the viewscreen.

"Yes! We got them!" said Eugene.

From within the fireball, two alien ships reappeared and flew directly toward them.

"Fire at will!" Jacob shouted.

Freedom glided through the debris and fired. The Orias ships' tails began glowing.

"Change course. Move us away!" yelled Jacob.

A blaze was emitted from the alien ship.

The next moment, an explosion on the bridge threw the admiral to the floor. Darkness engulfed him, and the air filled with smoke. He sat up and looked at his wrist. It was bleeding. He got to his feet and froze. The two Orias ships had returned their attention to the perimeter. "I thought they'd destroy us," he muttered. "Report," he ordered Tessa.

"Sir, we were hit by an electromagnetic charge as powerful as five of our torpedoes. If we hadn't steered away . . ."

"What about the Orias?" Jacob asked, taking a seat and spinning toward the viewscreen.

"My scans show that there was minimal damage to the Orias ships. But the second torpedo did more damage than the first."

The admiral eyed her. "Any theories?"

"I suppose proximity to the alien ships might have more effect. But I suggest..."

Jacob turned to Eugene. "What was our distance from that ship when the second torpedo hit it?"

"Sir, our second torpedo hit it at forty thousand kilometers."

"And damaged it?"

"It appears so, but that Orias ship is still functioning. We need more da—"

The admiral cut him off. "Open a channel," he told the communications officer.

"Channel open, sir."

"Freedom to the Imperial Fleet, do not engage the Orias upfront. Attempt to get less than thirty thousand kilometers from them, then fire."

A blast blinded everyone. Turbulence hit Freedom.

"What happened?" demanded Jacob.

"Sir. Jupiter. Jupiter. I-It's gone. They have . . ." cried out Eugene.

"Engage thrusters. Follow those ships! Do not let them reach the perimeter," Jacob ordered. He stood up from his chair and approached Eugene. "Continue to maneuver, but don't fire. Don't draw any attention to us. Tell me when we're about twenty-five thousand kilometers away from the Orias ships."

Eugene nodded. Freedom glided forward.

Jacob returned to his chair. "Chart the locations of all the alien ships and put them on one side of the viewscreen."

"Yes, sir."

The view in front of him changed. Jacob watched the Orias ships heading toward the perimeter. They moved in a circular fashion as if connected by invisible spokes. It looked like a giant wheel moving through space.

"Their pattern is interesting. Four ships appear to be keeping us busy while these six head toward the perimeter," said Tessa.

"Yes," replied Jacob.

"Sir, the fleet is taking heavy damage," reported Eugene.

"Patience."

"They're ignoring the fleet," said Tessa. "As if we were . . ."

"Mosquitoes," finished Eugene.

"Mosquitoes are extinct," said Tessa.

Jacob jumped to his feet and opened a channel. "Attention, everyone! Six Orias ships are heading toward the perimeter. Focus on one ship. Just one. Destroy their pattern. Fire now! Now!"

"What are you suspecting?" asked Tessa.

"I think the six ships will combine their energy and create a very powerful blast."

"Sir! We're twenty-five thousand kilometers from the Orias wheel," reported Eugene.

"Increase speed. Pick one ship and fire. Give it everything we've got!"

Freedom's weapons blasted through the hull of one of the alien ships, pushing it off course. Freedom fired again, and the Orias ship blew into pieces.

"Yes!" cheered Eugene.

Suddenly, another horrific explosion filled the viewscreen. Jacob's shoulders slumped and holding his head he waited for the bad news.

"Sir, it's Marion," said Tessa. "It took out one of the Orias ships."

The admiral smiled.

Suddenly, the alien ships broke their pattern and turned toward the Earth ships. Two of them flew in the direction of Freedom. Torpedoes blasted through Freedom's tubes, disabling one of them, but the second spacecraft dodged the torpedoes.

"Evade! Evade!" shouted the admiral.

"Sir. I'm . . ."

A bright light blinded everyone. Freedom shook,

throwing everyone off their seats. Multiple blasts occurred simultaneously. Alarms blared. Smoke filled the bridge.

When Jacob opened his eyes, he saw a huge crack in the roof. He turned. The viewscreen was fractured, and the Orias ship was powering up again. He scrambled to his feet and rushed towards navigation. He entered the coordinates and engaged the thrusters. "Come on! Come on!" he said, pressing the keys several times. But Freedom moved slowly. "Tactical, tell me we have weapons!" he yelled over the top of the screaming alarms.

The alien ship's tail turned red.

"Tactical?" Jacob asked.

A blaze hit the alien ship, and it turned to dust. Another tremor hit Freedom. Jacob grabbed the console and saw Marion fly past them. "Whew, that was close," he muttered, making way for Eugene, who took control of the helm. "Report."

"Decks 5 and 6 have been heavily damaged. Six crew members have been injured. No fatalities so far. We still have power, engines, and life support."

"What about the fleet?"

"They have destroyed three Earth ships; two ships have taken heavy damage but the rest of the fleet is engaging the enemy. The Orias ships have turned their attention back to the perimeter. Three ships are engaging us, and the other four have formed the same wheel-like pattern. They're heading for the perimeter."

"Damn."

"I think it's time to change strategies." Tessa breathed heavily.

The admiral eyed her. "Do we have orders from Earth?"

"No."

He looked at the screen. "Those four ships might be our last hope."

Saturn

Argon gritted his teeth. He didn't like their odds. There was still no word from Imperial Command, and Titan was silent as well. People were dying. People he knew. He returned to his chair and opened a channel to Freedom. "Admiral Donavan, this is Argon Keston. Permission to join the battle."

"Negative. Stay there."

"Sir, if my readings are correct, the fleet has taken heavy damage. We can help."

"The fleet was ordered to engage the enemy; the squadron ships are to remain as backup. Those were our orders. We stick to them until the Imperial Command says otherwise. Is that clear?"

"Sir, with all due respect . . ."

"Argon. Stay there. That's an order!"

Argon banged the console. He sat back and listened to the communications between the ships. He almost jumped when he heard another blast. He got up and stood in the middle of the cockpit. If he defied orders, he'd be thrown out of the fleet, and his career would end before it had even started. But if he didn't act, he risked the lives of everyone he loved. What mattered most to him? He returned to his chair and reached out to his squadron. "This is Argon. I'm going to defy orders and join the fight. If you choose to stay back, I'll understand."

"Argon," said Micah in his husky, heavy voice. "How long have you known us?"

Byron said, "If we don't join the fight, everyone could die."

"Oh, that's comforting," Argon muttered. He pushed the buttons, and the engine roared to life. The tail of the small fighter glowed in the yellow mist. Atlas slowly glided through the rings of the planet, leaving a long trail of dust behind it. Another three ships followed.

"Commander Waters to Cadet Argon," Anastasia's voice crackled on the commlink.

"Yes, Commander?"

"What are you doing?"

"Commander, I can't just sit here," Argon said. "They need our help!"

"I understand, but we have our orders. Turn back."

Argon huffed. "With all due respect, I can't sit here and watch people die!"

"Cadet, you're out of line!"

There was no point in arguing. Argon ignored her messages and charged ahead. He felt as if a sword loomed over him; he was damned if he did, he was damned if he didn't. He was a man of action, and every fiber in his body told him it was time to act.

As they neared the battlefield, the size and shape of the Orias ships mesmerized him. "Let's begin with omega sequence," he suggested. Pairing with Byron, Argon flew closer to one of the alien ships.

"Break the wheel?" asked Byron.

"I agree."

They got nearer to the four ships.

"Distance twenty thousand kilometers," said Byron.

"Close enough," Argon replied and fired.

Two torpedoes hit the alien ship, blasting through its hull. Atlas bounced and dipped, but Argon quickly regained control and reduced speed.

"Did you see that?" Byron shouted.

"Yeah! Too easy. I thought we would need more torpedoes."

The Orias ships broke their pattern and turned their attention to the smaller ships.

"Here they come!" yelled Byron.

Argon swayed Atlas away and pushed the engines. The Orias ships followed him. Byron came from behind and fired. Atlas jolted moving away from the blast. Argon turned around, and pursued the two alien ships following Byron. Aiming for the tail of the Orias ships, Argon called,

"One, two, three, fire!"

The blast from the two Orias ships was enormous. Hundreds of pieces of metal spread through space. Atlas dipped and shuddered. A huge section of debris headed straight for it.

"Whoa!" Argon cried out, whirling the ship out of harm's way. A piece of debris hit the wing of Atlas. The spacecraft jolted. Alarms blared. Argon punched a few buttons and brought the ship under control.

"Wow. How did you do that?" Byron asked.

"I aimed for the tails," Argon replied and opened a channel to the fleet. "Attention, everyone. This is Argon. We've discovered a flaw in the enemy ships' design. To disable them, target the tails at close range. Just be careful not to get too close."

Argon was about to contact Freedom when he noticed two of his squadron members were on a collision course. "Clio and Micah, what are you doing?"

"You know what we're doing," Micah replied.

Argon saw two Orias ships pursuing them.

"They're going for the death maneuver," said Byron with a hint of distaste in his voice.

"It won't work. Abort. Now. Abort!" Argon yelled.

"How would you know? We've never tried it before," protested Micah.

"This is not the time nor place," Argon said.

"He will not listen to you," Byron said calmly.

Atlas steered past two Earth ships, chasing an Orias ship. It maneuvered under Freedom and headed for Micah's location. Clio and Micah were heading straight for each other. The end of the Orias ship following them began to glow.

"They're going to fire. Change course now!" Argon shouted.

"Wait for it," Micah said.

"I'm coming in."

"Argon, don't. I can do this without firing a single shot."

"You're going to get killed."

"Argon, trust me."

Argon shook his head and reluctantly decreased speed.

Clio and Micah were getting close. Too close. The Orias ship was right on their tails. If they miscalculated, it might cost them their lives.

"Micah, they're charging their weapons," Byron said. "You should act now."

"One, two," Micah counted. "Now!"

Both squadron ships turned away. The Orias ships fired. The massive beams missed the small ships and hit each other. The blast was gigantic. It created a turbulence wave so strong that every ship in the battlefield shook.

"Woo-hoo!" shouted Micah.

"Yippee!" yelled Clio.

Argon shook his head in dismay.

"That was uncalled for!" Admiral Donavan yelled over the communication system. Argon ignored him. Then Anastasia's voice echoed in the cockpit. "Commander Waters to Cadet Argon. Commander Waters to Cadet Argon."

"Yes, Commander. We have them. Just three more to go."

"Argon, Emmeline detected another ship," said Anastasia. "It masked its signature. It's heading for the perimeter. I'm sending you the coordinates."

This was unbelievable. "Affirmative," Argon said, feeling his heart rate rise. The console beeped. He entered the coordinates. Atlas swayed along the perimeter and headed away from the battlefield. Byron's ship wasn't far behind it.

In a few minutes, they saw a new Orias ship. Argon felt uncertain, and his heart leaped to his throat. Why had this ship come in later? Why not join the battle? Did it have a different purpose? Could he stop it?

"There it is," said Byron.

They fired phasers to sway the alien ship away from the perimeter, but it kept moving. They targeted the tail, but it was resilient.

"We need to get closer," said Argon. He pushed the

small ship. When he thought he was close enough, he pushed the button to fire the torpedoes. Nothing happened. "Oh no! No!" he cried out and pushed the button again.

"Weapon's system malfunction," announced the computer.

"Byron, my ship is damaged. Tell me you have torpedoes."

"I'm out!"

Byron fired phasers. They did little damage, and the alien craft kept moving toward the perimeter. "It's not working!" he shouted. Byron ship's gained speed, moving closer to the Orias ship. Argon pushed Atlas and caught up with him. At least he could fire phasers. They had to stop them; at any cost. They fired again. The Orias ship jolted a bit but kept moving.

"This one is different!" Byron called.

Argon banged his console. "Tell me someone has torpedoes!" he shouted. "Hello! Anyone? We need help!"

The ship's tail turned red.

Atlas's proximity alert went off. Argon turned to his scanner. There was a reading he couldn't understand. "What the hell?" he muttered. His eyes widened as realization dawned on him. "Byron, move away. Move. Move now!" he shouted, hurriedly changing course.

Just behind Atlas, Prometheus appeared. The hefty scorpion-shaped spacecraft flew past the small ships. Two torpedoes blasted through its tubes. The Orias ship turned to dust.

"Yes!" cheered Argon.

CHAPTER 2: DISTANT COUSINS

PERIMETER

Prometheus destroyed the last two Orias ships, winning the battle. Cheers echoed over the communications system. Argon jumped with joy. He ran his hands through his hair, and his eyes filled with tears. He sat down, placing a hand on his chest. It had been a close call. He then realized his situation. He had disobeyed direct orders, a sense of dread filled him. But then he thought what would happen to him was not important. He had done what was needed. His home and citizens of Titan were safe.

Freedom and Prometheus used tractor beams to gather the pieces of wreckage. Once the debris was secure, the next step would be to study it and learn more about these aliens.

Atlas joined several other ships in the queue and waited for the gates to open. They had been lucky today; six out of ten ships had survived. Two of them were heavily damaged and were being towed back to the space station.

Atlas tagged along with Prometheus, and Argon marveled at the latter ship's beauty. The major part of the ship was an elongated section, which looked like a submarine without its starboard or aft fins. From the middle of this section emerged two broad wings, which curved backward. It had ten decks and a crew of 120. It was loaded with the finest technologies and weapons. As it looked somewhat like a scorpion, there was a debate regarding its name. The engineers argued that the ship should be called Scorpion, but the scientists disagreed, and their argument had won. Prometheus was a prototype of an experimental technology that could mask its presence. It could duplicate energy signatures and sneak behind other ships. Only at visual range could the enemy see the actual ship. Hence the name Prometheus, the trickster.

The gates opened. One by one, they all returned to their realm. The small fleet moved toward the majestic Titan. Argon put Atlas on autopilot and sat back in his chair. He never knew why, but looking at Titan from the outside always made him nostalgic.

The space station was as big as one of the craters on the moon, about 75 kilometers in radius and far heavier than anyone could imagine. Comprising of ten decks, it was like a city in space, a hub for research and military activity. It had two parts, the outer section and the inner section, and housed over twenty thousand colonists. Most of the civilian quarters were in the outer section. The eighteen ports supported by the outer section allowed trade ships and the Imperial Fleet to dock.

The inner section was the heart of the space station and was linked to the outer rim by six strong, bulky tubular passageways. The bridge, engineering and research labs, and all essential departments were in this section. The Crystal Lab was the crown jewel of Titan. It was an astrometric lab with powerful equipment used to build star charts and study the origins of the solar system, galaxies, and other celestial bodies. Five entertainment sections were an attraction for a constant influx of tourists and colonists. The four conservatories were on Decks 1, 4, 6, and 9. In total, fifteen cargo bays were available in both sections to store several resources including food and fuel.

The large ships flew toward the docking ports, and Argon and his squadron glided under Titan and entered the hangar deck. The hangar deck was an open space with clearly marked landing areas. The autopilot slowly set Atlas on Dock 52. Shutting all the systems, Argon got off his chair and rushed out of the cockpit. The exit door opened outward, and he rushed down the ramp. The hangar deck was overflowing with excited people talking in loud voices and celebrating. Excitement ran through his veins, and he looked for his friends.

Byron rushed towards him.

"We did it!" Argon cried out.

"Yes!" Byron said happily.

They hugged and patted each other.

"That was amazing!" said Byron.

"I know! I know! I never thought it would be so thrilling…"

His friend smiled. "Not bad for our first one!"

Argon thought about it, "Thanks for having my back," he said.

"My pleasure."

Byron was a strong, tall young man with straight silver hair. He had gray eyes, a square face, and a heavy jaw. Byron and Argon had been born only months apart, had gone to school together, and had just finished their training as cadets of the Imperial Command. But their goals were different. Byron had joined because one day, he wanted to be part of the tribunal and run the Imperial Command. Argon just wanted to fix his ship, Raven, and fly into the unknown. He was a pilot, born to fly, born to be free. Micah and Clio joined them. They embraced each other. Argon felt happy, he felt he had done something good in his life. Something that made a difference to his people.

Argon stood on his toes and peered above the crowd. She wasn't here. He'd thought she would come.

"Argon!" called a voice.

He turned and saw Selina, his sister, dodging groups of excited people.

"Argon! Argon!" she screamed as she reached him. The nine-year-old girl clung to her brother like a cub hanging onto its mother's belly. Selina had long blonde hair tied in two piggy tails and bright hazel eyes.

Argon looked into her eyes, and his fears melted away. She was his angel. He didn't care what happened to him. He took her in his arms and held her close.

"You won! You won!" she said excitedly.

"Yes, we did!"

"I'm so glad you're back!" Selina screamed over the noise.

"Oh, darling!" called a soft voice.

Argon turned, and there his mother stood, her hands close to her chest, her eyes filled with tears of joy, her face shining with the smile he would remember until the end of his life. She stepped forward and embraced him.

Aceline stood out from everyone around her. Her thin body hid underneath her purple outfit, and she had high cheekbones, long eyelashes, and long wavy hair colored in the most beautiful shades of lavender.

When he was a child, Argon hadn't minded his mother looking different from other women, but as he'd grown older, it had begun to bother him. Many times, he had attempted to tell his mom to change, at least her hair. It was eye-catching, and he felt embarrassed. But he realized soon enough that he couldn't do anything about it, as she was adamant about maintaining her appearance.

"Hello, Mrs. Keston," said Byron.

"Oh, Byron, thank you for looking out for him."

"No problem."

"All officers report to meeting room six," the computer announced. "All officers report to meeting room six."

Argon already felt like the celebration was over. He would have to face the consequences of his actions. With a heavy heart, he handed Selina to his mom.

"I don't care what they say or do. I'm proud of you," said Aceline.

"Thanks, Ma."

Argon watched as his mother, and sister disappeared into the crowd.

"We've got to go," Byron said.

Argon nodded and cast his eyes around. There was one more person he wanted to see. He had so hoped she would come, but she had not.

TITAN, DECK 6, MEETING ROOM 6

From the hangar deck, they took the elevator to Deck 6. The elevator was big enough to hold ten people and moved smoothly. Its walls were painted with broad strips of gray and white. Six bright lights hung overhead, and the floor was carpeted. The doors were made of glass. Argon observed the different levels as the elevator moved.

Byron excitedly shared his plans for the rest of the day. But Argon felt his pulse rise as the elevator reached Deck 6. The glass doors slid open, and they entered the corridor. To their left were the curved glass windows that opened into space. To their right was a smooth maroon wall. The corridor was lit by long strips of lights on both sides. Today, the corridors were overflowing with people, as the crews from all the ships were pouring into the station. They walked toward a hefty door.

Argon stepped forward and said, "Keston XALPHA245."

"Authorization granted," said a robotic voice.

The heavy doors opened, and they marched ahead. They were now in the heart of the inner section where only authorized personnel were allowed. The crowd grew thinner, and silence fell around them. As they walked, they glanced at the figures behind the opaque white doors to their right. Titan's internal security system comprised a small army of robots. They looked like ghosts, standing in rows, waiting to be awakened.

"I wonder if we'll ever use them," Byron said.

Argon slowed down to stand in front of one of the doors. He glared at the blurry figure. Even though it was powered down, he felt its eye on him. "I hope we never do," he muttered.

They entered meeting room six. The room was a well-lit spartan hall with a large elliptical-shaped black table in the middle. Several comfortable chairs sat on the spotless gray carpet. Three large windows opened into space, offering a partial view of two of Saturn's moons. Argon rubbed his hands together, looking for the admiral.

Suddenly, he became aware of a shadow. A group of captains approached the young men and thanked them for their bravery and support. Argon felt happy and surprised. He'd expected to be criticized.

Anastasia stepped forward. "Good job, you two."

"Thank you," Argon said.

She looked him straight in the eye. "Next time, wait for orders."

He smiled sheepishly. It was obvious Anastasia would favor the Titan Squadron and she had a soft spot for people who lived on the space station. "I'm sorry if I crossed a line."

"You did."

Captain Mykel Lockhart stepped beside Anastasia. "Thanks for holding the fort," he said, extending his hand in a calm, gentle manner. The captain of Prometheus was a smart, tall man with sharp features. His thick brown hair was parted to the right and bright blue eyes hinted a mix of kindness and shrewdness.

"T-the pleasure was all mine, Captain," Argon replied, feeling his pulse rise. "Y-you cannot imagine how happy I am to meet you!"

Mykel smiled. "I'm glad to meet you too."

"Captain," said Byron, extending his hand.

Captain Lockhart looked a bit jaded to Argon, or perhaps he wasn't as young and vibrant as when he left the solar system. That was four years ago, and he had been looking forward to seeing the Prometheus and meeting the man in person. Argon had followed the captain's career, and one day he dreamt of being like him.

Argon rubbed his hands together. It was difficult for him

to contain his excitement; he was meeting his hero. "Is it true you've never lost a mission?" Argon asked.

"Yes. I've been lucky, and I have a fantastic crew." Mykel replied smiling.

"So, what about Prometheus?" asked Argon.

"An excellent ship. It's done pretty well for its third mission. Although I think it needs refurbishment."

"What about the masking technology? Was it of any use to you?" asked Byron.

"It works well. We didn't need to use it until today."

Argon smirked.

"Did you encounter any other alien life?"

"Except the Orias, we have encountered no intelligent alien life."

Anastasia announced that the meeting would commence soon. Argon wished she hadn't.

Mykel looked them in the eye. "Cadets, if you ever need anything, let me know."

Argon and Byron glanced at each other. "Can we get a tour of the ship?" they asked in unison.

Mykel laughed whole-heartedly.

The meeting commenced. Admiral Jacob Donavan congratulated everyone, and he updated the group about their current situation. Four Earth ships had been destroyed. They had lost eighty-nine men and women. But there was no damage to the perimeter. Next, he announced a small celebration at 2100 hours at Midnight Orchid. It had been organized to honor those who'd laid down their lives to protect their home and those who'd fought and survived. Jacob shared with them that alien debris would be moved to Cargo Bay 16, and an engineering team would be assigned to study it. Then the topic shifted to repairs. Out of the six ships, only two were totally operative.

"Argon, I expect you to help fix Freedom."

Argon nodded. He felt a knot in his stomach and was still unclear about where he stood.

When the meeting was over, Argon found Jacob staring

at him. Everyone else left, and the men sat in silence for a while.

"You disobeyed a direct order, Cadet," Admiral Donavan said finally.

"I'm aware of that. But something had to be done," Argon said, feeling a lump in his throat.

"I know. I understand we need all the help we can get," Jacob eyed Argon. "This time, you're off the hook. But that doesn't mean I don't have my eye on you. Under my command, never break the rules again!"

Argon gave him a cheeky smile.

TITAN, DECK 2, CRYSTAL LAB

The Crystal Lab was a spacious hall with multiple workstations along the wall. Two observatories were linked to the lab by narrow passageways. Each workstation was about two feet wide, fitted with the latest computers. The data and processing unit was a large rectangular structure that stood in the middle of the lab. Two rooms were located opposite the main glass door. One belonged to Dr. Kent, and the other was a meeting room.

Dr. Kent was the head of the science department, and currently four students, including Emmeline, were his interns. They were on Titan to get their training to become astrophysicists.

Emmeline Augury tried her best to focus, but she could sense everyone's eyes on her. Especially Sela Kimber's. Since Emmeline had returned from Observatory One, Sela had been watching her. She was a fellow cadet, one of Dr. Kent's favorites. Emmeline wanted to sneak away to meet Argon, but she was worried that if she left, Dr. Kent would get mad at her.

Emmeline was the most infamous cadet on Titan because she wanted to do things no one else would do. She was a plain girl whose nose was usually in books and computers. Her long black hair was always tied in a French braid. She had soft, expressive brown eyes, an oval-shaped face, and a long, thin nose. Today, like most days, she wore a white full-sleeve t-shirt with a light-gray jumper. Most days, Emmeline could be found hidden in a corner, glued to her desk, scanning, analyzing, and categorizing cosmological findings. This is why she was way ahead of other students, but this affected her personal life. She sometimes got so engrossed in her work that she forgot where she was. Just two months ago, she'd forgotten to attend her own twentieth birthday party, a mistake that had angered Argon so much that he hadn't spoken to her for two days.

Emmeline felt like she was invisible to the rest of the team most of the time. But she realized she actually preferred that because today, she was the center of attention. Without Dr. Kent's authorization, she had snuck out of the lab to go to the observatory and study the cloud. She knew she was drawing unwanted attention and criticism to herself, but she couldn't help it. She had to see it. The Orias cloud was fascinating. It was a mystery. It raised several questions in her mind. Where had it come from? What was its source? What was on the other side? She had to know.

The doors to the lab opened, and Richard and Zack entered. Emmeline looked enviously at them. They had been to the bridge, working side by side with Dr. Kent. Emmeline liked her corner in the lab, but she didn't want to be buried there. One day, she wanted to work on the bridge. Work without restrictions, without apprehension.

Dr. Kent entered the lab, and Emmeline's heart jumped to her throat. She watched him closely.

"Emmeline, my office."

She glanced at Sela and saw her mouth curved into a smile. She lowered her head and followed her boss. He was her teacher, someone she cared for and admired, but at the same time he intimidated her. She entered the office, and the doors shut behind her. He sat silently in his chair. For several moments, his eyes remained fixed on her. Dr. Kent was much taller than Emmeline. His thick gray hair was parted to the right. He had small, dark, angular eyes and always wore a black stand-up-collared shirt, custom-tailored trousers, and black shoes.

"I was trying to help," Emmeline said before he could speak.

"No. As always, you were trying to prove you are better than anyone else."

Emmeline bit her lip. She never felt that way. Instead, she wanted to be like others. "I thought the cloud . . ."

"Have you completed the analyzes of the nebula we found two weeks ago?"

"Err. Well, I'm halfway through."

"Not good enough. It should have been done last week."

Emmeline rubbed her palms together. "It has hundreds of elements."

"Don't make excuses," snapped Dr. Kent. "You are wasting your time looking at things you shouldn't. You should follow procedures and orders. They are there for a reason. And why did you call Commander Waters? You should have contacted me. You weren't supposed to be in the observatory in the first place."

"Someone had to be. I didn't have the time. The fleet . . ."

"The fleet is none of your concern. You should stay away from it."

"But the Orias are an amazing phenomenon. Interesting. Enigmatic! The research involving the cloud . . ."

"In which you will play no part."

Emmeline felt her heart crush into pieces. She couldn't understand him. "But I already began the analyzes on the cloud," she protested.

"I know. Send me that data, and I will see if it's any good. Trust me it is for the best."

Emmeline felt repulsed. She wanted to finish and send her findings to the Astrophysics Society on Earth. It was her theory, and they were her findings. For the last year, everything she had done had been scrutinized, rewritten, and forwarded. Then another thought came to her mind, it was her fault. She deserved it.

"That's all," said Dr. Kent. "I want the analyzes on the

nebula completed tonight."

Emmeline returned to her desk. She felt like crying, but she controlled herself. They already thought she was weak. Since she'd joined this group, they'd had their eyes on her, waiting for her to fail, and she felt like she did every day. When she'd started working here, she'd thought she could finish her projects quickly and move on. She had worked harder than anyone else. She had done in days what took everyone else at least a month. But it seemed her enthusiasm had worked against her. Even after all her efforts, she hadn't gotten the credits she needed to complete her qualification. She was far away from being where Dr. Kent was, but these initial steps were proving harder than ever. No matter what she did, Dr. Kent was never pleased. In a way, it was her own fault. Her mind drifted to an incident a year ago. It was her fault, and she had to suffer.

Everyone left except Emmeline. Tears rolled down her cheeks. The doors opened. Her face flushed when she saw Argon. She quickly wiped her eyes and approached him. "Hi. I'm so sorry. I should have come to the hangar. Are you okay? Is everyone okay?" she asked.

"I'm good, and everyone made it back safely. Well, everyone we know. What happened to you?"

"Nothing."

Argon looked at her with his kind but steady eyes. He knew. "Are you coming to the party?"

"I-I can't go. I have to finish something."

"Why can't anyone else do it?"

"Because it's my responsibility. I should have done it ages ago. It's my fault."

"That's what you said last week. And you can't beat yourself up for every mistake you make."

"I know," Emmeline whispered. "I'm sorry. Let's meet at Midnight Orchid tomorrow for breakfast."

Argon smiled. "You'd better show up."

"I will."

"Okay. What about the *other* thing?" Argon asked in a low voice, looking around to make sure they were alone.

"Nothing much, but I'm hopeful." Emmeline smiled and cherished the feeling that she could share anything with him. "Would you like to see it?"

He nodded, looking excited.

Emmeline placed her right palm on the wall below the bureau. It moved outward and slid to the right. Among all her books, notepads, and space charts was a red bag. She unzipped the bag and handed a sleek black tablet to Argon.

"Wow," Argon said, touching its smooth surface. "It's beautiful. I thought this thing was ancient." He looked at his own reflection in the plaque.

"I thought so too," admitted Emmeline. "But this is what I found after its rock shell fell off."

Argon flipped it over and observed an image of the sun rotating anticlockwise. Otherwise, it was blank. "That's it?"

Emmeline tapped the image of the sun. The plaque beeped.

The image of a sun with a face vanished and several nonsensical words revolved around in a clockwise fashion.

"Wow," Argon whispered. "This is amazing, but what do these symbols mean? They don't look like alphabets."

"It's a cipher."

"Another riddle?" Argon's shoulders slumped. "Do you know how to decode it?"

Emmeline sat on the chair. "Honestly, I don't know."

"Are you sure there's something on it?"

"There should be."

"Emmeline, this is fascinating, but I don't think you should waste your time. You already have so much to do. And you never know. We might need you."

She bowed her head. "I can't just let it go."

"You think the myth is true?"

Emmeline eyed him. "It's not a myth. They found this plaque in an expedition in the early twentieth century. Then, somehow, it found its way to my family."

Argon smiled. "Yes, I know, and I also know that your ancestors loved fairy tales."

"That's not funny."

Argon smirked. "I would love to sit with you and hypothesize about this plaque, but we have other pressing matters. The Orias could attack at any time. We need everyone, including you."

Emmeline's face turned grim. She didn't know whether she was needed. She saw that her gloomy mood was making Argon uncomfortable. She reached forward and grabbed his hand. "Tell me, how was it? How did it feel? The battle?"

Argon looked thoughtful. "Exciting and terrifying."

TITAN, DECK 3, MIDNIGHT ORCHID

Midnight Orchid was a venue with a bar and seating arrangements for over two hundred people. It was spectacular, with windows that curved upward to form half of the roof. The floor was covered with white carpet, and the vast hall was decorated with many varieties of plants and flowers, including orchids. Tables were arranged along the windows, giving the colonists a beautiful view of the heavens and Saturn's moon, Titan. The lights were dim, the music light and calming.

Anastasia stood with a glass of champagne, feeling like a bit of a phony. She hadn't fired a single shot, and yet she was being commended. The tribunal of the Imperial Command had praised her and Jacob. While the admiral had taken in all the glory and compliments, Anastasia thought the cadets and the fleet deserved the honor more. She watched as Evan, Adrian, and Cyr mingled and were soon joined by Micah, Clio, and Byron.

"Nice party," said a familiar voice.

Anastasia turned and tried to give an assured smile to Dr. Kent. She noticed that Emmeline wasn't at the party, probably being punished for being innovative. Sometimes, Anastasia wished she had some control over the science division. She knew at the bottom of her heart that the friendship between the admiral and Dr. Kent influenced a lot of decisions made in the Crystal Lab. It was politics, maybe. She didn't know who pulled the strings in that lab. From her dealings with him she felt that Dr. Kent was selfish, shrewd, powerful, and hungry for glory.

"You did a fine job," Dr. Kent said.

Anastasia smiled. "Where's Emmeline?" she asked.

"I don't know. I don't control my students."

"Oh, really? Is that observation without bias?" said Anastasia, knowing she was asking for trouble.

"It is. I'm a fair man. But I know Emmeline is a crybaby. All of my students work equally hard."

Anastasia felt like snapping, but she let the comment slide.

"Frankly, you don't understand her. You don't understand me," said Dr. Kent.

"Tell me, Dr. Kent, what do you want?"

"To be one of the finest scientists and all the glory that

comes with it."

"All Emmeline wants is to be an astrophysicist."

"Well, she's not ready."

"That's your perspective," said Anastasia. Dr. Kent was about to reply, but Anastasia held her hand up. "We're at war and putting down young people like Emmeline will not help us. Remember, all your distinctions, titles, and glory won't matter if Titan is destroyed."

Dr. Kent's face hardened.

Anastasia continued, "In other words, if Titan falls, you fall with it."

Anastasia was relieved when Dr. Kent left. She didn't completely understand the story between Emmeline and Dr. Kent, but she knew he was punishing her. She knew why? One year ago, Emmeline conducted an experiment without authorization which led to considerable damage to the lab, engineers and computers on the bridge. It was wrong of her. But it made no sense to her that Dr. Kent was punishing Emmeline for being innovative. His own career was full of taking risks, defying orders and working harder than anyone else. How could he not see that Emmeline had the same qualities? He was young once.

She shook her head and walked to the window. As she watched the sparkling sky, she felt a shadow over her shoulder. She gulped. She had been formal. She had been avoiding him, but she couldn't anymore. Now that he was back, she felt she was losing control again. The past never vanished, nor did the memories of your first love. She turned to look into Mykel's soft eyes. He always looked at her that way. Why wouldn't he stop?

"Hey. Good to see you again. How are you?" he asked.

"I'm well. How are you?" she replied, trying not to pay attention to her beating heart.

"Good, good. And your daughters?"

"Doing well and with their father on Earth."

"That's good. How's Martin?"

"He's well," Anastasia answered. He didn't know.

Maybe it was best not to tell him. This wasn't the time. It was for the best. "How was your trip?"

"Oh, long. You and I need to take a day off to discuss it. I have so many stories you're going to love."

Anastasia tried not to blush, "As the captain of Prometheus, you will be debriefed."

"That wasn't what I meant," Mykel replied.

Feeling her discomfort rise, Anastasia changed the topic.

The doors opened, and Argon stepped into Midnight Orchid and joined his friends. Born and brought up together on Titan, they were thick as thieves.

Micah was the first to speak. "Hey, man. Great shooting!" Micah was heavier than the rest of the party and had short, curly red hair and round blue eyes. He was a playful young man who spent most of his time in nightclubs or gambling. He never took life too seriously. Argon was sometimes envious of his carefree life.

"Thank you for supporting me," said Argon.

They all raised their glasses. Argon, Micah, Byron and Clio had been there for each other as long as he could remember. Of course, Byron was his best friend, but Micah and Clio were people he could depend on, rely on, and he trusted them with is life.

"What's with the maneuver?" said Byron.

"We had to try it," said Micah.

"It was dangerous and unnecessary," said Argon.

"We got two ships at once," Clio replied, "And we proved that it can be done." Clio was a skinny young girl with long red hair and steel-blue eyes.

"One for the history books," Micah said, raising his glance to her.

Argon bit his lips. He sensed a growing friendship between the two, and he was happy for them. "Just don't do it again."

"Look who is talking. You defied the admiral's orders," remarked Clio.

Micah glanced at the admiral. "Be careful of that guy. People say he's gone a bit...nuts." His voice was almost a whisper.

Argon didn't know where Micah got his information.

"Oh, yeah, that's true," said Clio. "He hates it when people don't listen to him."

"I think that's normal," stated Byron.

"No," said Micah. "They say he takes it as a personal insult."

"Guys, I think you're wrong. Admiral Donavan is one of the most respected, most decorated, and bravest officers in the fleet," Argon said.

"No one denies that," Clio whispered. "But he has turned . . ."

Argon was confused.

"We don't know the entire story, but the bartender is friends with one of the officers on Freedom. He says the long space trips have taken a toll on him."

"Really? I thought it was because his wife left him," said Clio.

"That happens. Long distance relationships rarely work." Byron shrugged.

"Yeah, you and I are mature enough to understand that," mocked Micah.

"Okay. Stop." Argon said raising his glass. "Today was a day that changed our history forever. Over eighty people died, and I honor their sacrifice for their home. But I am glad we all made it back. To friends forever!"

They bumped glasses and finished their drinks. The group of young people had known each other as long as they could remember. If one got in a fight, they all got in a fight. If one was struggling, all of them reached out to offer support. They planned trips together; they ate together; they were inseparable. Until recently, when Argon had expressed his wish to fly into open space and Byron wanted to go to Earth.

Titan, deck 3, Midnight Orchid

Long after everyone had left, Dr. Kent and Jacob sat together and had a drink, just as they always did after one of them had been away for a while. Usually, it was the admiral, but Dr. Kent didn't mind.

"I'm glad you made it back," said Dr. Kent.

"Thank you," Jacob answered, but he didn't feel right. Something was off. Since last year, everything was off.

"How's your wife?" Dr. Kent asked.

"Still wants a divorce."

"Sorry."

Jacob shook his head. "She knew what I was when we got together. It's been forty years! Forty years! Doesn't time matter to people anymore? Why can't things stay the same? It's sad that people back down on their word. It's really terrible, and there's no law to prevent it."

"Jacob, out of forty years of marriage you have been away most of the time. What's the point in staying with someone you don't care for? The question is, does she love you? Do you love her?" asked Dr. Kent.

"That doesn't matter," Jacob argued. "In my view, once you commit to something, you stick with it, no matter what!"

"Okay. How was your voyage to Proxima Centauri?" Dr. Kent asked, changing the topic.

"It was great," said the admiral, and began sharing stories about his voyage and the challenges he'd faced.

An hour went by, and then Dr. Kent began talking about Phoenix, an experimental particle ray that he wanted to set up in the Crystal Lab, which used up considerable power.

"That's impractical and very dangerous, Chris," Jacob told him. The truth was, he was scared to present the project to the Imperial Command. They needed something tangible, a working design, not something that wasn't based on facts. He also thought that Chris sometimes used their friendship to push his projects forward. That was selfish of him.

"I think we can do it. I've run some simulations, and I

think we can control the power flow," said Dr. Kent, showing the admiral his new design and data. "With everything going on, it took me six months to develop, but I think it will work. "

Jacob went through the designs and data. He had to admit to himself that it looked good, possible. Chris was an excellent scientist, but he was unrealistic. He wanted things to move fast, but Jacob felt it was time to slow down. "Looks similar to your previous design," he said without interest. Why wasn't Dr. Kent interested in discussing his problems? All he ever talked about was this stupid experiment. Scientists never changed.

"It's different," said Dr. Kent. "Now I can explain to the science committee and arrange for a demonstration."

"You're playing with fire," Jacob said warningly.

"There is always risk in trying new things…"

"You do not have a reliable power source. It might damage, Titan. We need Titan, especially during this time."

"Agreed. But we also need powerful weapons. If this works, it can be used to defend our world. You can convince the Imperial Command."

The admiral looked thoughtful. "I don't think we have time for scientific experiments."

"Come on," said Dr. Kent. "We need to think out of the box. And we're friends, and you promised you'd help me out."

"Yes, we are friends, but I can't be biased."

"What is the problem?"

"We do not know if it will work."

"I can put up a demonstration to show that Phoenix works," argued Dr. Kent.

"But you don't have any data except that dreadful incident a year ago. It might have costs us a lot you know." Jacob replied. He started thinking of a way to redirect his friend. He couldn't approve of such a nonsense project. It would hurt his reputation. Dr. Kent was a fine scientist, and his student Emmeline was good enough, but Jacob was a better judge of what was right and wrong. He was a better judge of everything, it was up to him to make sure his friends and those under him did not make mistakes.

"Jacob, I helped you map your voyage and upgraded the science lab on Freedom, and we've given priority to analyze all your findings," Dr. Kent said. "Without our help, your ship wouldn't have the latest technology."

"The Imperial Command approved that."

"You are not making any sense. You want data. I can't get that without a demonstration, and you won't get me permission to do one. It feels like you don't want my work to go ahead."

"Don't be ridiculous, Chris," Jacob scoffed. "You can't get attached to a project."

Dr. Kent's face turned gloomy. "Fine. I'll reach out . . ."

"Okay. Okay," Jacob caved. He couldn't let Dr. Kent reach out to the science committee himself. That could be disastrous. Staying in control was everything. "I'll speak with Vince. And you should focus on the war."

TITAN, CARGO BAY 16

Emmeline couldn't rest. The alien debris haunted her like a bad dream. After work, she returned to her quarters to get some sleep, but she couldn't. So, she made a decision, despite knowing the risk she was taking.

She pressed the codes on the panel to open the doors of Cargo Bay 16. As soon as she stepped inside, the lights turned on. She found herself surrounded by enormous pieces of debris standing on large stands. She felt as if she had landed on an alien planet with huge, strangely shaped buildings.

It reminded her of her childhood. The first time her grandpa took her for a hike. It was in the northern hemisphere, and she could still feel the cold and remembered deep and dangerous trenches. The mountain was enormous and looked welcoming during the day. But once they had to hike at night, and the rock above her looked somewhat like the debris. She shook her head dismissing the memory, grabbed her scanner and got to work.

She had no idea what the time was when she heard the door open. She hid, remembering that she was here without authorization. Dr. Kent would be mad at her. Anastasia could send her back to Earth.

"Who's there?" asked a familiar voice.

Emmeline peered out and spotted the chief engineer of Titan, Lieutenant Cyr Storm. She knew Cyr wouldn't be that mad. "Hi," Emmeline said in an embarrassed tone.

"What are you doing here?" asked Cyr.

"Ah. Ahem. Err," Emmeline replied, stepping away from the debris. "I was doing some preliminary scans."

The engineer was shorter and more muscular than Emmeline and was a proud Asian woman. She was hot-headed and blunt, and she ran the engineering department with military precision. Her staff both feared and respected her.

Cyr checked her pad. "You're not assigned to study the debris."

"I'm not assigned to anything."

Cyr stared at her. "You're not supposed to be here."

"I know. I just thought . . . It doesn't matter."

She was about to leave when Cyr said, "How long have you been here?"

Emmeline looked at the clock and balked. "It seems all night. I thought the faster we got the information, the better. What if they come back?"

Cyr smiled. "Okay. Tell me what you found, and we can work together on it."

Emmeline jumped with excitement. "Thank you! I want to be useful. I know I can be." She trailed off when Cyr folded her arms. "Doesn't matter. Okay. This is what I found. The hull of the ships is made from an unknown material. The alloy is organic and light, but it's very strong. However, the ships use most of their power for fighting."

"They're designed for war."

"Yes."

"But how are they powered?" Cyr asked.

"That's a good question. I don't know. I haven't found a

power source. On the other hand, remember the cloud?"

"Yes," said Cyr. "You said it was a doorway."

"It's a conduit, and these ships can travel through them. My preliminary analyzes show it's a spatial distortion."

"Meaning?"

"A rift in space. But it's not a natural phenomenon. Something or someone has the power to open those conduits and send the Orias through."

"Wow. Can we go through the cloud?" Cyr asked.

"Yes and no," replied Emmeline. "It's a doorway that opens on both sides. We can certainly try to fly through it. But I wouldn't recommend sending a ship. Until we figure out how to open or close the conduit, it would be best to send a probe."

"Okay. I'll add that to the recommendations."

"Thank you," she hesitated for a moment, "I think you need to see something else." Emmeline's heart started racing as she remembered the first time she'd noticed it.

Cyr followed Emmeline to the end of the cargo bay, and they stood before a two-foot-tall piece of debris. Emmeline crawled below it, and Cyr followed her.

"What are we looking at?" Cyr asked.

Emmeline took in a long breath. "That."

Out of the wreckage poked a large claw. It reminded Emmeline of the dinosaurs that had ruled the Earth before mankind.

"There's another one," Emmeline pointed out. Four sharp claws protruded from a second piece of debris to their right. Emmeline gulped. "And I found a leg," she said, pointing to the limb lying near a section of the wreckage.

"Oh, wow. These things are huge," Cyr muttered.

"Yes. Possibly six to seven feet tall."

Cyr fell silent.

"I analyzed both the debris and the remains of the Orias. They're identical in several aspects. It's probably a species where both the pilot and the ship are alive and made up of the same biological material."

They crawled out and got on their feet.

"Okay," Cyr said slowly. "What else?"

"I'm not an exobiologist, but there's something peculiar about the Orias DNA," Emmeline said.

Cyr smiled. "It's alien."

"Yes. But the Orias DNA consists of traces of DNA that match the DNA of animals on Earth."

"What? How could that be possible? Which one?" Cyr asked.

Emmeline felt her stomach twist. "It could be reptilian." The first thing that came into her mind was the crocodile. They still lived on Earth, but their numbers were decreasing.

"Are you telling me the Orias are linked to a species on Earth? Does that mean an Earth-based species somehow evolved and turned into these creatures? If I remember correctly, humans have reptilian DNA. Could they be related to us?" asked Cyr without stopping to draw breath.

"Okay, slow down," answered Emmeline. "Yes, we have reptilian DNA. At this point, I don't know if they're linked directly to homosapiens or any other species. I can detect the traces of reptilian DNA in this debris but not anywhere else."

"Not in that leg?"

"No."

Cyr became thoughtful. "Oh, my God. Have you told this to anyone else?"

Emmeline shook her head. "I'm not an exobiologist or a doctor, and I'm not using a medical scanner. We need to confirm these facts before we tell anyone else."

Cyr nodded.

Emmeline hoped she understood. She thought about the hook-shaped claw and gulped. "It looks like Adrian's noblemen from hell might have originated from Earth."

Chapter 3: Nemesis

Titan, Deck 4, Argon's Quarters

Argon sat up in his bed, breathless. He held his head, thinking about his dream. *Not again*, he thought. Since they'd detected the Orias, he'd been having recurrent dreams about Titan's destruction. The unsettling feeling never left him. For a moment, he wondered if he should speak to someone. But he dismissed the thought almost immediately. As soon as he stood up, the lights in his quarters turned on. He walked to the window. The gigantic moon had changed color again. Titan's photochemical haze, rich in organic material, gave the moon a smooth, featureless orange glow. It was always an interesting sight. Beyond the moon were only the stars — steady points of light in the blackness.

As if she sensed his discomfort, his little sister Selina walked into the room with her bear. She yawned and crawled into Argon's bed. "No more nightmares if we stay together," she said as she closed her eyes.

Argon smiled. Last night, he'd spoken with his father, who'd congratulated him on his win but also cautioned him. He'd asked him not to antagonize the admiral. It could affect his career. He didn't know what to think; he thought he had done what was right and what was needed. He couldn't let more people die. He returned to bed and tried to sleep. Selina put her arms around him, and her presence gave him comfort. It was good to have a family.

TITAN, DECK 6, ASSEMBLY HALL

Jacob didn't enjoy training new cadets. They thought they were heroes who were going to bring balance to the world and could do the impossible. In Jacob's view, they were ignorant, naive children with excessive hormones running through their veins. The hall was spacious, with a circular track for running and warm up. The hall also had a boxing ring, large fight stimulation modules, and a firing range.

It was early, and Jacob felt tired. He had been on a long voyage and couldn't remember the last time he had taken a vacation. But he had a duty to perform. He was their leader, and leaders had to make sacrifices.

He felt his frustration rise and glared at Argon, Byron, and Clio as they stood at attention. Three more squadrons had arrived from Earth. Jacob liked them better. They were experienced and disciplined and highly recommended by the Imperial Command.

He glanced at the time. There was one cadet missing. Micah. Jacob greatly disliked that young man. He was obnoxious, disobedient, careless and most of all a risk taker.

The doors hissed open, and Micah rushed inside, ignoring the fact that there were still flakes of confetti in his hair. He hurried to stand beside Clio.

The admiral walked toward him. "Had an enjoyable night out, Cadet?"

"Excellent, sir. You should try it."

Jacob took in a sharp breath. "Cadet, you stink!"

"Well, we're going to train anyway, so why shower?"

"What you do in your own time is your business, but when you report to duty or training, you show up sober! Do you understand?" Jacob demanded.

Micah nodded but couldn't suppress a burp.

Everyone burst into laughter.

"Quiet!"

The hall became silent again.

"Cadet Micah, fifty laps around the hall."

"Yes, sir!"

Without hesitation, Micah began running. Jacob was amazed. He had expected him to argue, plead, or make a sarcastic remark. But instead, he accepted his responsibility and followed orders. The admiral watched him closely. Maybe he could tame this one.

"Now, I know some of you have just completed your training, but it's basic, and you have limited experience," Jacob began, addressing the rest of the group. "I'm going to prepare you for battle and for victory!"

TITAN, DECK 4, ARGON'S QUARTERS

When he returned to his room, Argon's body was aching. Six hours of training was too much, but he felt good. Initially, he'd had his doubts and wondered what the admiral could teach them. But it was an excellent experience, and Argon felt he had learned more today than he had in the last six months. The most interesting aspect of the training were the new maneuvering skills.

Argon showered and picked up his pad, going through the list of repairs required for Freedom. First, he had to attend a meeting on Deck 10.

The door to his quarters opened, and Selina entered, jumping up and down. "Lunch break! Lunch break!" she yelled.

Argon embraced his little sister.

"I'm hungry," she complained.

He realized she was supposed to be at school. "Well, Ms. Elena would have made some wonderful lunch."

"No. I want to eat with you," Selina insisted.

"Honey, I have work to do."

Her face became pale. "I hate this war. I hate it. Everything has changed. Everything is changing!"

"Where's Mom?" Argon asked, changing the subject to distract her.

"Something really odd, old, and smelly arrived by space mail yesterday," Selina told him. "She's been in the archaeology lab since then. I think Mom forgot about us."

Argon chuckled. "I'm sure she didn't. What would you like to eat?" he asked as they walked out of his room.

Titan was home to many people. Its creators had made efforts to make the living quarters as comfortable as possible. His family had been allocated a big living space. It had three bedrooms, a living room, and a kitchen. The living room had an oval dining table and a few comfortable white lounge chairs. Four curved windows opened into the cosmos. The floor was covered with thick gray carpet. Machines in the kitchen prepared all food and beverages.

As Argon prepared lunch, he glanced at the table and remembered his father. Just a few months ago, they'd had family lunch almost every day. Those had been the good old days.

TITAN, DECK 6

Since his mother was still at the lab, Argon dropped Selina at school. It was a colorful rectangular hall. Several desks stood in rows, and each was equipped with a transparent screen. He watched as Selina took her seat and waved him goodbye. She touched the screen, and it came to life.

"Welcome back, Selina. How was your afternoon?" said the computer.

"It was great. Argon made me lunch."

"That's lovely," said the computer. "Let's look at what you can do today."

Selina nodded, clapping her hands.

Ms. Elena entered the hall and welcomed everyone.

When all the children settled, Argon approached the teacher.

"How can I help you?" Ms. Elena asked.

"I came to drop off Selina," replied Argon.

Ms. Elena looked confused. "But she should have been here all along. I'm sure she didn't miss school this morning."

"She got out during lunch break and returned home."

Ms. Elena looked surprised. "Again? How?" she asked, glancing toward the child.

"I don't know!" Argon said. "Look, I'm worried that one of these days, she'll wander off somewhere. You shouldn't let her leave."

"I didn't. As a matter of fact, she can't," said Ms. Elena. "The computer monitors the exit, and it doesn't allow children to leave. They don't have authorization."

Argon was shocked. "Then how did she leave?"

Ms. Elena shrugged her shoulders.

"Let's ask her." Argon approached his sister. "Darling, how did you leave the school?"

Selina pointed to the door.

"Was it open?" asked Argon.

"Nope."

"Did you leave with another parent or guardian?" asked Ms. Elena.

"No."

"How, then?" Argon said.

"I told the computer to let me go, and it did," Selina replied simply.

The teacher and Argon exchanged worried glances. "You told the computer?" said Argon.

"Yes."

Argon scowled. "Selina, what did I tell you about making up stories?"

"I'm not making up a story. I wanted to leave, and the computer let me!" said Selina. She grumpily turned back to her screen.

Argon folded his arms.

"I'll keep an eye on her," said Ms. Elena.

Argon nodded. But it bothered him. How could Selina just leave school whenever she wished? She was nine and didn't have access or the skills to manipulate a computer. It was impossible. It could be a glitch, but it had happened before.

TITAN, DECK 6, MAIN MEETING ROOM

Argon rushed into the meeting room and was glad when he saw that the meeting had not yet begun. He found a seat near Byron and turned on the screen in front of him. It displayed the agenda for the day.

The meeting room was spherical, with a large screen behind Anastasia's chair. The room had maroon walls, and the floor was covered with white carpet. A couple of plants stood along the wall.

Argon noticed Mykel Lockhart, who was sitting beside Anastasia. They spoke in low voices. Suddenly, Anastasia beamed and laughed. Argon was a bit surprised. He hadn't seen her so happy, not since her family had left. Then his eyes found the admiral who sat alone, looking unimpressed and glaring at the officers around the room. Although he admired the man, he felt uncomfortable around him. Was it because he defied orders? Or was it something else? He didn't know.

The lights in the room dimmed, and Anastasia began the meeting. "Thank you, everyone, for being here. Admiral, what is the status of the fleet?"

"At the moment, all the ships, including my own, are undergoing repairs," Jacob responded. "We've recalled ships to Earth, but it will take them at least a month to return. Some of them might take longer."

"What else can we do?" Anastasia asked, looking at Adrian and Evan.

"How about installing generators to erect an extra shield around the perimeter?" suggested Adrian.

Everyone nodded.

"Good. How long will that take?"

"At least a month," replied Evan.

"You have fifteen days," Anastasia told him.

"Ma'am?"

"You heard me. Fifteen days."

"But…"

She regarded Evan intently.

"We will try our best," Adrian replied.

Then she turned to Argon. "Is your squadron ready?"

"The Titan Squadron is ready."

"And have more arrived from Earth?"

"Yes."

"How many?"

"Including the three squadrons that arrived yesterday, we now have sixteen ships like Atlas."

"And who will lead the squadron?" Anastasia inquired.

Argon turned toward the admiral.

There was a slight hesitation, but then he said, "For now, Argon will lead them."

Argon's heart sank. He didn't like it. It was too much responsibility. The training, the repairs to Freedom, and now the squadron. He'd expected to be disciplined and demoted. Everyone knew the admiral didn't like insubordination. Why was he picking him as the leader? Did he expect him to defy orders again or was it to keep an eye on him?

"I think you're the right man for the job," said Mykel.

"Thank you, Captain," Argon replied uncertainly.

"Ask me if you need help," Mykel added.

Argon nodded, trying to smile.

Anastasia turned to Cyr. "What else?"

"After the completion of the ship repairs, the engineering staff can help build shields around the perimeter."

"Admiral, is there any way we could speed up the process of building new ships?" asked Commander Waters.

"We're building twenty ships, but it will take months."

Argon agreed. Even though the Challenger colony was advanced, each ship took at least a couple of months. He wished they could speed up the process, but he didn't know how.

"And we should consider a diplomatic angle," Admiral said.

The room became dead silent. War brought Argon no joy, but he wasn't blind.

"We tried that. It doesn't work," Anastasia responded in a calm tone.

"That's what I told the Imperial Committee."

"Did you mention that over eighty people died?" asked Argon.

"Yes, I did. It had no effect. They believe that to prevent further deaths, we should attempt to make peace with this species. And I agree."

"What if they don't want peace?" Cyr demanded loudly.

"Regardless, we should try diplomatic methods," replied Jacob.

"What if we all worked together?" suggested Mykel.

"What do you suggest?" Dr. Kent asked.

"I think all the captains should come together and speak with the Imperial Committee," said Mykel.

Argon liked the idea. Maybe they could convince them. He still couldn't understand why the Imperial Command couldn't see the Orias as a threat.

"I agree. Please gather as many supporters as you can," Anastasia said. "Now, Dr. Kent, what do we know about these Orias?"

"The debris contains elements we've never seen or encountered before," Dr. Kent said. "As we suspected, the Orias are made of the same biological material as their ships. We're doing the best we can. It's a slow process. We're at a very early stage . . ."

"Doctor, I understand you want to know more about this species. What I want to know is why they're attacking Titan and how we can defeat them," said Anastasia.

The room fell silent.

Dr. Kent smiled patiently. He looked as if he'd been expecting the question. Argon often thought the doctor was more than he appeared, but he despised the man because he treated Emmeline badly.

"I think we need to study this species," the doctor replied slowly. "Knowledge we gain could help us in our future encounters."

Cyr cleared her throat. "I think the doctor is right. Maybe his team can help us locate what could be a data module. If we can find any logs, flight patterns, or planets this species has visited that information might be helpful."

"What do you think, Dr. Kent?" asked Anastasia.

"If there is such a module, we should find it."

"Okay, I want that wreckage studied and analyzed. Rip it apart if you must. Any other ideas?"

"I have an idea that might seem a bit . . . outrageous," said Mykel.

Argon felt excited.

"Before the Orias fire, there is a considerable increase in energy levels from within their ships," Mykel explained.

"Yep. And their tails glow," commented the admiral.

"Maybe we can take advantage of that," said Mykel.

"How?" asked Cyr.

"During our attack, we discovered that at a close distance the tails are vulnerable to our phasers and torpedoes. Perhaps we could reprogram our torpedoes to detect that increase in energy and target them."

Everyone looked at each other.

"That's a great idea," said Anastasia.

Argon was blown away. He wished he had come up with it.

"How do we test this theory?" Cyr asked.

"We can only test it in battle."

"Can we do it?" Anastasia asked Edward, the tactical officer.

"Yes. We can begin immediately."

"Can we do the same for our phasers?"

"I don't think so," said Edward. "But we can definitely get started with the torpedoes."

"Good. Do it," said Anastasia.

The meeting was about to adjourn when Cyr spoke up. "One more thing. I feel it's important to share this. While we were going through the debris, we found parts… of the Orias."

Everyone remained silent.

"Emmeline did the early scans and found a DNA pattern that matches reptiles on Earth."

Anastasia turned to Dr. Kent.

"W-What?" asked Argon.

"That's unbelievable!" said Adrian.

"That is preposterous! Are you sure?" yelled Jacob.

"No, it's not preposterous!" argued Cyr. "Orias might have similar origins to reptiles on Earth. It's a clue that this species is somehow linked to our planet."

"That has nothing to do with the war," argued the admiral.

"How do you know?" argued Dr. Kent.

"We're wasting our time!"

Ignoring the admiral Cyr said, "I've contacted an exobiologist from Earth, Dr. Isaac Finch. I've gotten approval from the Imperial Command for him to travel to Titan. Since he could help us win this war, his paperwork went through quickly. Delta Dune is his designated pilot, and she should fly him in tomorrow. Dr. Kent, are you happy to work with him, or should I ask Emmeline?"

Argon tried not to show his amusement. His eyes drifted toward Anastasia, who gave him a quick glance.

Dr. Kent nodded. "I'm fine with that."

Anastasia stood up. "This is excellent progress. Keep working. We need to get some answers. There are three other stations like Titan guarding the perimeter. Titan is the most powerful of them all. Why attack us? Why now? I want answers."

"Maybe now they have the means to do so?" Cyr suggested getting to her feet.

"Or they found out that there are other neighboring species and want to explore," said Dr. Kent, collecting the pads in front of him.

"If they're explorers, they shouldn't attack," Argon pointed out.

Anastasia smiled and raised her left hand. "All excellent theories. Let's get to work."

Everyone got to their feet and began to leave.

"Maybe Titan has something they want, and we're not aware of it," Evan suggested, chuckling.

Argon stopped dead and felt a sense of doom looming over him. Something on Titan. Something they want. *Could it be it?* He wondered. He thought about the plaque Emmeline had found. She'd been studying it for several months. Could the Orias and the plaque be connected? No. It wasn't possible. Many artifacts and historical objects of unknown origins were brought to Titan from all over the realm. Why would the Orias want Emmeline's plaque?

Evan sensed his concern. "Argon, what is it?" he asked.

"Nothing, nothing," Argon answered, feeling his pulse rise. What if there was a connection?

Two Months Ago

Titan, Deck 10, Docking Bay

Argon toiled alone in Hangar 23. It was quiet, and he liked it that way. It was way past midnight, and he still was fixing the AI of Raven. It was an old ship that his dad's friend had given to him and challenged him to fix as a joke. He had taken up the challenge, and many times regretted his decision. It had been two years, and still Raven was under repairs. The delays had been mostly because life got in the way. He had to study for his exams, get combat and pilot training, and then as a part of his qualification he had to spend six months on Earth for a project. But Argon could still remember the day the ship had arrived. He'd thought it was beautiful, though his father often referred to it as garbage.

Raven could easily hold over twenty people, but it wasn't a cargo ship. It was made for long flights and had a powerful engine. In the last two years, Argon had integrated every technology he could to upgrade it. Technology and parts were readily available on Titan, usually from the local recycling shops, or he could get them from engineering. Being good friends with the chief engineer had its benefits.

"Unable to comply," the computer said for the fifteenth time.

Argon rolled his eyes and stretched his back. He was getting tired. Deciding to try just one more time, he made slight adjustments to the server and wondered if increasing the computer's capacity and integrating another power server would do the trick. He pushed the button again.

"Raven online," said the computer.

"Yes!" Argon shouted, but then he heard a wheezing noise, and all the lights shut off. "Oh no," he muttered.

Frustrated, he left the ship and glared at the vessel. It was gray and broad at the end, narrow in front. Its exterior wasn't smooth like Titan's; it was covered with square bumps. Argon heard footsteps and turned to see Emmeline. He smiled. It wasn't unusual for her to stay awake so late. She must have been working, and as usual, once she was done, she'd come to find him.

"How's it going?" Emmeline asked, looking at Raven.

He liked that she was interested in technology and ships, and always keen to know what he was working on. "Not too good," he told her.

"You'll get there."

Another plus point. For the last two years, Argon's father, mother, and friends had regularly told him to give up on fixing Raven. Emmeline said the opposite. But today, he felt tired and jaded. "Maybe this is all I can do with it."

Emmeline folded her arms and asked, "Okay. Tell me how far you've come."

He knew what she was doing, but she always wanted to hear it again, and he liked to tell her. "I've updated the engine, the computer, and the server. Byron and I pulled out all the old interiors and refurnished it. Micah and Clio helped us fix all the holes in its haul. We fixed the landing gear. Now it has operational weapons. I had to beg Commander Waters for approval. She didn't want a private ship to be armed, but I convinced her."

"Wow, you've practically rebuilt it."

"You're right," Argon replied, remembering that Emmeline had helped him fix the engines.

"Looks like the AI is the last thing you need to fix," Emmeline said.

"Yeah, I don't know. Maybe I should ask for help. It's not working."

"Maybe you could ask Lieutenant Storm."

Argon wondered if Titan's chief engineer had the time, but when he thought about it, he realized they all had a lot of time on their hands. Things on Titan were rather quiet.

"Did you have dinner?" Emmeline asked.

"Not yet."

"Care to join me?"

He smiled. He wouldn't miss the opportunity.

TITAN, DECK 10, DOCKING BAY

"Are you sure about this?" asked Delta as she prepared to launch Astra.

Delta was a little older than Emmeline and her best friend since childhood. She remembered meeting Delta in one of the cottages in the mountains of northern hemisphere. She was hiking with her grandpa, and Delta was with her father who was a pilot delivering supplies in the region.

Delta was pretty, with long hair in shades of blue. She wore a body-fit red top with black pants, which looked like leather. Delta was a high-spirited pilot who flew a small cargo and passenger ship called Astra.

Emmeline sat in the co-pilot seat. "We can't be sure about anything until we get there."

Last night's dinner with Argon had gone well, and she was ready for her trip today. She'd told him about what she was doing, and he'd seemed worried. Once again, she'd had to remind him he didn't need to worry about her.

"Thanks for planning another adventure. Hauling cargo and passengers from Mars to Titan or to other colonies is no fun at all. I need a break!" Delta laughed.

"That's your job. Do you want to keep Astra or not?"

"Of course, I do, and it pays well. I can't imagine a day without my ship."

Astra was much older than its pilot. It had once belonged to Delta's father, and when he'd died, she'd inherited it. With its fourth-generation engine, it was much slower than the current ships and wasn't built for long-distance space travel. Astra was divided into three parts. The pilot's cockpit was attached to a small sitting area. Behind the sitting area were twenty chairs for passengers. If needed, the chairs could be folded to make space for cargo. The cargo bay was located between the propellers and the sitting area. The cargo section had a large door that opened outward and turned into a ramp.

Delta was Emmeline's best friend, but recently, whenever they were together, Emmeline couldn't help but feel envy. Delta never worried about a thing. Emmeline, on the other hand, felt trapped. Her days were spent doing administrative jobs, making sure all data from the scans was accurate, cataloged, and documented. It wasn't a terrible job, but she never thought she would be doing this forever. Everything she did was cross-checked and reanalyzed by Dr. Kent. She wanted to go to the next stage, but he seemed to want to keep her where she was. In a way, it was all her fault. She'd made a mistake, and she had to suffer the consequences.

The engines fired up, and Astra came to life. Emmeline began entering the coordinates and mapping a flight plan.

"Where's the fun in that?" Delta asked.

Emmeline eyed her.

"I know Earth is that way." Delta pointed her thumb to her left.

"I'm just following procedures."

"Darling, you need to spend more time with me."

Emmeline smirked.

The doors to the docking area opened. Then the shiny opaque shields of Titan dematerialized.

"Astra. You're clear to launch," said the operator on the intercom.

"Thanks, Samuel. I'll see you later."

A short laugh crackled on the radio. "Safe journey. I'll see you girls when you get back."

Emmeline sulked. Everyone liked Delta. Boys flirted with her and wanted to be around her. Emmeline just wasn't good at any of that. She liked Argon a lot, but she still held back. She thought that if she was stuck forever on Titan, he would stay as well. This worried her. He often mentioned flying away, and she didn't want his feelings for her to hold him back. Of course, she could join him on the same ship, but for that she needed her qualifications. She rolled her eyes; everything depended on her getting her credits.

Astra left Titan, swaying away from the giant space station. Emmeline looked at it. It filled the entire window. It was more than a station. It was a hub for interstellar exploration and trade and a refueling center. Soon, Astra raced full speed toward Earth.

"So, do you want to tell me where we're heading?" Delta asked.

"Earth."

Delta rolled her eyes. "Yeah. Earth is big. Where on Earth?"

Emmeline gulped and bit her lip. She remained silent for a while and then, in almost a whisper, said, "Sector 1001."

Delta's face turned stony. "What? Do you mean Quarantine Sector 1001? Why the hell would you want to go there?"

Emmeline lowered her eyes.

"Oh no. God! I can't believe I fell for it. Again! Not the fairy tale."

"It's not a fairy tale!"

"I don't understand you. Since you found that stupid ancient junk, you haven't been the same."

Emmeline crossed her arms. She feared that if she said anything more, Delta would turn around and head back to Titan. She had worked hard for this opportunity. She had spent the last three weeks lobbying three people to get into Sector 1001. She'd had to beg Dr. Kent to approve her leave.

"Emmeline. There's nothing for you in Sector 1001," Delta said. "There's nothing for any of us. What was it called? Oh, yeah. You mentioned it last time. New York. There's nothing there. The place is a tomb. Everything is dead!"

Astra's cockpit became silent.

"Not everything is dead," Emmeline replied softly.

Delta took a deep breath. "I'm sorry. I don't mean to be rude. But that place makes me sick. I hate it. I don't want to go there. We're not meant to be there. Something horrible happened, and I feel like that horror lives in its shadows."

Emmeline said nothing.

"A couple of months ago, I had a passenger," Delta continued. "A meteorologist who was being sent to conduct a standard survey of Sector 1001. He said it was fine during the day, but at night, he saw shadows and heard cries. As if something unnatural had survived the catastrophe. He believed demons lived in Sector 1001."

Emmeline rolled her eyes. "Demons don't exist! How can someone believe such stupid stuff?"

"People believe in what they want to believe in. Look at you! You believe in fairy tales and myths."

Emmeline remained quiet.

"I hate Nemesis!" Delta cried.

Emmeline didn't share Delta's obscure theories, but she loathed Nemesis as much as any other human being did. She wished it had never existed. Oh, if only she could turn the tides of time.

It had been 150 years ago, but it had left everyone scarred. It had shaken the planet and wiped out half of Earth's population.

The comet Nemesis had not been detected soon enough. Just a day later, and Earth would have been a bit further away. Just a day. But it wasn't to be. It had come out of nowhere. The military hadn't been ready. The scientists were helpless. No one had suspected anything.

Once detected, spaceships had been sent to destroy it, but they'd all failed. Nuclear weapons had been launched, blowing it to pieces. Half of the comet had perished in space, but the remaining half had split into two sizeable pieces that had gotten caught in Earth's gravitational field. One had impacted the North American continent, and the other had headed for Asia.

The two interstellar objects had struck the planet almost simultaneously. The impact had shaken the ground and created two mushroom clouds that spread for miles. Everything burned — streets, cities, countries, and homes. Everyone within a forty-mile radius of the impact had died instantly. The impact had created ridges in all directions, fracturing the ground and burying buildings and bridges.

But Nemesis was not done.

The sun was lost for days, and dangerous gases like sulfur and carbon monoxide had filled the air. The planet had become hotter, and radiation levels increased. The air turned to poison, and half of the planet's population died. Plants, animals, and anything else living in the affected regions had not been spared. Radiation poisoning had affected most of the survivors, deciding their fate in the coming months.

Help had arrived, but it hadn't been enough. The military had isolated all sources of radiation and locked them down using shields. The bodies of those who'd died were left behind. There'd been too many to carry or bury.

Almost ten years later, the sky had turned blue again. But it had taken over sixty years for humankind to get back on its feet, and the planet was still recovering. When the air had become breathable again, man had dared to visit and study the impact sites, which extended for miles. Those areas were still under lockdown. One of those areas was Sector 1001.

Something good had come out of the tragedy. It had forced humanity to build the perimeter. Once they'd built the perimeter, they'd focused on building space stations like Titan that were strong and powerful enough to destroy any rogue asteroids, comets, and anomalies threatening Earth.

"Why would you want to go there?" Delta asked.

Emmeline's thoughts returned to the present. "To look for it."

"Emmeline, it's just a story."

"I don't think so. When I was seven years old, my grandpa used to tell me stories about a mythical device. Its creators were unknown, and so were its whereabouts, but Grandpa was certain it existed. As a child, I always thought it was just a story. His father shared this family secret about a device that was ancient and magical. Although, his father thought it was folklore, Grandpa decided to look into it. He started asking questions and soon found out about a plaque. He discovered through interviewing his family that the plaque could be a map of some kind. Of course, it was all hearsay."

"A map to where?"

"I don't know. But he speculated that the plaque was the key to finding this mythical device."

"What do you think?" asked Delta. "Scientifically . . ."

"At first, I thought it could resemble the Tablet of Destinies. It's an ancient device of immense power mentioned in Greek Mythology."

"But that's fiction."

"I went through Grandpa's notes and logs about this device or plaque and couldn't find anything tangible. I've been studying my family's diaries for the past year."

"Yeah, I know. The ancient garbage." Delta sighed. "Why are you wasting your time?"

"It's not junk," Emmeline insisted. "The diaries are over five hundred years old. Most of them are personal logs. Some of them are computerized, and others are handwritten. Fortunately, the handwritten ones have been well preserved. I've spent a lot of time digitizing them. You can't imagine, it's like watching them living their lives. It's fascinating to hear how different their lives were than ours."

"Did they mention about Nemesis?"

"Oh, yeah. It was a cruel life. Our family had lost almost everything... but we were better off compared to others. We were fortunate not to be cruelly exposed..." She stopped and closed her eyes on remembering the horrors described by her ancestors.

The cockpit became silent.

"Did you find anything important related to the myth?" Delta asked.

"Last month, I found an entry in one of the diaries dated in the 1900s. It describes a plaque."

"Hold on," Delta said. "In the 1900s, they didn't have digital tablets?"

"In archaeology, a plaque or tablet was an ancient medium of writing."

"Ah, I see. What were they made of?"

"Clay, rock, or metal."

"Okay. What about this plaque?"

"It's made of rock and was found when a bunch of explorers sailed to a frozen continent called Antarctica," Emmeline explained. "As soon as they returned to their homeland, they sold it to the highest bidder. Fortunately for us, the highest bidder was a lady of some power."

"You found her diary?" asked Delta.

"Not hers, but her son kept written notes and made drawings of the plaque. There are a couple of them in the diaries. Then he married and had a daughter. The plaque was passed on for generations."

"Wait a minute. You told me the diaries you have belong to the twentieth century. This plaque appears to be ancient," Delta said.

"I think it was bought by our family in the nineteenth century and remained with us for generations," Emmeline replied. "Down the line, a young girl found it in the basement of her father's old home. Her name was Beverly Watcher. She was the first person to study it with a historian."

"Did they find anything?"

"No. To the best of the historian's knowledge, it wasn't of any known origin. But he noted the plaque had a figure which looked like a sun and seventeen circular indentations on it. He couldn't interpret what it meant."

"So, this Beverly lady had this plaque all this time but found nothing?"

"No. I think, at some point, she gave up," Emmeline replied. "Remember, they had very limited resources in the nineteenth century. No one cared about it until the twenty-third century. Out of curiosity, Alexander Hendrix, one of my ancestors began studying it."

"And?" Delta asked.

Emmeline gave a weak smile. "And there is the greatest mystery of my family. After that, Alexander and the plaque both disappeared."

"What? How could someone just disappear?"

Emmeline had many theories, but she was reluctant to share them. Unfortunately, his disappearance had earned him a reputation as a traitor because he'd vanished with important information about Nemesis and he was wanted by the Imperial Command. Emmeline decided to keep this information to herself for now. "I agree. People don't just vanish into thin air. I studied his personal logs, and I traced his disappearance back to Sector 1001."

"Did he die on impact?"

"No. He and his family were traveling at the time and survived the catastrophe. But he was a planetary geologist."

"So?"

"Who led one of the teams elected to study Nemesis."

"Ah. Now, that is interesting," Delta replied. "What did he find?"

"That's the thing. No one knows," Emmeline responded. "He worked for five years on that project, spending every day collecting, analyzing, and cataloging his findings. He and other teams reported hundreds of elements found in Nemesis. Then one day, he just disappeared. So, did most of his data and the plaque."

They became silent for a moment.

"Maybe he found something. Something he shouldn't have had. He reported it to the government, and they killed him. Or perhaps it was the government who built Nemesis and targeted it at Earth," Delta speculated.

Emmeline folded her arms. "We don't have that kind of technology. And why would our government destroy its own world?"

"You're right," said Delta. "But you have to admit, it's bizarre."

"There is another possibility," Emmeline continued.

"What?"

"He didn't want anyone to know what he'd found."

"Why? Why would he do that?"

"I don't know. It's just a thought."

Silence dominated the cockpit for a few moments.

"Well, thank you for the history lesson. Alexander is possibly dead. The plaque is lost. I don't give a damn about Nemesis. So why are we going to Sector 1001?"

"Two months ago, I put together Alexander 's entries, his data and his logs," Emmeline said.

"And you found nothing. Again! Did you check his rock collection?"

"I did. Nothing unusual there."

"But you found something. I can sense it."

"While others disregarded his personal logs as mere words, I could not," said Emmeline. "One thing I realized from his diaries was that the guy loved solving puzzles and uncovering hidden clues. He also liked to create puzzles and leave clues for his daughter to find. I ran all kinds of encryption algorithms on his logs. I searched for any encrypted keywords or hidden texts. Found nothing. Then I came across a poem written by him to his dear wife, stored in a vacuum document protector."

Delta nodded.

"I did all kinds of tests on it."

"Enough. Tell me you found something."

"I think you should see it to believe it."

Delta raised her eyebrows and gave a mischievous smile. She placed Astra on autopilot, and they left the cockpit.

They sat at a small table. Emmeline reached for her bag and took out a silver box. Then she took out a triangular glass object.

"What are you doing with a prism?" Delta asked.

"Just watch," Emmeline said. "Astra, turn the lights off."

The room turned dark, and Emmeline placed the silver box opposite to the prism. Then she pushed a button on the silver box. A sharp beam of light passed through the prism, and a band of colorful light appeared from the other side.

"Okay. Now impress me," Delta remarked.

"As you know, when white light goes through a prism, it splits into seven colors."

"Yeah. Everyone knows that."

"The wavelength and the refraction angle determine the ratios of colors we see in the rainbow," said Emmeline. "Don't worry. I will not bore you with the details." She reached for her pad and punched in a few numbers. There was a slight variation in the colors of the rainbow.

The document protector looked like an A4-size glass frame. Emmeline placed her palm on the document protector. It came to life and began glowing. Sentences began appearing on the glass, and it recited the terms and conditions of opening this preserved document. Emmeline waited for it to finish, then said, "I agree."

The frame slowly opened from three sides. The thin plastic film covering the document moved like a book opening. Emmeline gently picked up the letter and placed it in the path of the multi-colored beam. Suddenly, the old-looking paper turned golden and glowed.

On it appeared a message: *The secret to the stars, their end and the beginnings, lies in the crypt of your ancestors.*

"Wow!" Delta cried out, leaning forward. "How did you do that?"

"I found it by accident. I'd been trying for days to find a clue about this plaque. Frankly, I'd given up. Four weeks ago, I was sitting with my desk lamp on, and the rest of the room was dark. I was drinking tea and placed my glass between the lamp and the document, and it began glowing. At first, I could only see the letter *S*. It took me a while to figure out that it would take a prism to unlock the entire message."

"So, it appears only when exposed to a certain spectrum of light?" asked Delta.

Emmeline nodded. "Yes. A very specific spectrum. As you know, infrared and ultraviolet rays always form the borders of a rainbow. Infrared is the highest, and ultraviolet is the lowest. In this case, the distribution of the wavelengths had to be exact." She referred to the pad. "Infrared at 800, red at 700 nanometers, orange and yellow at 650 nanometers, green and blue at 500 nanometers, and violet at 400 nanometers. This distribution ends with ultraviolet at 300 nanometers."

"How did you find this?"

"It was hard," Emmeline admitted. "The computer must have run a million algorithms. But once I had it, that appeared."

They sat wordlessly, looking at the glowing letter.

Delta faced Emmeline. "This must be really important. What are the odds of this spectrum of light hitting this letter?"

"None unless someone was looking for it."

"What do you think it means?"

"I think the message is straightforward. Let's go to Sector 1001 and look in my ancestors' crypt."

TITAN, DECK 10, MIDNIGHT ORCHID

With Emmeline gone to Earth, Argon felt more alone. Then he found out that Selina had escaped school. He tracked her down to Midnight Orchid. She didn't seem to be bothered by the attention of a group of traders visiting the space station. Argon wasn't worried because the bartender was his friend and promised he would look out for her.

Argon didn't rush his little sister away from her new friends. Instead, he watched as she chatted away to them. He was a bit surprised since her teacher had told him she was very shy. *Perhaps she didn't like her teacher*, he thought.

Soon, Selina left the group and ran to embrace Argon. He didn't scold her, though a part of him told him he should. She was on Titan, and she was wearing her communicator. She was safe, but he was still worried.

"I know. I know. I shouldn't have left," Selina said. "But school is so boring."

Argon smiled. It was almost time for her to go home anyway, so they walked toward their quarters.

As soon as they entered, they found Aceline walking up and down the living room. "Darling! Where were you?" she said, picking Selina up. "Please don't do that! Your teacher called and told me you were missing."

"Mom. You shouldn't worry. As long as I'm on Titan, no harm will ever come to me."

Argon studied his mother's worried face.

Selina looked from one face to another, "Believe me. As long as I am on Titan, no harm will ever come to me."

Argon smiled. "You're right, Selina," he said. "But you shouldn't leave without telling the teacher."

"You do," she argued.

"We're adults."

"So, I'm treated differently because I'm a child?" Selina sulked. "I am not just a child!"

Argon changed the subject. "Tell me, Selina, how did you get out."

Selina made a face as Aceline put her down.

"I'm not telling you! You don't understand. You will never understand!" she cried out, turned and walked into her room. Aceline and Argon looked at each other.

"Mom?"

"I don't know. I don't know what to say… she is what she is."

Argon bit his lips. Is Selina telling the truth? Could she just tell the computer to do what she wanted it to do? Of course, the odds of any harm coming to Selina on Titan were low, but how did she know she was safe? Wasn't she afraid?

CHAPTER 4: SECTOR 1001

ASTRA

Delta reduced speed as Astra flew past the Challenger colony.

Emmeline cast her eyes over the colony that stood between Earth and the moon. It was over 100,000 kilometers away from Earth, a sort of midpoint between two planetary bodies. From above, the colony looked like an enormous snowflake. The middle section was round, and from it, five long cylindrical passageways spread in all directions. At the end of each passageway were two smaller extensions. These were ports for spaceships. Three of the spaceports were occupied. Emmeline remembered watching the stars with her grandpa as a child, trying to identify all the constellations. From Earth, the Challenger colony looked like a shiny dot.

Emmeline looked ahead. The big blue planet dominated the viewscreen.

"Why do we have to go through this every time?" Delta complained.

Emmeline smiled.

Ships going to restricted areas on the Earth needed a permit. These sections were not tourist sites, and civilians were prohibited. Most of the quarantine sections were hubs for environmentalists, scientists, and medical researchers. Although Emmeline already had a permit, the guard ships would check their credentials.

There was another place that was restricted to civilians, and no matter how much she tried, Emmeline would never get access. But why would she want to go to a criminal facility?

Enforcement of law and order by the Imperial Command was common practice. The punishments for law-breaking were severe, but treatment of prisoners was mostly humane. Still, there were exceptions. Emmeline's eyes rolled up, surveying the cold northern hemisphere. There, somewhere, was the Specter colony, a prison created for criminals, its computers designed to deliver merciless sentences.

Astra slowed down when two guard ships blocked their way. Delta opened a channel. "This is Astra. We have authorization to land and visit Sector 1001."

Emmeline always wondered who'd designed the guard ships. They looked like huge gray eggs with a round red area right in the middle. She narrowed her eyes and saw the pilot through the red glass. The guard ships were heavily armed, but she didn't understand the logic behind guarding these sections. Why would people want to go to that area of Earth? It was flooded with radiation, had low levels of oxygen, and had been barren for over hundred years.

The robotic voice on the commlink said, "Checking credentials. Please wait."

Emmeline surveyed the bright white light surrounding the planet. Nemesis had forced humanity to think outside of the box. It had taken them years to build the generators, and the amount of energy required for this endeavor had been tremendous. But it had been worth it. Emmeline had not shared this with anyone, but Alexander Hendrix and her grandpa had speculated that the mythical device was a source of extreme power. If she succeeded in finding it, it could reduce their dependence on fuel, alloys, nuclear power, and solar energy. Exploring deep space would be much easier. It could change everyone's life, including hers.

"Credentials approved. You can approach Sector 1001.

Please be aware that Sector 1001 is an abandoned and hazardous area. Please wear protective gear. In case of emergency, contact the nearest guard ship. You are not allowed to stay in the area for over ten hours. When your time is up, leave immediately. If you fail to do so, the guards will escort you out of Sector 1001. Do not take any objects out of this region without conducting a thorough scan."

"Oh, shut up," muttered Delta, but the guard ship didn't.

"Be cautious. To avoid detention outcasts and criminals, sneak into Sector 1001. If under threat, immediately contact the nearest guard ship." The robot recited all the safety precautions and measures.

Emmeline waited patiently.

Soon, the guard ships cleared the way, and Delta guided Astra closer to the white shields. A flashing bright light appeared, and a gate opened.

The computer announced, "Welcome, Delta Dune and Emmeline Augury. We hope you have a pleasant stay." Then it fell silent once more.

Delta guided Astra through the huge spiral gate and entered the Earth's atmosphere. Astra shuddered. Emmeline grabbed her chair and heard something rattle. She glanced at Delta, but she didn't seem worried. Astra rocked, and a loud beeping noise echoed in the cockpit.

"Ah, don't worry," Delta said, increasing speed.

"That's a bad idea," Emmeline warned her.

The ship vibrated. Emmeline could hear the engines screaming. What she saw next scared her even more. Bright beams of yellow light surrounded them; the temperature rose inside the cockpit. Astra jolted. "Delta?" said Emmeline.

Before Delta could reply, Astra crossed the troposphere and flew smoothly miles above the ground.

"All good," Delta replied, smiling.

Emmeline relaxed.

It was early in the morning. Astra flew over the Pacific Ocean, and the sun shone over the horizon in the cloudless sky.

Emmeline saw tall buildings in the distance. Several small craft hovered about the buildings like bees. *Life moves on*, Emmeline thought.

SECTOR 1001

Astra approached Sector 1001, and sadness washed over Emmeline. She could only imagine the horror of the people who had witnessed the incident.

Soon, they approached another whitish dome. As Astra flew closer, Delta eased it down toward the circular gate. "Here we go again."

Two guard ships approached them. While Delta dealt with the guard ships, Emmeline looked beyond the dome. This was her second visit to Sector 1001 in the last two years. Her father did not approve, but she wanted to solve this family puzzle. She wanted to know if the fairy tale was true.

She eyed the barren landscape. It stood solemn, even under the beautiful cloudless sky. The comet's impact had created such an inferno that, although it had touched the ground miles from here, it had turned everything to dust.

It was a sorry sight. A few buildings stood strong, others half broken and fallen to pieces. The structures that had survived bore the wounds of the hit and had turned black over time. A few streams of muddy contaminated water flowed under the three crippled bridges. Emmeline eyed a small army of robots working near the riverbank. The cleanup was ongoing. She didn't know if it would ever be successful; no one did.

The circular gates whizzed open. Delta eased Astra into the sector, and Emmeline felt as if she had entered an alien world, a strange world. The dome extended for miles and was built not only to stop people from entering the area but also to minimize the aftereffects of the impact.

Scientists estimated tons of carbon monoxide had been released into the air. Nemesis had also damaged four nuclear reactors, releasing toxins. These shields had been erected on the seventh day of impact to secure all the areas affected by it. At first, the shields hadn't been effective enough to contain the gases. It had taken a while to improve them, but finally, repeated efforts had paid off. From what Emmeline had heard, similar procedures had been carried out on the Eastern continent, and people had salvaged what they could.

Emmeline felt a bump when Delta set Astra down on the banks of the Hudson River.

"We can't land in the city," Delta explained. "Too much rubble."

"Okay," Emmeline replied and turned to the panel. "Oxygen levels are normal. Atmospheric pressure is normal. There are no dust storms for now. Radiation levels are 150 Sv. Safe, but I recommend we wear suits. Carbon dioxide levels are high. Our helmets should protect us. It's hot out there, almost 110 Fahrenheit."

"All clear?"

"All clear."

"Let's go," Delta said, putting Astra in surveillance mode.

They left the cockpit and entered the cargo bay. Emmeline opened the closet and grabbed her suit. She unbuckled her jumper and stripped down to her underwear. Delta did the same. The suits very much looked like wetsuits and were made of thick but soft glossy material. They were designed to protect their wearers from chemical agents, radiation, and harsh changes in the atmosphere.

Emmeline looked at herself. The suit was tight, curved around her rounded hips. She felt the material sticking to her skin. She glanced at Delta, who she thought looked marvelous.

"You have a figure," Delta remarked.

Emmeline ignored her. Delta took every opportunity to remind her to wear better clothes. But she couldn't be bothered.

She tapped her fingers on the small screen embedded near the wrist of her suit. The screen came to life and assessed her vitals. It measured her heart rate, blood pressure, body temperature, and respiratory rate. Then it shifted to the surrounding environment. It calculated levels of oxygen, carbon dioxide, nitrogen, dust, radiation, and so on. Emmeline put on her helmet and pushed the green button on the screen on her wrist.

"Helmet active," said a voice inside it.

The transparent screen of the helmet displayed the same information. Emmeline picked up her backpack. It was a flat black bag and was made of hard material. She pulled out a pad and turned it on.

Delta came to stand beside her. "Well?"

"It's a long walk, about ten kilometers from here."

"That won't be a problem."

"Oh?"

"I arranged for transport," Delta replied gleefully.

They stepped into the loading bay. Emmeline stopped dead in her tracks when she saw two motorcycles. Her jaw dropped, and a surge of excitement ran through her body.

"Well, what do you think?" asked Delta.

One bike was red, the other blue. They looked heavy. The metallic cover hid most of the parts except the wheels and the exhaust.

"Oh my God!" cried Emmeline.

"What do you think? Aren't they wonderful?"

Suddenly, dreadful thoughts clouded Emmeline's mind. "Delta, what were you thinking?"

"Yeah, that's the enthusiasm I was looking for!" Delta scoffed. "This is what I get for hanging out with a nerd."

"That's not it. You know I love bikes! Where did you get these? They look old. They must be expensive!"

"They still make them, although these are older. I got these at an auction on the eastern continent about two weeks ago. Great bikes with a fantastic combination of speed and comfort. Not made for racing, but they can go up to 100 miles per hour with their 750cc electric engines. I must work really hard for the next few months to pay for them, for Astra's fuel too."

Emmeline's jaw dropped. "You spent all your money? You're nuts!"

Delta shrugged. "What can I say? I like my toys. Anyhow, it's my birthday gift."

"Your birthday is six months away!"

"Hey, don't spoil the fun," Delta argued.

Emmeline fell silent.

"And don't tell Mom."

Emmeline rolled her eyes. "Why did you have to buy two?"

"I bought the second one at half price," Delta said, smiling as if this justified it. "Once we're done here, I'll store them on Titan for a while, then sell one bike for a profit."

"Where will you ride them?"

"You know me. I'll find a road somewhere," Delta said, winking.

Emmeline smiled and chose the blue one.

"Hope you still know how to ride," Delta teased.

Emmeline eyed her. She had grown up around three men who were enthusiastic about machines. She didn't remember playing in a backyard or with dolls. No. At the age of nine, she remembered her brother teaching her how to ride his bike. They'd never stopped since then, not until she'd moved to Titan two years ago.

"Astra, prepare to open the loading bay," Delta said.

Emmeline smiled, got on the bike.

Astra announced, "Loading bay doors opening."

The huge brown doors opened outward. Light flooded into the cargo bay. Emmeline saw the dusty, cracked, and rocky path ahead. She pushed the red button, and her bike came to life.

"Preparing for departure," stated Astra.

Loud noises echoed inside the craft. Beep. Beep. Beep. The lights turned green.

"Here we go!" Delta shouted.

The bikes raced over the ramp and left a trail of dust as they charged along the riverbank. Emmeline could almost hear her heart racing over the roar of the engine. She felt bumps as she rode the bike over the cracked road, and a broad smile spread across her face. She had forgotten what having fun felt like.

As they neared the bridge, Emmeline saw that the road ahead was covered with rubble. The bike bounced over the rocks. Sweat trickled down her forehead, and her breathing quickened. But the speed was exhilarating. Excitement like she hadn't felt for days returned. She felt several bumps but stayed in control of the motorcycle. Emmeline swayed her bike around a few flipped vehicles, and Delta raced her bike to ride alongside her.

"Having fun yet?" Delta asked.

"Delta, you're the best!"

"Tell me something I don't know!"

The bikes raced ahead, then turned to the bridge. Emmeline realized that at some point, the bridge had been a marvel of steel and cables. She saw six lanes, separated by pale white lines. The tall towers holding the structure together cast shadows over the road. She looked to both sides and imagined how beautiful the city must have looked when it had been alive.

"Hey, stop daydreaming!" Delta shouted as she rushed ahead.

Emmeline increased speed. Part of her wanted to remove the helmet and feel the fresh air. But that wasn't possible just yet. A huge tilted vehicle sat in the middle of the road. She swerved her bike around it and gained speed. She spotted a large gap ahead. The tower to her left had crumbled, and the other side of the bridge was tilted. "Delta?"

"It's not big. Come on. We can do it," Delta replied and picked up pace.

Emmeline wasn't sure. It was risky. But she liked it. Emmeline watched Delta's bike leap over the gap and land on the other side. A wave of excitement hit her. Emmeline increased speed, and her vehicle bounced over the gap. "Woohoo!" she shouted.

The two bikes entered the city.

Sunlight hardly penetrated the jungle of broken structures that loomed over the vehicles. The path was broken and blocked in several places. It was hard to maneuver the bikes around the obstacles. Emmeline's helmet regularly reminded her of the polluted air and high radiation levels. But she was having so much fun, she didn't care. She just wanted to keep riding.

After thirty minutes, they reached the coordinates and came to a stop in front of a collapsed iron gate. Emmeline turned off the engine, and dead silence surrounded them. There was no breeze. Not a bird, leaf, or flower in sight. The city was gray, dead, and lifeless. The damaged gate, the burned trees, and the half-fallen roof of the house scared her.

Once inside the premises, Emmeline parked her bike in front of a partially collapsed main door. She got off and looked at the ground. The cement bore huge potholes. But that wasn't what caught her attention. She kneeled to touch the tiny green leaf sprouting out of the ground. Against all odds, it had somehow survived. *Life finds a way*, she thought.

Inside, Emmeline stood in the living room with her feet apart, surveying the old rusted building. She reached for her backpack and grabbed a square-shaped scanner. Her eyes slowly moved from the half-fallen ceiling to the weather-beaten walls, which were riddled with massive holes. The white paint had almost disappeared, and the bricks beneath it were exposed. Her heart filled with warmth as she reached for the broken wooden crib that stood in a corner. She studied the data her scanner had collected. She sulked. Nothing. There was no crypt here. But she didn't give up. She kept scanning and walked around the ruins, trying her best not to touch anything.

Although she left the building empty-handed, Emmeline felt content. She felt the house was at peace, happy to be left as it was. It held great memories of her family, especially her grandfather. She smiled to herself.

"Anything?" Delta asked, appearing from behind the structure.

"There's a structure under the house, but there's no crypt," said Emmeline. "What about you?"

"Only dirt, cement, and rocks. The other side of the house is a big pile of gravel and nothing else. Let's check again. Then we can count this house out."

Emmeline was confused.

Delta's thin lips stretched into a wide smile. "Don't you remember? You told me there was another house, older than this one."

Emmeline recalled her grandfather telling her about the other house. Fear rushed through her body as she also remembered he hadn't liked it. No one in her family did.

"Are you coming?" asked Delta, heading into the house.

Emmeline looked at her. Her heart was beating faster than ever. "Give me a moment, will you?"

Delta gave her a quizzical look but turned and disappeared into the house without questioning her.

Emmeline grabbed her pad and went through the entries in the diaries — not her grandpa's but the ones that had been written long before he'd been born. No one knew it, but Emmeline had discovered encrypted entries in several of the diaries that dated back to the early twenty-first century. Her grandpa hadn't found them because he hadn't thought to check if they were encrypted.

After her grandfather's death, Emmeline had acquired all documents relating to her family. Some had been found in the basements of her relatives, others in a vault sealed by her ancestors. It had been hard to get them, but because Emmeline was a descendent of the Augury family, these documents belonged to her by law. It was in the vault where she had discovered numerous diaries and personal logs. The unidentified writer lived in the twenty first century and had encrypted most of the logs. She'd had a friend decode them.

"The other house . . ." she muttered. Was it true? She

wanted to be sure. She stopped pushing buttons when she found the entry:

The other house has a deadly secret. I have seen it, felt it, and witnessed what it can do. It is so unbelievable. I cannot even tell it to my father or my wife. There is nothing to do but hope and wish that it is never discovered.

Blood drained from Emmeline's face.

When Emmeline and Delta left the house, they rode their bikes north. As she drove to her destination, Emmeline could feel all her hopes fading away. Her father was right. It was all a wild goose chase. There was nothing here. On the other hand, investigating might give her the closure she needed to move on. Her attention was drawn to the deserted, dusty road. She tried to recall all the information about the old house. It was a preserved family heirloom and had been used as a guest house for several years. Most of the time, the family had lived in the city house.

From the encrypted logs, Emmeline remembered one sentence: *Old sins cast long shadows and hide in the dragon's wake.*

She didn't understand what it meant, and she had no one she could ask. This anonymous writer had mentioned the dragon quite a few times. But when Emmeline had checked human history, she'd discovered that dragons were legendary creatures, a part of folklore.

The sun shone brightly in the sky, and the air was thin and dry. The temperature rose, or at least it felt like it. Emmeline slowed her bike down when she saw Delta dodge a few potholes in the middle of the road. She followed her, swaying her bike to and fro. When they cleared the potholes, she increased her speed to match Delta's.

As they approached their destination, both of them slowed down. It was a similar picture, but there were no big skyscrapers here. On both sides of the sandy road were skeletons of cement and steel. The houses were long gone. One or two poles stood where Emmeline supposed there had once been fences. The bikes moved effortlessly along the snake-like road. They turned and found that the road ahead was engulfed by tall, crooked, burned trees that bent inward, leaning toward the ground.

"How much further?" inquired Delta on the intercom.

Emmeline looked down at the display. "It should be coming up now." A moment later, she glanced up, and her jaw fell open in surprise. Under the clear blue sky stood a big house.

"Wow! This is beautiful. I don't believe it's still standing!" said Delta.

Emmeline smiled automatically, but she knew it was barely standing. The historical society had decided to preserve all heritage buildings that were structurally sound and environmentally friendly. This included private properties. Fortunately, her ancestors had put in the effort to refurbish the house. But despite their efforts, over the years, the building had begun to crumble, and her father wasn't doing anything to keep it standing. To Emmeline, it seemed he wanted to bury their history deep beneath the ground.

The girls slowed their bikes as they neared the iron gates.

Emmeline stopped her bike beside Delta's. "What are the radiation levels?"

"Minimal," replied Delta.

They removed their helmets. Emmeline was glad for the chance to breathe fresh air. Titan was great, but the air there wasn't natural. Nor was the gravity. Emmeline had lived most of her life on Earth, and although she had been on Titan for over two years, she still missed the natural beauty of her planet. Earth had changed, while in the past most of the parts in the northern hemisphere would be covered in snow, now it hardly snowed, and most of the population had moved either to the north or the south. When she was young, she spent every summer with her grandpa in his cottage, in Canada. While her brothers taught her how to drive a bike, she learned a lot about space crafts from her grandpa. His old rusting private ship was one of the best things she had learned to fly.

A low humming dominated the air.

"Security shield?" inquired Delta.

"Yeah," Emmeline replied, looking at the house. She could see that the wall facing the gates was shattered in places, and the west wall had partially collapsed. The new alloy used to stabilize the house was clearly visible. She walked toward the panel near the gate and punched in the codes. The humming noise stopped, and the old rusty gates slowly opened inward. The girls drove onto the premises. As they got off their bikes, the security shield closed behind them.

Emmeline looked at the old building and wondered how it had lasted so long.

Delta had already started scanning. "We have five hours to get out of here."

Emmeline nodded and began working.

Delta slowly strolled in the opposite direction. "I think we should be careful," she called behind her. "Most of the structure is compromised. It could collapse at any time."

Emmeline heard her and kept walking. Delta was right; her scanners told her that one day, the house would collapse. Her heart sank, she wished it wouldn't. It reminded her of the old castles made of large stones. They stood the test of time, and a part of her wished the same for this house. She touched the wall, and she knew it wasn't logical, but she felt a connection to it. Her scanner began beeping loudly. Her eyes widened in surprise. "Delta!" she called out.

Delta came running toward her. "What?"

"It's unbelievable," Emmeline whispered, pointing her scanner toward a large pile of rocks. Beyond them were traces of human remains.

They walked over the sandy ground and climbed over the heaps of old rock that had molded together with time. Emmeline stood in the middle of a cluster of crooked brown trees. The ground was covered with rocks, mud, and sand. She slowly moved ahead, leaving the trees behind. The scanners beeped loudly.

"Okay, yes, there are human remains here." Emmeline turned to her right. The beeping noise amplified. She moved her device back and forth. "Oh, this is a graveyard," she said.

Delta turned around to face her.

Emmeline didn't move from her spot. She was unsure of how she felt about walking on someone's grave. As if sensing her discomfort, Delta took a step back.

Emmeline got to her knees and kept on scanning. "Four, to be exact," she said in a soft voice.

"Agreed," Delta said.

"They died a long time ago," Emmeline drawled.

"This is a crypt," said Delta. "If Alexander was right, this is where the secret should be buried."

Emmeline felt uncomfortable. She didn't want to disturb someone's resting place, especially not her family's. Her scans had found cement, human remains, and nothing else. If the mystical device or plaque was buried here, the scanners would have picked it up, surely. She got to her feet.

"This is creepy," Delta remarked, looking at something.

Emmeline spun and looked at the vast wall, which was covered with a maze of dried twigs and branches. Big cracks emerged from the ground and spread across it. "This is the east wing," she said, remembering.

Delta eyed her. "The what?"

"The house has two wings, east and west. This is the east wing."

Delta rolled her eyes. "Did the diaries mention it was creepy?"

Emmeline managed a bleak smile and began scanning. Again, her scanner beeped.

Delta looked over her shoulder. "What?"

Emmeline didn't answer immediately. She compared her scans of the west wing to those of the east wing. Something wasn't right.

"What?" Delta asked again.

"There's something down there," Emmeline replied,

pointing toward the base of the wall.

"You mean a hidden structure?" Delta asked, checking her scans.

"Or a crypt," Emmeline said happily.

They entered the east wing. Emmeline's hands trembled, and her heart beat faster and faster. Her hands were sweaty. She didn't know if it was fear or excitement. She turned and paused. The scanner showed traces of copper. She looked up, and a chill ran down her spine. Her breath quickened. On the wall was a gigantic shadow. She knew it at once. A shadow of the mythical creature she had read about, the dragon. Her hands reached for her neck as she eyed it. The metal frame and the sculpture had disintegrated a long time ago, but the shadow remained.

"That's really creepy," Delta said, stating the obvious.

Emmeline nodded robotically. She knew what the scanners showed, but she felt as if the shadow was trying to tell her something. It was a warning. She remembered the diaries, and the constant hint by the writer to be careful in this house. For the first time since she'd begun this journey, she felt danger.

"There it is," Delta said.

Emmeline put her thoughts aside and joined Delta.

They stood near a collapsed staircase. Delta was scanning the wall. "The entrance to the crypt was from the first floor. But it's been sealed by the collapse of the staircase and this section of the house."

They walked through another doorframe and came to a stop between several racks. Emmeline looked down at the papers and the skeletons of rotten books. She bent over and looked through the collapsed floor. Then she looked up at Delta. "If I'm correct, if we climb down, we could get to the crypt this way."

Securing the rope, Emmeline was the first to climb down into the dark void. She assumed the basement was at least ten feet underground. When her feet set on the floor, she got the chance to look around. She saw a collapsed wall with a small opening at the top. Her scans showed that there was another room beyond it.

Followed by Delta, she crawled through the small opening and entered the dark room. The air was stale, but surprisingly, there were no odors. Her flashlight barely cut through the darkness. An icy shiver rushed through her. She felt like she was being watched. She took out her scanner and began scanning. The device detected nothing.

"Anything?" Delta asked.

Emmeline studied her face.

Delta looked calm and composed. "You okay?" she asked.

Emmeline moistened her lips. She could feel it but couldn't see it. Maybe this was why her grandpa hadn't like coming here. She remembered his words, "I don't want you to go there alone…ever… understood?" Maybe this was what her ancestor had found out. Maybe they'd felt a presence.

Emmeline turned her attention to the room. It appeared as if frozen in time. It was as big as the upper floor, covered with dust but protected from the calamities that had struck above. The walls were cracked. Framed paintings had fallen to the floor and turned to dust. The skeletons of two big couches sat in a corner. The carpet had degraded, and the old cement floor was visible underneath it. Three benches still stood, holding broken glasses.

Emmeline turned to the wall behind her. Her scanner beeped once, then twice. Then it went crazy. Using her hands, Emmeline cleared the dust off the wall and took a step back. On the wall was a picture of a dragon in a circle. Just like in the diaries. It looked like a logo. She turned to her scanner. On the other side of the rock, there were traces of stone, glass, and metal.

Suddenly, Emmeline felt a cold touch on her neck. She gasped and turned around. Darkness surrounded her, but she felt certain there was someone there. She glanced at Delta, but she didn't seem to sense it. Emmeline stood in dead silence, watching for a few moments, then turned toward the wall again.

"Did you find something?" asked Delta.

"Yes." Emmeline gestured toward the wall, trying to control her beating heart.

Delta scanned the area. "You're right. There's something behind this. But we can't blast through. We'd have to remove few stones." Delta touched the wall.

They used knives to cut through the concrete.

"This is odd," Delta pointed out. "Look at this. The cement here looks. . . new."

Emmeline leaned forward and saw that the cement they had just removed was whiter than the cement around the other stones. "You're right. Someone may have found the compartment and resealed it."

It took a while, but eventually, they were done. They removed four stones and put them on the floor.

Delta illuminated the interior with her flashlight. "Okay. This might be it."

Emmeline stepped forward and saw old cloth. She unfolded the cloth and saw something glowing under her flashlight. It was a rock in an airtight container.

"That's a special container, isn't it?" Delta remarked.

"Yes. Usually used by geologists to preserve samples," Emmeline answered. The sample had been well preserved, and the tamper-proof glass container was intact without a scratch.

"What's it doing here?" Delta asked.

"I have no idea. I was looking for the plaque. Let's take it with us." Emmeline handed it to her friend. Then she reached for the next object. In her hands, she held a plaque made of stone. It was rectangular, about thirty centimeters in length and twenty centimeters in height. On it were deep lines, possibly carved by a sharp object. The lines originated from a semicircle on the top and went sideways, looking like sunrays. Emmeline flipped it over and saw small circular indents in the left-hand corner. She counted them. In total, there were seventeen.

Stone made plaque (front and back)

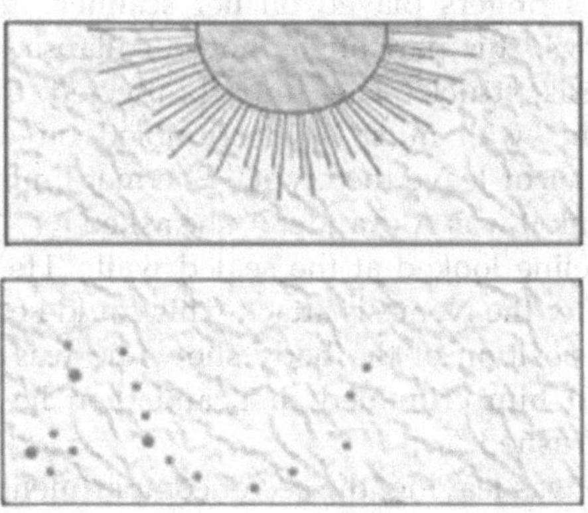

"I'll look around to see if there's anything else," Delta said before walking away.

Emmeline stared at the plaque as if waiting for it to reveal its secret. She heard a beeping noise.

"Emmeline. . ."

There was something in Delta's voice that terrified her. She turned and saw Delta at the far end of the hall, standing in front of an opening that might once have been an arch-shaped door. Now it was sealed by stones.

"There's someone here," Delta hissed.

Emmeline's heart pounded. She left the plaque on the floor and joined Delta.

"There are human remains, but these are less than a hundred years old," Delta explained. "Not like the ones we found in the garden."

Emmeline studied her scanner.

"But these aren't buried," continued Delta. "He died here."

The data started pouring in. "He was middle-aged," Emmeline said, watching the information light up her scanner. "The skeleton has multiple fractures. It has been. . . smashed." She scanned the area above the arch. "He might have died when the wall collapsed."

Delta's fingers played on her scanner. "According to these readings, this part of the house collapsed a few years after Nemesis struck. The impact affected the structural integrity. This wall must have crumbled on whoever was trying to enter or leave the crypt." She met Emmeline's eyes. "Do you think it was Alexander?" she asked.

Emmeline looked at the sealed wall. "He disappeared five years after the Nemesis attack. This could be why."

"The position of the body shows he was leaving. The stone behind him crumbled first, and then he was thrown ahead and crushed."

"If he was leaving, the secret compartment would have been left open," Emmeline argued.

Delta nodded. "Maybe he resealed it and was on his way home."

Emmeline felt sad. "He should have been careful." She stood quietly, wondering. The one ancestor who'd known about the plaque had died trying to find it, and when he found it, why did he reseal the compartment and leave? Why didn't he take it with him? Why did he leave a rock sample with it? She didn't know.

A robotic voice echoed, "Emmeline Augury and Delta Dune. You have exactly two-and-a-half hours to leave Sector 1001. I repeat: you have exactly two-and-a-half hours to leave Sector 1001. If you fail to comply, the guard ships will escort you out of this region. If you fail to comply or accompany the guard ships, an official investigation will be launched."

Before it could continue, Delta answered back, "Guard ship. This is Delta Dune. Don't worry, we'll be leaving soon."

"Affirmative. Thank you for acknowledging my message. I will keep a lock on your signal."

"It could be someone else... a thief?" Emmeline

wondered.

"Only one way to find out," said Delta.

Emmeline felt her stomach twist.

Delta kneeled. "Okay. One of the bones is just beyond these rocks. Should we get it?"

"Is it safe?" asked Emmeline.

"We could use the laser cutter. I'll lower the intensity of the beam. If we can get a bone, we can get a DNA match and find out if this was really Alexander."

"If it is, we'll come back for him. I'm not leaving him here."

Delta smiled. "Of course."

It took a lot of patience, but slowly, the red beam cut through the thick stone. Delta bristled at the repeated warnings from the guardships. When Delta was done, Emmeline cleared the rubble. Wearing protective gloves, she picked up the sample collector which looked like a pair of tweezers. She carefully grabbed the piece of bone. The top of the sample container whizzed open, and she placed the bone inside it. "Seal," she said. The container sealed.

"It's the fifth distal phalanx, from the small toe of his left foot," Emmeline said, turning to her scanner. "The dryness and the humidity in the atmosphere have slowed down its degeneration."

"Good for us," Delta said. "Are we done?"

Emmeline looked around. She'd hoped the plaque would tell her something, but it was just a rock with lines. She had no idea how to decipher it. "I think we're done."

It took them a few minutes to pack up and reseal the secret compartment. The presence Emmeline had felt didn't return, but it left her curious. She wondered if she could ask her father or her brothers. She pushed away the thought immediately. Her questions would lead to more arguments and her father telling her she was wasting her time.

Before leaving, she cast one last glance at the crypt and wondered what other secrets it held.

Astra flew out of Earth's atmosphere and approached the spiral gates, which opened with a bright flash.

The robot spoke again. "Thank you for your visit. Please come again. Your cooperation is greatly appreciated. Please remember, if you need to visit other parts of the planet, you do not need a permit. Have a pleasant journey. We hope to see you again."

ASTRA

Delta needed little assistance flying back to Titan, so Emmeline loaded all the data onto the computer. Hours passed as Emmeline worked. As time flew, she felt her excitement grow. She forgot all about the crypt and the presence she had felt in the house.

"What the. . .?" she muttered when she looked at the chart detailing the compounds that comprised the plaque. Minerals like calcium, aluminum, and zinc were common in rocks on Earth. That was no surprise, but there was something odd here. Among all earthly elements, Emmeline had detected something completely unexpected. Her fingers danced across the panel. Then she waited for the computer to finish. A detailed analyzes of the compounds popped up on the screen. Her eyes widened, and her mouth dropped.

"No. No, that can't be possible," she whispered to herself. She turned to the computer and redid the analysis.

Emmeline didn't know how much time passed before Delta joined her.

"Anything exciting?" Delta asked, taking a seat beside her when Emmeline didn't reply. "Why are you not analyzing the plaque? That's what we came for."

"I'm done with that."

"Okay. What's this? It looks like a geological report."

Emmeline nodded. "Yes, it is. Alexander created it."

"Why are you looking at it?"

Emmeline shook her head. "Something isn't right."

"What?"

"Something doesn't add up."

"What doesn't add up?"

Emmeline turned to her friend. "You know that comets are mostly made of dust and ice. The heart of a comet is called the nucleus which is made of hard rock. When the remaining part of Nemesis entered Earth's atmosphere, several small rocks separated themselves from the parent body, forming a meteoroid shower. Remember how I told you that Alexander was one of the team leaders assigned to study Nemesis? They collected several pieces of the meteorites that originated from the comet."

Delta nodded.

"The meteoroids were covered with a shiny black crust created by excessive heat while they descended through Earth's atmosphere," Emmeline continued. "Most of them were calcium-aluminum-rich meteoroids. What's not commonly known is that eighty-two percent of meteoroids contain a dark-gray matrix of small mineral granules called chondrites. These chondrites aren't found in rocks on Earth. The chondrites in the meteoroids originating from Nemesis were made of magnesium-rich olivine, surrounded by iron sulfide. But the teams found several isotopes of oxygen, mainly O-17, carbon, silicate, iron, and over a hundred amino acids."

"Okay. This is scary," Delta said mockingly.

"I haven't gotten to the scary part yet. When I analyzed the plaque, I found something very disturbing." Emmeline paused. Her hands were shaking. She had done the analysis four times to make sure she hadn't made a mistake.

"Emmeline, what?"

"The plaque is made of the exact same compounds that were found in the meteoroids from Nemesis. Same isotopes, equivalent number and percentage of amino acids. The levels of carbon, silicate, and iron are identical. I also found traces of the same chondrites that were found in Nemesis in the plaque. Delta, the plaque and Nemesis are connected!"

On autopilot, Astra neared Titan and swayed toward the

giant colony. Sunlight penetrated through the windows of the craft and fell over Emmeline's backpack. Suddenly, streams of yellow light emerged from the backpack. The yellow glow filled the ship and then died out.

Chapter 5: The Unexpected Visitor

Titan, Deck 1, Anastasia's office

Anastasia sat in her office, checking daily reports submitted by all departments. Her office was an average-sized space with a ceiling that offered a view of the heavens. The unblinking stars looked as if an artist had methodically painted each one with planned precision. The windows showcased vast corridors that linked the outer rim with the inner rim of the space station. As it was nearing midnight, the passageways were empty. The station was dead silent.

Nothing had changed. Things on Titan were near perfect. As usual, Anastasia worked late while others were already in bed.

She scrutinized proposed projects requiring approval from the Imperial Command. In the long list, she wasn't surprised to see that Dr. Kent had resubmitted the Phoenix project. She wasn't a scientist, and she didn't like Dr. Kent, but she had to admire his persistence.

Over the course of half an hour, she read through and approved ten projects from her crew. They were low risk and needed limited resources. She knew the authorities would promptly approve them. On the long list, she saw a name that brought a smile to her face. Prometheus's Captain, Mykel Lockhart, had submitted a project called Poseidon. *You always knew how to draw attention*, Anastasia thought to herself.

Her excitement grew as she read through the project proposal. During its voyage toward Earth, Prometheus had detected a surge of gravitational waves in a binary star system about thirty light years from their position. They couldn't isolate the source. There was no sign of a supernova. The two stars in the system were not the cause of the waves. There was a possibility of two black holes orbiting each other or merging could create the wave. But Prometheus's crew hadn't been able to detect a black hole. From her own experience, Anastasia knew it was a challenge to detect and isolate them. The other issue was that Prometheus was too far away. Due to their obligation to return home, Mykel had transmitted his findings to the Imperial Command and put in a request for the Poseidon project.

It was a high-risk project. It needed a lot of resources and crew and would take Prometheus ten years to complete. Anastasia's heart sank. Ten years was a long time. But Mykel had been gone for years, and he often left to chase new mysteries. She could still remember the day he'd left for the first mission, and she didn't stop him. She didn't want to hold him back. And personally, she was as ambitious as him and didn't like anyone holding her back. That day had changed their lives. They drifted to different sectors of space, hardly having time to speak. Then she got married, and it felt like Mykel and their love had faded away in the darkness of space.

Anastasia like most nights couldn't sleep or rather, didn't feel like it. From the corner of her desk, she picked up a photograph of her girls, who lived on Earth with her ex-husband, Martin. Like everyone who chose this profession, she'd had to make sacrifices. For her, the hardest part had been choosing her career over the man she'd married.

Anastasia had been the commander of Marion for ten years and had not only raised her kids but also tried her best to maintain a good relationship with her spouse. It hadn't been perfect; it had been hard work. And she thought she wasn't a good mother; she shouldn't have had kids. Managing a ship and family had been a challenge that had left her weary, heartbroken and lonely.

Then she decided to salvage what was left of her life. Tired of living on a spaceship, she'd finally taken a major step and decided to give up space exploration. An opportunity to command Titan arrived, and she took it in a heartbeat. It had been a good decision for her family and her relationship. But none of it had lasted.

Over the years, the kids had become more attached to their father because she never had time for them. Last year, Martin had insisted on moving back to Earth, but Anastasia hadn't wanted to go. She'd found herself asking how much more she should sacrifice. She'd already given up her freedom, her need to explore and discover new things. Should she give up another command? No. She'd decided she couldn't leave Titan; it meant too much to her. Being in command of the most powerful station in the system gave her a sense of power over her life. It gave her control. It gave her life meaning.

Martin had left Titan with their teenage girls, and Anastasia hadn't tried to stop them. This had led to a divorce, and she wasn't surprised. Martin blamed her career, but Anastasia knew better. Yes, her career had been a factor, but there was something else. She realized now how little love had existed in their relationship. There'd been mutual respect and communication but no chemistry; the spark had been long gone. She didn't want to live with a man who she didn't love anymore.

Anastasia's girls were thriving on Earth, though they missed their mother. She wanted them back with her, but their happiness and safety mattered to her more than anything else. A year had passed, and she could see that they were building their lives. They had made friends and attained some stability. They were no longer confined to the boundaries of a spaceship. Tears filled her eyes as she looked at her kids' picture.

Sacrifices, she thought.

TITAN, DECK 1, BRIDGE

Anastasia left her office and soon found herself on the bridge. The lights were dim, and the command center was completely silent except for the intermittent beeps of the consoles. She remembered living on Titan as a child, and her mother was friends with the commander and often brought her here. Never had she thought, one day she would command it.

She could already imagine her routine for tomorrow, and sulk. The three crew members on night shift appeared to be busy on their consoles. Without a word, she turned and left the bridge.

The doors of the elevator slid open on Deck 4. Anastasia strolled silently with her head bowed. She turned left and entered passageway three, which led to the outer section. She paused and turned to look out of the windows, staring at the glowing perimeter. She'd thought she was done with exploration, but for the last year, she hadn't been able to shake the feeling of nothingness. Maybe exploration wasn't done with her.

TITAN, DECK 10 HANGAR DECK

After docking Astra in the hangar, Delta and Emmeline walked toward their quarters. The deck was silent, and all the craft stood under dim lights.

"Are we going to discuss this?" Delta asked in a low voice.

"Let me think about it."

"If Nemesis was linked with a plaque that existed centuries ago, people should know about it."

Emmeline faced Delta. "I know," she said. "I know. I'm worried too. But we can't go to the science committee without more answers. We need to investigate how and why these two things are related."

"Can't you just speak with Commander Waters?"

Emmeline shook her head. "I thought about that, but without more information, it's useless to involve her."

The doors to the elevator opened, and they stepped in.

"How long will it take you to decipher it?" Delta asked.

Emmeline felt annoyed. She'd thought that discovering the plaque would lead her to the mythical device. Instead, it had just made things worse. "I don't know how to decipher it. I need time. I need time!"

Delta grunted, shaking her head. "Alexander was branded as a traitor because he falsified data and then disappeared without a trace. Now you have the plaque, which is somehow linked with that damn comet. This doesn't look good. We have to be careful."

Emmeline wanted to tell Delta that it was all a lie, Alexander would have never done such a thing. But the truth was she didn't have all the facts and history told a different story. Imperial Command did not take disobedience lightly and when it came to the Nemesis, it spared no one. She remembered her grandpa telling her the months of scrutiny the family had to go through after he disappeared. They had confiscated all his data, his work, locked down his accounts and raided the house. But found nothing. Since he had vanished without a trace, and no one knew what happened to him, he remained on the wanted list of the Imperial Command. The link between Nemesis and the plaque wasn't going to make it easy. She didn't know how to deal with this information.

The elevator halted on Deck 4. They stepped out and were greeted by a small group of people. They walked through the corridor, and Emmeline came to a stop at door 04-114. "This is me."

Delta looked up and down the corridor. "So, we keep this between us?"

"For now. Let's wait until I find out more."

"Fine." Delta was about to walk away, but she stopped.

"Emmeline, I'm sorry. I should congratulate you. I'm glad you found evidence that a part of the myth could be true."

"Thank you."

"But let's be careful, very careful."

TITAN, DECK 4, EMMELINE'S QUARTERS

Emmeline punched in the codes, and the door opened. Despite all the excitement of her journey, she was glad to be back home. She put her backpack on the chair near the door, then stretched out on the couch.

Her quarters were a small compact space. Her living room was rectangular with three large curved windows. The walls were light gray and decorated with paintings of stars and galaxies. Two vases holding different types of lilies rested on a rectangular metallic table pushed against the wall in front of the couch. On the table were three photo frames: pictures of her parents, her brother, and her grandparents. To one side of the door were six shelves holding several books. To the other side was an orchid plant she had smuggled from the nursery bay.

Emmeline got to her feet and peered out of the window. The giant clouds of Titan danced through the sky, giving the moon a mixed glow of orange and red. The clouds drifted aside, revealing a view of the frozen rocks on Titan's surface. She wondered about the information she had collected, but her mind was too tired to comprehend, so she decided to get some sleep.

It wasn't until the buzzer went off that Emmeline realized it was 0700 hours. She rubbed her eyes and stretched on the bed. The buzzer sounded again.

"You have a visitor," said the computer.

"*Yes, I know!*" Emmeline thought, getting on her feet.

"Emmeline, it's your father. Please open the door."

At first, she froze. Last time she checked, he was on Earth. When did he get here?

"Oh damn," she muttered, picking up her backpack. She opened her closet, pushed her clothes aside, and placed her right palm on the wall. A rectangular panel moved outward, then smoothly slid sideways. She put the backpack inside and said, "Close."

The small panel closed. She shut the doors to her closet, quickly checked her appearance in the mirror, and ran back into the living area. She pushed the green button to open the door and found her father, Arthur Augury, standing in front of her.

"Hello, Daddy," Emmeline said, trying not to show her anxiety. She gave him a warm hug.

Arthur's face quickly softened. "All right. All right now," he said as they parted. He entered her quarters, and the door shut automatically behind him.

Arthur was a polite and wise but hot-headed man in his sixties. Emmeline had inherited her father's facial features but not his hair, which was silver and curly. Arthur towered a few inches above her and had a significantly larger build. Today, he wore a long white coat, which almost touched his feet, over a blue turtleneck shirt and white pants.

"How's Mom?" Emmeline asked.

"She misses you and wants me to bring you home," her father told her.

Emmeline just smiled, not knowing how to respond. There was so much going on Titan and in her life, she wasn't sure she wanted to go back home. "So, what brings you to Titan?"

"As if you don't know."

Emmeline shrugged her shoulders.

"You went to Earth without telling me. And then just left! Without visiting your parents?"

"Dad, I'm not a little girl anymore. I don't have to tell you where I go. I wasn't on vacation, otherwise I would have come to see you."

"You went to Sector 1001."

"So now you're spying on me!" Emmeline exclaimed,

outraged.

"You leave me no choice. Elliot has filled your head with junk. I'm trying to fix the problem."

"Dad, please don't say that about Grandpa."

Arthur walked up and down the room. "You're out of your senses. Why do you want to follow this stupid story? This myth about this mythical device. It doesn't exist, Emmeline!"

"I'm just following my in—"

"It was the greatest mistake of my life to give you those diaries," said Arthur. "I should have burned them!"

"Burn generations of family history?" Emmeline demanded.

Arthur faced her. "Generations of fiction!"

"Dad, I know you don't believe in myths. Nor do I, but I think. . ."

"You're wrong!"

"Dad, I just want to see where this goes."

"It's going nowhere. You are wasting your time and your energy. Focus on completing your credits, finish your work with Dr. Kent, and return to Earth," Arthur ordered. "We've been waiting for you. It seems you have forgotten us!"

Anger stirred inside Emmeline; she didn't want to leave Titan. She loved her family, but there was nothing for her back home.

"You're just like your grandfather," Arthur said. "Reckless and stubborn. He let the family business die and left his old wife and grandchildren behind to go on a ship that was destined for doom."

"Grandpa was an explorer, and he followed his dream," Emmeline countered. "The ship was destroyed in an ion storm. It was a tragedy. Accidents happen!"

"He was stupid."

"He was your father."

"Yes, and he left us."

Emmeline drew in a deep breath. "Dad, just accept the truth. You are angry at him because he followed his dreams when you didn't!"

"I couldn't dream. I had a family to feed."

The same argument again, thought Emmeline. "No, you didn't. When I turned eighteen, like everyone, I got access to our assets and the vault. We would have been fine without you or my big brother, Warren. We have enough assets to feed the next two generations, even if neither of us earns a dime. Yes, you developed the business and took it to the next level by collaborating with the military to make spaceships. But Grandpa and our ancestors built the foundation of the company."

Arthur was about to argue, but Emmeline stopped him. "Dad. If you want to give up the business and go on an extended vacation, do it! Warren can take care of everything. You have trained him well. Take a ship and go, but don't speak ill of Grandpa. And speaking of Grandma, you weren't even around when I was taking care of her. And you know what? She asked Grandpa to leave, to follow his dream. She had become ill, and it was her wish to stay back and die on Earth in her home!"

Silence fell in the quarters.

Emmeline said after a few moments had passed. "I don't wish to make an enemy of my father. What's come over you? What's going on? Just tell me."

Arthur slowly sat down. "I'm terrified. I feel like I'm losing you too."

Emmeline's heart sank.

"I miss you. I miss having you around. The house is too quiet. I am scared. You're too much like Elliot," Arthur continued. "I'm worried that you'll destroy everything you have. I've read those diaries too. I've thought about all the deaths, mistakes, mishaps, and destruction. I know the misery exploration and curiosity brought to our family."

Emmeline lowered her head. *It also brought progress*, she thought.

"Especially the ones that have no name," said Arthur. "The anonymous journals."

"The ones from the twenty-first century?"

"Yes. They made so many mistakes. They stuck their noses where they weren't supposed to. Did you know that one of them was accused of murder?"

Emmeline smiled slightly. "Accused but not convicted."

"It gives the family a bad name."

"Dad, that was centuries ago. No one remembers."

"People remember, and traits pass down through generations."

"You're worried about nothing."

"Really? What about Alexander?"

Emmeline eyed him.

"Since you've become so interested in his life, I did a bit of digging," said Arthur. "He was appointed as a leading planetary geologist to study Nemesis, and he falsified data. He stole data from another team, altered it, and then disappeared with the original findings. It's believed that he hid a very important finding during his survey."

"What was it?" Emmeline asked remembering the dead man under the fallen staircase.

"No one knows. They say he corrupted his team, and they went rogue as well."

"Did anyone find out why?"

"No. No one. They couldn't understand him. He was given the opportunity of a lifetime. Just imagine what glory it would have brought us! But look what he did. He went rogue and destroyed his life! And he was a criminal."

"Dad, shouldn't you check facts before condemning a man? From the dairies it appears Alexander was kind, hardworking, and loyal to his field and colleagues. He wasn't a well-renowned scientist, but he was dedicated to his wife and family. Has it occurred to you that such a man wouldn't become a crook without a very good reason?"

Arthur straightened up.

"I'm just saying we should learn more about what actually happened," Emmeline told him.

"The way I see it, Alexander discovered something, and it was huge. He wanted all the fame and glory, and that's what led to his doom."

Emmeline stayed quiet.

"What are you thinking?" Arthur asked her.

"You will not like it," she said.

"Tell me anyway."

"What if he found something crucial, but before he could get to it or gather more facts, he died?"

Arthur raised his eyebrows. "You seem very sure of his death."

Emmeline eyed him. "Dad, he lived a long time ago, and if he was still alive, don't you think if he wanted fame and glory, he would have come forward with his discovery?"

Arthur looked uncertain.

"Don't worry, Dad. I will not do anything stupid."

Arthur narrowed his eyebrows. "I know you already have."

Titan, Deck 7, Training Hall

After her father left, Emmeline couldn't rest. His words bothered her. She looked at her schedule. She had training with Argon and then several tasks in the Crystal Lab.

She got ready, and before she headed to training, she stopped by the Medical Bay 1 and asked the technician there to do a DNA test on the bone she'd found in Sector 1001.

Emmeline rushed inside and found Argon already doing laps around the hall. She was so happy that she could train with him. He was her friend, or something more. She didn't know; she didn't want to know. She liked the way things were between them. She thought her life was already full of complications, friendship was a safe ground.

Emmeline found Argon very attractive, and she could see the physical changes in his body since he had finished Imperial Command training. He was smart, intelligent and ambitious, like her. What Emmeline loved most about him was that he never stopped her from being herself. If she loved doing something, he joined in. They played games, listened to music, and most of the time had breakfast together. She believed one of the reasons she liked Titan was because he was here. He listened to her talk about stars and comets for ages. Other boys expected her to do things for them, but Argon asked nothing of her. On some level, that bothered Emmeline.

"Sorry, I'm late," Emmeline said as she arrived.

Argon stopped running and approached her. "Emmeline, you need to be on time if you really want to learn how to fight."

Emmeline threw her bag in a corner. "Honestly, I don't think I need to."

He rolled his eyes, "What did you say?"

"I don't need to learn how to fight. I have you," she said, smiling. She knew what would happen next.

His face softened. "Very flattering. It will not work with me."

"Are you sure?" she teased.

"Yes. If you want your credits, you will need to complete the training. Like it or not scientist and military personnel on Titan or on any other ship have to get basic combat training."

She smiled.

"Now let's start warm-up."

After the warm up, Emmeline trained with Argon using a disruptor. It was a standard hand weapon used on all ships and space stations. Anyone preparing for space travel was required to gain basic knowledge of using weapons to defend themselves in case of emergencies. For pilots and cadets of the Imperial Command, the training was hard and long. For scientists, it was short, just enough to get them acquainted with weapons and basic defense strategies.

Holding the weapon, she felt maybe Argon should have started her training with something else.

"Computer, initiate safety protocol," said Argon.

"Affirmative."

An invisible shield separated the shooting range from the rest of the training hall. The shooting range was in the far corner of the hall. Emmeline stood in the fourth lane at the end of the long, wide red stripe printed on the floor. She looked at the smooth black wall in front of her. This felt dangerous and wild, and she couldn't picture a scenario where she would these skills. Violence was something she had never witnessed or experienced. But she knew this was just the beginning. Once she had learned to use this weapon, Argon planned to teach her how to use the flux rifle, a weapon that looked like a gun but was ten times more powerful than the disruptor.

"Initiate training," Argon said.

The target appeared in front of her. Three red circles in a square. Emmeline gulped, stood with her legs apart and held the cold weapon in both hands. It was very light. As soon as her right thumb pressed the button in the middle, multiple small lights glowed for a second, and it made a hissing noise.

The computer stated, "User identification: Emmeline Augury. Status: trainee."

"Okay," said Argon.

Taking a quick breath and closing one eye, Emmeline tried to concentrate. Then she fired. The small beam hit the wall meters above the target.

Argon eyed her. He stepped closer. "Your hand should be parallel to your shoulder. Don't be afraid. Now try again."

Her heart was beating fast. Sweat gathered and smeared her palms. "I don't like this."

"No one likes to kill, but sometimes, it becomes necessary. Remember, someday you might have to protect yourself."

"Argon, I don't think this is necessary."

"Emmeline, it is. Trust me."

Cringing, Emmeline did as she was told.

"Keep your eyes on the target," Argon said. "Don't move your hand backward." He lowered her hand a bit.

She pushed the button hard and slightly lifted her hand. The beam hit the wall way above the target.

"Target missed," said the computer.

She fired again and again, but none of the shots hit even the outer edges of the target. A rage grew inside her. She stomped her feet, lifted her hands in anger, and tried again. The beam of light went sideways, hitting the target in the next row. "Ah! I hate this!" she shouted.

"Try this," Argon said, giving her a knife.

Emmeline glared at him, wondering if he was trying to be funny. She said nothing, handing the disruptor to him and taking the knife.

"You know how to throw it, right?" Argon asked.

"Yes. Grandpa taught me," she boosted. Why did he think this was funny? It wasn't.

"Well. Let's see."

Emmeline held the edge of the sharp side and threw it with all her might. The knife fell to the floor before it even reached the target.

Argon burst into laughter.

"I don't believe this!" Emmeline shouted as she marched toward the fallen knife.

"Oh, this is going to be so much fun," Argon muttered.

"I hate you!"

TITAN, DECK 2, CRYSTAL LAB

Training had been frustrating, but it had also been a wonderful distraction. It had refreshed Emmeline's mind. The day was passing quickly, and with a long list of things to do, she didn't think she would have time to look at the plaque. She'd just finished working on integrating all the cosmic findings documented by Freedom into Titan's computer. Freedom had just returned from its voyage to the Proxima Centauri star system, which was over four thousand light-years away. The phenomena were incredible, and Emmeline could understand why Dr. Kent wanted them cataloged right away.

When she finished cataloging two thousand items and

transferring thirty-two billion terabytes of data, she stared at the console, asking herself where to begin. She approached Dr. Kent, who said that the first thing he wanted to study was the origin of the gravitational waves Freedom had detected ten light-years beyond Proxima Centauri. The intriguing fact was that Prometheus had also reported the waves, but in a different section of space. Just like Prometheus, Freedom hadn't been able to determine the source. Where had the waves come from?

She spent two days studying the data. When she had the time, Emmeline pulled up the data about the plaque. First, she checked her analyzes again. Astra's computers were old, so she thought perhaps she had made a mistake. After an hour, she reviewed the bars. No, she was correct. The composition of the plaque and Nemesis matched perfectly. If she could find out the origin of the plaque, maybe she could understand how it was linked with Nemesis.

She looked around. It was late at night and she was alone in the lab. Emmeline grabbed the plaque. It was made of grayish rock and weighed around one and a half kilos. Its surface was rough. She focused on the seventeen indentations on the back of the plaque, then noted the lines coming out of the semicircle at the top. Placing the plaque under the scanner, she scanned both the front and back of it. Then she put it back in her bag and turned to the screen. She highlighted the visual lines and said, "Computer, save pattern one."

"Saved."

She observed the indentations on the plaque and isolated them. "Computer, save pattern two."

"Saved."

"Encrypt files and access to all data of Project MYTH."

"Affirmative," said the computer.

"Analyze patterns one and two."

As the computer analyzed the patterns, Emmeline concentrated on reading to identify more tests and analyzes that she could run to unlock the secrets of the plaque. She sat back, thinking. Had Alexander hidden the plaque because it was linked with Nemesis? Or had he just hidden it because he'd thought it was important? Perhaps he'd known about the mythical device. Emmeline would never know. But what she knew was that decrypting the plaque would not be easy. She also needed to study the meteoroid Alexander had preserved. Why had he done it?

"Pattern two identified," said the computer.

Emmeline sat up straight. "Show."

"Pattern one is the constellation Draco. Seen from Earth, Draco is the eighth largest constellation in the night sky and occupies an area of 1,083 square degrees. The constellation consists of seventeen stars and lies in the third quadrant of the northern hemisphere. It is visible at latitudes between ninety and minus-fifteen degrees. It was discovered and cataloged in the second century as one of the forty-eight constellations. Draco's brightest star is Etamin. Draco is located 148 light-years from Earth."

"Pause," Emmeline said. She knew all about the constellation, but how did it relate to the plaque or the mythical device? She had no idea. "Computer, analyze pattern one."

"Analyzing," responded the computer.

She rocked her chair back and forth until the computer spoke again.

"This pattern was not found in the astronomical database."

"Okay. Try historical databases."

She waited.

"This pattern was not found in historical databases."

Emmeline chewed her lip. "Search all databases."

The computer became silent again. "Unable to comply. The request is too broad. There are too many references in the database."

"Computer, merge patterns one and two, then search."

"Searching . . ."

Emmeline waited.

"No results found," said the computer.

Emmeline rolled her eyes.

Annoyed because she'd been unable to find anything, Emmeline invited Argon to play hover ball in the gaming room. For the next hour, she felt happy and excited. After their game, they sat on the floor of her quarters and had dinner. Argon talked about his day, and Emmeline listened intently. He had finally figured out how to fix Raven's AI, with Cyr's help. He was so excited. Listening to him, Emmeline completely lost track of time.

TITAN, DECK 10, DOCKING BAY

Lieutenant Commander Adrian Olson didn't know why, but he found himself in the docking bay. He was done with his shift on the bridge and was about to head to Evan's quarters. But for some reason, he had taken a different route.

He'd heard Astra was leaving again, and he was worried. Since Delta's father had passed away, Adrian had felt responsible for looking after her. Not that she needed it. She was independent, strong, and smart; she didn't need a protective big brother. He didn't want to be her brother, anyway. He wanted more, more than just a friend. Unfortunately, he felt he was nothing more to her than just another guy. She could have had any man or woman on the station, and yet she stayed alone. For the last four years, she'd spent most of her time working.

AUTOMATE, a robotic forklift, drawled down the hall, carrying a massive box labeled "Pl – DRILL 2." Adrian could only speculate the weight of the drill. The forklift turned toward the ramp of Astra and disappeared into the cargo ship.

Adrian walked toward Astra, and his heart skipped a beat when Delta came to meet him. She looked radiant; her blue hair tied up in a high ponytail.

He gulped nervously. "Hey. You're going again?" he asked, then cursed himself.

She gave him a sly smile. "Yes. The Vesta colony needs a new drill."

Vesta was a mining colony in the asteroid belt between

Mars and Jupiter.

"What happened?" Adrian asked.

"You know they're mining platinum. The engineers pushed the drill a bit hard and damaged it."

"Ouch."

"Titan is the closest to the asteroid belt and is currently holding three drills. They need it as soon as possible. They fear that if they don't continue drilling and mine the mineral soon, the Imperial Command might pull the plug."

"Wow, that would be bad," said Adrian, trying to understand why he was having this conversation.

"Well," Delta said. "I'm going to drop this baby off and pick up the damaged one."

"I'm sure Lieutenant Storm can fixed it."

"Yep. Titan's got one of the best engineers in the system. What are you doing here?"

"Uh . . . I was just on my way to Lieutenant Weeds quarters. We're off to watch a movie."

A playful smile appeared on Delta's face. "The Lieutenant's quarters are on Deck 4."

"Oh. Well, it's a nice day for a stroll."

AUTOMATE reappeared. "Delta Dune. The cargo has been loaded," it said.

"Thank you."

"You are welcome."

Delta walked toward another container. "AUTOMATE, move this one to my personal lot, number 106."

"Affirmative," said the robot.

"What's in there?" Adrian asked curiously.

Delta folded her arms. "Something exciting, hot, and not available on the market."

Adrian arched his eyebrows, watching as the robotic forklift slowly lifted the container and began moving away. "Oh, come on!"

"Adrian!"

"Oh, all right," he said, looking at the container.

"Well, I'm off," said Delta. "This is going to be fun."

"You're always looking for the next adventure, aren't you?"

Delta lowered her eyes. "I am," she answered.

For a second, Adrian thought that she blushed, but he wasn't sure. He watched her as she disappeared inside Astra. The ramp lifted and closed behind her.

Sometimes, Adrian wished he had someone he could discuss his feelings with except Evan. Technically he outranked Evan. They worked on the bridge; they were friends and colleagues. When it came to Delta, deep down, he knew his friend was telling him the truth, but he wasn't ready to accept it. Not now, not for the last four years.

Adrian hadn't been lucky. His parents were separated. That wasn't unusual, but his family was complicated, and no one kept in touch with one another. All he knew was that they were alive. His father was a farmer, and his mother was on the Challenger colony. He heard from his mother now and then, but the conversations only ever lasted a minute or two and were always all about her. Her day, her work, her friends, and how her husband had betrayed her. It was the twenty-fourth century, but humans still bickered about these things.

Adrian was the youngest son, and his two brothers had left home a long time ago. When he'd taken up a position on Titan, his mother had complained. She hadn't wanted him to leave her and had told him he was being selfish. But he'd never felt wanted anyway, and he couldn't understand why she was pressuring him to stay while letting his brothers leave home. Around her, he felt like he was a tool, something to use, not to respect or love.

It was different on Titan. Adrian had joined as an ensign, and in the last four years, he'd worked his way to become second in command of Titan. He served at the helm and was a trained pilot. He'd always dreamed of flying a ship or doing something exciting, like Delta. He'd been so excited when he'd got the license to fly a craft. Unfortunately, Titan never left orbit, so he felt that his pilot training was a waste.

At first, Adrian had found Anastasia intimidating and demanding, but the more he'd gotten to know her, the more he liked serving with her.

Adrian couldn't complain. His life was much better than it had been four years ago. He was surrounded by people who liked and respected him, and he had earned that. He could be himself with them. They didn't mind him reading ancient books and citing them now and then, although Evan never stopped taunting him about his choice of literature. But in the last year, seeing one ship after another leave and getting to know more young cadets like Argon, Adrian had felt like he was meant to do something more significant. Something good, more than just daily routine stuff. Adrian felt he should get out of this system, explore, make new friends, join a new crew. He'd always wanted to be a pilot and had trained for it. What was he doing here?

Adrian knocked and waited for Evan to open the door.

"There you are. Come in."

Adrian entered Evan's home on Titan. There were clothes everywhere, and he smelled perfume. The curtains were drawn. The lights were dim. Three plates of half-eaten food sat on the small glass table. "What the hell do you do in here?"

"Is that what you're wearing?"

Adrian looked down at his uniform.

"We're off duty. You should try different clothes. How about this?" Evan asked, showing him a colorful shirt.

"No, thanks."

"You're late. Dorothy and Claire will be waiting," said Evan.

"W-what?? I thought the two of us were going,"

"Stop complaining and just come with us."

"No."

"Adrian, you need to talk to girls. Girls other than Delta. We're off in five minutes. Are you sure you want to go looking like that?"

Adrian sulked and stepped into the bathroom and took a good look at himself in the mirror. He looked a bit tired, but besides that, he looked fine. He glanced at the wall and scowled. He stepped out of the bathroom and said, "You still have it?"

"What?"

"The stupid framed picture of the queen."

"Hey! She was the greatest singer of all time, and this is my quarters. I'll do whatever the hell I want to do with the place. Let's go."

"Don't tell me you made dinner plans too," Adrian complained.

"Adrian, live a little, my friend. Live a little."

One Week Later

Titan, Deck 6, Archaeology lab

The day went faster than Emmeline had hoped. The only time she had fun was when she trained with Argon. Since Argon had finished his exams, he had more time on his hands. He was teaching her self-defense, and she liked it. It was good to feel powerful.

Emmeline had received the DNA test results. It was Alexander Hendrix. It made Emmeline happy to know that she had found her long-lost ancestor. But she was unsure if she should tell her father. She didn't know how to resolve this or who she could speak. She wanted to seek Argon's advice. She had other things on her mind, like the plaque. Her failure to decipher it bothered her, and after trying several times on her own, she decided to seek help.

When she left the lab at dinner time, Emmeline walked cautiously, wondering if she was making the right decision. She had no choice. She'd searched through the databases and run hundreds of tests on the plaque, all in vain. She knew the plaque was ancient, and she hoped an archaeologist could help her. The computer told her Aceline Keston was in the archaeology lab.

When she entered the enormous hall, Emmeline immediately felt nostalgic. The archaeology lab was very different from the Crystal Lab. Her Lab looked like an advanced spaceship, while the archaeology lab made her feel as if she had traveled back in time.

On several benches sat hundreds of artifacts, fossils, and rocks. Emmeline noted that the walls had several shelves, most of them occupied by samples. The wall in front of her had a screen showing Earth. She noticed several blinking red dots on the globe. The picture changed to show a star map. Again, a few lights flashed. Emmeline assumed it showed where the samples had been found.

She slowly walked between the long desks. The surfaces of the desks were white, glowing due to the lights below. She came across a skeleton. She leaned over and observed the head. She was unsure if it was human. It looked human, but the eye sockets were different. The cranium looked bulky and the jaw heavy.

"I can't believe it either. We're still finding them," said a familiar voice.

Emmeline straightened and saw Aceline. Suddenly, she felt embarrassed. She was so plain, wearing the same clothes almost every day. She had no idea how-to put-on makeup or even just lipstick. In front of her stood a woman in her fifties. who worked with artifacts, fossils, and dusty things all day, but she looked so fresh. She was dressed in a white blouse and black stylish pants. The fact that she was Argon's mother didn't make things easy. If Emmeline married Argon, Aceline would be her mother-in-law. She tried not to imagine what that would be like.

"Where did you find this one?" Emmeline asked.

"It was discovered last year, buried under ice at the South Pole," Aceline replied. "I got this two months ago, and it's almost ready to go to storage. Now I'm waiting for Prometheus to arrive."

"Why?"

"It found a planet where the crew discovered prehistoric rocks and bones of a species we've never seen before."

"Should we be taking other species' remains?" Emmeline asked.

"Oh, don't worry," Aceline said dismissively. "They're long gone, and I don't believe in ghosts."

Emmeline smiled. Nor had she until she'd felt the presence in Sector 1001.

"But something tells me you're not here to talk about relics," said Aceline.

"I am here to talk about this," Emmeline said, handing

over a pad. It contained the two patterns she had isolated from the plaque.

Aceline arched her eyebrows and tapped on the pad. "Fascinating," she mumbled, walking away from Emmeline and over to her desk.

For the next ten minutes, Emmeline watched Aceline walk up and down the hall, humming and smiling to herself. She hoped Aceline would realize she was still in the lab.

"Where did you find this?" Aceline finally asked.

"In the northern mountains on Earth."

"Really?"

Emmeline said nothing.

"Have you brought the original with you?"

"No."

Aceline placed the pad on the desk and looked at the image as if memorizing it. "You want it translated?"

"Yes. I've looked through the computer, but it couldn't interpret it. I think it's something that wouldn't be in a scientific database."

"I've never seen anything like this before," Aceline admitted. "These lines are interesting."

Emmeline wasn't sure. "I know you're busy, and I hope this doesn't take up too much of your time . . ."

"Ahh, I'll do it."

Emmeline was pleased and extended her hand.

"Why so formal? Come here, my dear." Aceline stepped forward and hugged her.

Emmeline didn't know how to react. Soon, they parted.

"Okay," said Aceline. "Now I need to get home before I forget! Goodnight."

One Week Later

Titan, Deck 1

Anastasia strolled through the corridors of Titan. Even though it was early in the morning, Titan was already buzzing with activity. Three big cargo ships were getting ready to leave the solar system, and Titan was their pit stop for supplies. Anastasia's job was to make sure the ships got everything they needed for their long journeys. They were the first ships to head off to the Torus colony, which was twenty light-years away from Titan. The doors opened, and Anastasia entered the busy docking bay.

She watched as men, and women rushed across the large hall. Huge boxes were being moved by Automated Hovering Carriers (AHC). These were rectangular floating platforms designed to move the cargo from one place to another. She watched as six barrels of fuel floated just above the floor and slowly moved toward Docking Port 5. Satisfied that her people could do the job; she headed to the bridge.

A familiar voice called her from behind. "Good morning, Commander," said Lieutenant Cyr Storm.

"Good morning. How are you today?"

"I'm good, thank you. Did you see my report?"

"Yes, I did. Excellent work."

The doors to the elevator opened, and the women stepped in.

"Right. Thanks," Cyr replied. "Are you sure you don't want me to look into anything else?"

Anastasia regarded her. "Computer, stop elevator." The elevator stopped. "What's going on?" Anastasia asked lowly.

Cyr hesitated. "Titan is running . . . perfectly. It's been a year now, and not even a transformer needs fixing. All systems are working perfectly."

Anastasia smiled. "That's a compliment to its engineer. You've taken good care of Titan."

Cyr forced a smile. "There was some excitement last week," she said. "We detected cosmic dust in the armory. There was a small hole in Titan's hull. It was exciting, especially because my staff fought over the job. To keep them busy, I asked them to check all the systems to make sure the cosmic dust hadn't done any more damage."

"Excellent," Anastasia commented wondering if finding holes was exciting.

"Commander, I need to tell you something. I'm going nuts."

"Why?"

"There's nothing to do," Cyr said. "Everything is the same. Every day is the same. Titan is running so perfectly; I don't have anything new to do."

"You'll find something."

"More space dust?"

"I'm sure this is just temporary . . ."

Cyr shook her head. "No. It's not. I haven't told you the entire story. After my team finished cleaning up the space dust, I found myself hovering over a console. The tactical console. I wanted to fire a torpedo just to make sure it worked."

Anastasia's face hardened.

Cyr cleared her throat. "Freedom is planning another deep space mission in the next couple of weeks. They're looking for an engineer. I'm thinking about taking the job."

Anastasia felt as if the environmental systems had stopped working. The elevator felt warm, and her palms grew damp. "I see. Are you sure?"

"Lieutenant Baker is an excellent engineer," Cyr said. "He'll take good care of Titan. I'll make sure he does."

Anastasia did not smile.

"Please. Titan is fantastic, but there's nothing more to do or learn here."

"If that is what you want, Cyr, I will support your application," Anastasia said woodenly.

"Thank you!" Cyr replied.

"Computer, resume," Anastasia said, looking at the

door. She gritted her teeth. She wasn't happy to let Cyr go and fought the urge to ask her to stay. But then she asked herself if she was being fair. Because when she looked deep inside herself, she didn't want to stay either.

TITAN, DECK 1, BRIDGE

"Everything is ready to go, Commander," said Adrian from the helm.

"Good," said Anastasia. "Open the gates."

They watched quietly as the three ships left the system. As the ships disappeared from view, Adrian secured the perimeter. "Commander, I'd like to run a diagnostic of the perimeter," he said.

"Do it." Anastasia watched the dead space, feeling sorry and sad. Not because they were going, but because she couldn't.

TITAN, DECK 2, CRYSTAL LAB

As usual, Emmeline was the last to finish up. When she was done, she looked blankly at the screen.

The doors opened. "Ah, there you are."

Emmeline jumped. She calmed down when she saw it was Aceline. "Hi."

"Hello, how are you?"

Emmeline beamed, "I am well, thanks."

"I'll get straight to the point," said Aceline. "I have studied the images of the plaque you gave me and also the data you collected. You didn't find this piece of rock in the mountains," She studied Emmeline's face. "Darling, look. If you don't want to tell me something, that's your business, but this rock could be really ancient. Maybe centuries, even millennia old."

"What?" demanded Emmeline. "You're telling me this could be from the ice age? The stone age?"

"The ice age, I believe. We've recorded over five significant ice ages throughout our planet's history, and the most recent one ended around eighteen thousand years ago. While many other species perished, humans adapted to the changing conditions by developing tools, hunting, building fires, and tribes. You see, my dear, there were no alphabets or languages at that time. Man didn't even know how to speak." She paused. "When there was no language, there were drawings. Doodles, you and I would say. But it was their way of communicating."

"What are these doodles?" Emmeline asked, pointing towards the lines.

"It's an interesting finding." she said, "What do you think they are?"

Emmeline nudged her head, "They look like sunrays..."

"Yes... that is what I thought. And I ran hundreds of algorithms to test this hypothesis. But then I started thinking... maybe it was something else... I got an idea when I heard Anastasia play the piano in her quarters."

Emmeline raised a brow.

Stone made plaque (front)

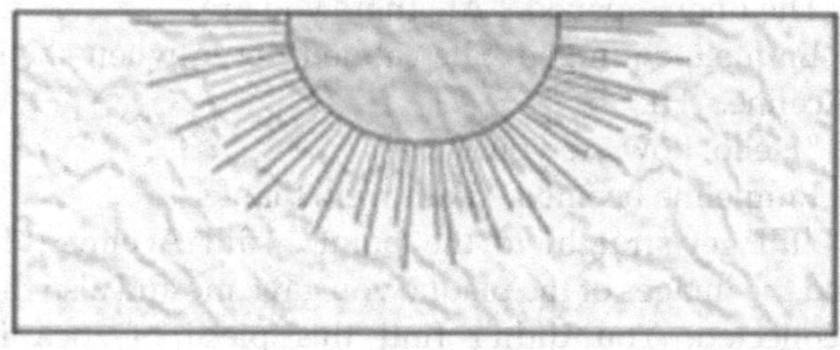

"What if... this is a diagram of a musical instrument with three-level keys..."

Emmeline stood straight. She hadn't thought about it that way. "What do you mean?"

"Usually, such drawings describe the sun, the moon, the mountains, and the rivers. Some are about animals. But these . . . these could be tunes."

"Tunes?" Emmeline's eyes widened.

"Exactly. Although early man was smart, he wasn't smart enough to develop musical tunes and definitely didn't have the skills to develop codes. They had music, but they didn't know how to record it. Methods to record musical tunes were developed around the eleventh century."

"Wow," said Emmeline.

"Yes. Have you noticed the length of the lines?"

"Yes,"

"The shorter ones are 1.5 centimeters, the medium ones around 2 centimeters and the longest are about 2.9 centimeters. If you notice, it's very faint but the medium-sized lines are a bit lighter than the color of the stone..."

"I noticed that... but thought it could be because it is old."

"I agree. There are discolorations in several parts of the plaque. But let us assume that this is an instrument... that means the key to solve this could be a tune."

Emmeline folded her arms, "There are too many possibilities."

"Agreed. Then I remembered the seventeen indentations you mentioned, and you said it's a constellation."

"Yes. The Draco constellation."

"Then let us assume that this musical tune doesn't have over seventeen notes."

Emmeline's eyes widened.

"That narrows down the possibilities," she said, handing over a pad. "I have recorded all the possible tunes and the only way to test them is to play them near the plaque."

Emmeline stood feeling a bit dumb.

"We cannot know the tempo or the pitch of the tunes... but as I said, you won't know until you test it."

Emmeline looked through the list of tunes. "Thank you." She felt so grateful. They were different, but Aceline had helped her without judging or questioning her.

"I should thank you! This thing had me baffled for a week, and I loved it! Let me know if you have something else this challenging. I'll see you around, dearie!" Aceline said, turning to the door. Then she paused, looking hesitant. "You're interested in the future. I'm interested in the past. If it's not too much to ask, could you tell me where you found the plaque? I'd really like to study the actual thing."

"As soon as I finish what I'm doing, I'll hand it over to you," Emmeline replied. "I'm really grateful for your help. I was going to give up."

Aceline looked into her eyes. "You know that's a lie. Women like you and me never give up." Her lips spread into a wide smile. "I hope you have a tuning fork!"

Emmeline stood dumbfounded for a moment before she realized Aceline was joking.

TITAN, DECK 1, BRIDGE

As the computer continued to run diagnostics, Adrian lost track of time. Today, he felt excited. Helping those ships depart had given him hope that one day, maybe, he could go on a mission. Titan was great, but four years was a long time. He was so consumed by his thoughts; he didn't notice Evan sitting beside him.

"Hello there!"

"Ahh!" Adrian cried out. "What the . . .?"

"Yes, I am the ghost from your mythical . . ."

"Oh, shut up."

"It's midnight. Don't you want to sleep?" Evan asked.

Adrian shrugged. "I have the next two days off. I thought it would be better if I completed the diagnostic. That way, I don't have to worry about it."

"You could leave it for me."

"Nah, it's okay."

"Hey, what's this?" Evan asked, tapping a few buttons on Adrian's console.

"Don't!"

"Oh, my Lord," Evan said, looking at the video feed of the hangar deck. It was Delta. "Are you watching her?"

Astra had just returned after delivering another shipment from Vesta, one of the largest asteroids from the asteroid belt between Mars and Jupiter, currently a promising resource for mining platinum.

"Shush! No!" Adrian responded.

"You're stalking her?"

"You don't understand!" said Adrian. "I just wanted to make sure she returned safely. She took up the job of transporting miners from Earth to Vesta. That asteroid is unstable. I-I just wanted to make sure . . ."

"Adrian, you have to stop."

"It's not what you think. I'm just looking out for her."

"You've been 'looking out for her' for as long as I can remember," Evan said. "Time's up! Either you ask her out or let her go."

"I-I can't," Adrian said weakly. "I can't ask her out."

"Why not?"

"What if it ruins our friendship? I don't want to take the risk."

"Buddy, make your choice."

Adrian's face hardened, "Goodnight," he said coldly.

Evan stood up. Just then, a loud beeping noise echoed on the bridge. "What the hell was that?"

"I don't know. The diagnostic isn't done yet," Adrian said.

Evan took his station.

"It's a signal," said Adrian. "Something's out there."

"Out where?"

Adrian looked at him. "Beyond the perimeter."

TITAN, DECK 4, EMMELINE'S QUARTERS

Hours passed painfully, and Emmeline's head began spinning. She had been playing the tunes, but all her efforts were in vain. The plaque sat silently on the table besides the pad which played one tune after another. Her annoyance grew, and she covered her ears with a pillow and put her feet on the table.

"Oh, this is ridiculous," she muttered. Maybe it was all for nothing. Maybe Aceline was wrong. One can't always be right. She should focus on her studies, on her training, and spending more time with Argon. Instead, she felt she was wasting her time listening to an out of tune orchestra.

A tune rang out, and she felt the table vibrate. She looked at the plaque and thought it emitted a glow. She paused the music and then played it again.

"Oh my god!"

As soon as the music died, the pad fell from her hands. She moved away as a bright yellow light began to emerge from the plaque. First, the grayish rock began to crack. Then it withered away until only a black plaque with a smooth surface remained. As if she had opened a closed book, pictures emerged. At first, Emmeline saw what looked like the sun, then three circles. Soon, the entire plaque was filled with symbols she had never seen before.

"What is this?" she wondered out loud.

Her communicator buzzed, but she didn't want to look away. She was trying to understand what the plaque was telling her.

The communicator buzzed again. "Emmeline, this is Adrian."

"Adrian, I'm busy."

"I need you. There's something beyond the perimeter. I think it's an alien spacecraft."

Emmeline froze.

"Emmeline?"

"Yes?"

"I need you in the Crystal Lab. Now!"

"Give me a minute!" She picked up the plaque, put it in the backpack, and returned it to the safe.

TITAN, DECK 2, OBSERVATORY 1

Emmeline was puffing by the time she reached. She turned on the gamma-ray telescope and the thermal imaging system.

"Are you there yet?" asked Adrian through the intercom.

"I'm here. Transfer the coordinates."

"Transferring coordinates."

The large concave screen in front of her came to life. She stood on the console and began scanning.

"Have you tried hailing?" she asked.

"I have sent several hails; the ship is not responding."

She didn't answer him, and looked at the data.

"Emmeline," said Anastasia. "What have you got?"

"Hold on."

"Patch us through," Adrian said. "I'm losing it. The ship is going off my sensors!"

"Okay. I've got it!"

The screen blurred for a few seconds, then cleared. She could see a vague long black craft.

"I'm patching the image through to the bridge." Emmeline continued to tap on the panels. "Lieutenant, the reason it's vanishing from your sensors is because it's on the lower orbit of a gas giant approximately two light-years from our position."

"Wow."

"Yes."

"But we weren't looking for it," said Adrian. "How did Titan detect it?"

"I don't . . ." Emmeline was about to reply when a small flash appeared from the ship. "Maybe that's why. It just emitted some sort of energy blast . . ." Her voice trailed off.

"It's gone!" Adrian said. "I've lost it. Do you have it?"

"Hold on. I'm recalibrating the sensors." Emmeline's fingers danced on the panel. "Expanding search perimeters." She turned on the gamma-ray spectrometer. Several minutes passed.

"Emmeline, try infrared spectrograph," said Dr. Kent, entering the lab.

"Already on it," Emmeline replied. "I'm also conducting all standard scans, including UV. Adjusting sensors," she said.

"I will order the computer to take pictures using the telescopes so we can do a geospatial data analysis," suggested Dr. Kent. He began working on a console.

"Understood."

A few minutes passed.

"I'm having trouble keeping track of it. It's disappearing from my sensors!" Emmeline cried out.

"I'm losing it too!" said Dr. Kent, tapping the keys on the console.

They both looked at the screen. They couldn't see it anymore.

"It's gone! It's gone!" Emmeline cried out.

"Perhaps it has entered into the planet's atmosphere," Adrian suggested.

"Checking," Emmeline replied. There was a long pause. Then Emmeline banged the console. "My scans of the gas giant are inconclusive. I need more time, and we're just too far away. I recommend sending a ship after it."

"Hold on. Did you scan for debris? Maybe it was destroyed," asked Anastasia.

"If it was, it would have shown on my initial scans. But I'll check," Emmeline said.

Again, they all waited.

"Nothing," she reported when the checks were complete.

"So, it appears, emits some kind of beam, and then vanishes?" Anastasia asked.

Emmeline didn't know what to say. "It seems so. But why did it appear to begin with? Where did it come from?"

"Could it be a sort of communication?" suggested Anastasia.

"If it was why did it vanish?" said Dr. Kent

None of them knew it but a couple of days later, three similar ships would show up near the perimeter and change their lives forever.

CHAPTER 6: DNA NEVER LIES

PRESENT DAY

TITAN, DECK 2, JACOB'S QUARTERS

Admiral Jacob Donavan sat on a chair in his quarters and looked out at the stationary stars. After traveling for four long years, he was used to seeing the stars moving. The stillness gave him some comfort, though he wished the timing was better. The silence was welcoming and so was the environment. Titan's quarters were much better than Freedom's. Although he was the admiral, Freedom's quarters weren't built for comfort. The only other place he felt comfort was in his home. A sadness dawned upon him, it had too many memories and he didn't feel like going back there. Not just yet. He looked around. Maybe he could make Titan his home.

The possibility of an interstellar war with the Orias appeared to be inevitable, although some part of him hoped otherwise. Their first battle had gone well. Jacob knew Titan's citizens needed him. Titan was powerful, but under a weak commander it might perish. *Yes, yes it will perish*, he thought.

Freedom was a fine ship, but he felt he had to stay behind to fix things that had gone wrong, including his marriage. He shook his head in disbelief. After forty years, she wanted to leave him. He couldn't believe it. What hadn't he done for her? For some people, nothing was ever enough. You just had to tell them they couldn't have it, and he wouldn't let her have this. Enough was enough. He would not go through with the divorce. He believed in the vows of marriage, and she was bound to them, bound to him. That was it. Rules were rules; they were in it for life. *Rules must not be broken,* He thought.

Jacob had thought he could finish this last mission, return to Earth, work with the tribunal, and fix his marriage. It would have been simple if it weren't for the Orias. Now he was stuck on Titan, guarding the perimeter against this unknown enemy. He had to stay. They had no leader, no experience.

What had life come to? He could feel that the people on Titan were eager to fight. Argon and his squadron needed to be disciplined. That is why he had nominated Argon as the squadron leader. Responsibility will teach him discipline. The scientist including Dr. Kent need to follow rules and regulation better. He felt that Commander Waters was lenient and focused more on action than thoughtful strategies. She wanted Titan to join the fleet. *Silly woman.*

He knew their first attempt had failed, but still there were chances of a diplomatic solution. He rolled his eyes. The Imperial Command knew very little of what he had to deal with. He was the mediator, the linchpin, managing both sides. Thank God the members of the Imperial Command believed in him. Otherwise, the situation would have been worse. It was his duty to protect these people, not only from the Orias but from themselves. They didn't know better, so he had to show them. He thought about Anastasia's plan and the steps she was taking. But she wasn't him; he was better.

Titan, Deck 5, Engineering

When he entered engineering, Lieutenant Commander Adrian Olson was unsure if he was in the right place. Usually, it was a humdrum area, but today, it was loud and somewhat overwhelming. He thought about the meeting and the idea to put shields around the perimeter. It sounded very good at first, but as he planned the upgrade, he felt the burden of the enormous task.

Two months ago, he was thinking of leaving, doing something else. Now all he could think about was the Orias. Those ships, black, long, cylindrical and dangerous. The mysterious cloud. He couldn't believe how the situation had turned, and now Titan was on full alert. He sensed fear, but also excitement. No one liked war, but in a way, it was forcing them to be innovative.

The usual sound in engineering was the loud humming of engines, but today, the air was a mix of screeches, whirls, and beeps. Adrian looked up at the bridges and saw the engineering crew moving fast. A loud screech made him turn toward the overhead crane, which was carrying a large white cylindrical container. The machine stopped in the middle of the deck and groaned, and the container slowly moved downward. As he walked ahead, the container was placed on an Automated Hovering Carrier. A crewman tapped on a pad and walked along with the equipment as the carrier approached the exit.

Adrian strolled toward the four ten-foot-high green-colored cylinders, which were filled with fuel. They looked like four hefty pillars, forming the corners of a square. Around each fuel tank were two crew members, tapping on consoles and probably running diagnostics. Adrian felt a tap on his shoulder. He turned to look at Titan's engineer. Delta stood on her side.

"Okay, I'm super busy. What is it you want?"

"The generator."

They came to stand in front of a heavy white cylindrical object. Its top was pointed, and its bottom was flat. It sat above the ground on the hovering platform.

"Are you sure this is going to work?" asked Adrian.

Delta and Cyr looked at him.

"Well, in case of massive power failure, generators could be hooked up to the perimeter's built-in installation panels. Theoretically, it should work. Practically? Well, that remains to be seen," said Cyr.

"Okay, we'd better suit up," said Adrian uncertainly.

PERIMETER

The circular door above opened, and Adrian slowly climbed the ladder. He passed through the door; the lights turned on. He waited, and the door below him closed.

"Opening outer hatch," said the computer. "Caution. Opening outer hatch."

He checked his suit. It was working perfectly. Although he was trained for spacewalks, he hardly ever got the chance to do them. His heart beat fast as the door opened into the heavens. He held onto the ladder as the narrow cabin decompressed. Once the decompression was complete, the gravity boots were activated, and he slowly climbed up the ladder. He took a deep breath as he stood on the roof of Astra.

"All good?" asked Delta on the intercom.

"All good. All systems working perfectly. I'm moving toward the edge of the ship."

He felt the complete silence around him; it was refreshing. He imagined he was standing at the edge of a mountain, surrounded by the miracle of the cosmos. He always found taking the first step hard. Cautiously, he put his left foot forward, then his right, and he soon felt like he was walking on Titan. Except that the suit was heavier than his uniform.

"Commander Waters to Lieutenant Olson," came Anastasia's voice.

"Yes, Commander," Adrian replied as he slowly made his way toward the edge of Astra.

"Good luck."

"Thank you."

The intercom became silent, and Adrian stood at the edge of the cargo ship to look at the huge white jungle of crisscrossing poles. The massiveness of the pillars was unimaginable from a distance. He turned and squinted, but Titan was barely visible. The twinkling lights on its outer edges indicated its presence. Despite the suit, he felt cold and shivered a bit.

"Are you ready?" asked Delta.

"Wait a minute," he replied and looked up at the installation mechanism. He fired the boosters and propelled upwards.

"Easy now," said Evan on the intercom.

Adrian ignored him and kept his eyes on the installation mechanism. He glanced down and saw the edge of Astra disappearing from his view. Adjusting his trajectory, he flew upward along the vast wall and slowed his pace when he reached the structure. He turned off the booster and grabbed hold of one of the pillars. He observed the hexagonal installation mechanism with a cone-shaped interior. Gradually, he moved down the pillar and came face to face with the structure. Grabbing its edges, he floated around and stood on the edge of a slanted pillar just behind it. Now he was behind the structure.

"How does it look?" asked Evan.

"Looks good. I have to make sure it works," Adrian said. He looked at the panel. The installation mechanisms had never been used, and he couldn't recall if they had even been tested. His heart pounded in his chest as he reached for the smaller square panel and opened it. As he'd expected, there was a small switch. He flicked it, and the main panel opened outward. He gulped, looking at the bulky, round red handle. He grabbed it, pulled it outward, and turned it ninety degrees. He pushed it back in and felt a thud just below his feet.

"Lieutenant Weeds?"

"Hold it."

The structure vibrated. "What's happening?" Adrian asked.

"It's online."

"Great!" Adrian said, feeling relieved. He quickly closed

the panel. Still holding onto the pillar, he floated around and came to the front of the perimeter. He grabbed the edge of the installation mechanism and saw two blinking blue lights at the end of the cone.

"Astra, are you ready?" he asked, wondering if he was too loud as his voice echoed in the helmet.

"Yep, ready. You need to move away from the mechanism."

Adrian fired up the boosters. The gas from the boosters left a small trail behind him. He looked like a tiny, slow-moving speck on a massive wall. When he thought he was far enough away, he turned the boosters off and got hold of one of the pillars. Resting his foot on the edge of the pillar, he made sure he had a clear view of Astra. "Okay. I'm at a safe distance."

Astra's engines fired up, emitting a bright light. The small cargo ship's bow began to dip.

"Delta, be careful," said Evan on the commlink.

"Don't worry. I can handle this."

Adrian watched as the ship moved downward until it was almost parallel with the perimeter. The engines became silent, and the ship stood still for a moment. Then the bottom thrusters came online, and it moved toward the perimeter.

"Good. Just a bit more," said Evan. "Stop."

The thrusters turned off.

Adrian let go of the pillar and turned on the boosters. He slowly moved toward Astra as the doors on the roof of the cargo ship opened outward.

"Ready to launch perimeter generator 001," announced Delta.

Adrian reduced his pace as the generator emerged from the ship.

"Aligning the generator," said Delta.

"Take it easy," muttered Adrian.

The generator was held by four broad mechanical arms. Adrian watched as it fully emerged and moved slightly up and down as Delta tried to align it.

"Easy. Just a bit higher," Evan said, guiding her.

"I'm trying," replied Delta in a strained voice.

Adrian flew closer and placed his hand on the generator. He pushed himself, floated toward the hexagonal structure, and saw the generator's top enter the structure. "You're doing great," he said. "We're almost done."

Soon, the generator's pointy head disappeared into the hexagonal structure. Adrian felt a thud.

"Done. The generator is secure. Release clamps," announced Evan.

The clamps released, and the mechanical hands slowly moved away from the generator. Adrian waited as Astra closed the doors. He turned on the boosters and floated away from the perimeter. When he thought he was far enough, he again fired up the boosters and brought himself to a complete halt. "Okay, punch it."

"I am bringing it online, now."

Silence. Then two green lights blinked at the round end of the generator.

"It's online! Full power," said Evan.

Adrian smiled. "Woo-hoo! Excellent work, guys!"

"Hm. One done, just eighty-nine more to go," grumbled Evan.

Titan, Deck 4, Anastasia's Quarters

Anastasia studied the notes in front of her. She didn't know how much it could help, but history was a good place to start. She had learned a lot while in command of Marion, but she knew very little about war. Human history was full of it. Sitting on a comfortable chair, she admired the cosmos. The commander's quarters were no different than other colonist, but she had made it special and personal. The carpet was purple, with light cream walls on which hung carefully picked pictures. They were mostly of family, her children and her childhood on Titan. Just beside the window sat a piano. It was old and had lost its glow, but still she wouldn't part with it.

There was a small kitchen which she hardly used, and a good-sized bedroom which was messy because she didn't have time to clean up.

Anastasia focused on her work. She had made a list of techniques and maneuvers used to win and survive a war. She bit her nails and wondered if they would help. Then she picked up the next pad and studied her notes about their meeting with the Imperial Command. They had to convince the members to take the Orias seriously. She hoped to hear from the admiral about it.

Soon, she felt restless and knew what she had to do. She got up, walked to the piano and began playing. The music brought her a sense of relief, calmness, and her mind slowly centered. She hoped her playing didn't disturb other colonist.

The doorbell rang.

"Come in," she said.

She paused when she saw Mykel smiling at her.

"You still have it?"

"Some things are difficult to part with."

He stepped forward and admired the instrument, "I didn't see it last time I visited."

"I had to put it in storage when I left the system. When my family left for Earth, I brought it out of storage."

He sat beside her.

"Let's see," he said and played a tune she remembered very well. She joined in, and both of them played for a while. The music echoed in the room, and she felt like singing again after a long time. The music stopped and their eyes met.

"There is a crack over here," Mykel said, pointing out the wood.

"Well, you gave it to me twenty years ago… its bound to have a few cracks."

"It can be fixed."

"I know. But I like it the way it is." Anastasia replied, "What are you doing here?"

"We have a meeting in an hour. I thought I'd drop by for a cup of coffee."

She eyed him, wondering if she should do this. But given everything that was happening around them, she said, "Sure."

Soon, she felt she had made a good decision, though she felt that people were watching them as they walked down the corridor. Being the only commander was a lonely job, but when Mykel was around, she never felt that way. She still hadn't told him about Martin, and maybe with their current situation, she didn't need to. It didn't matter. They had bigger things to worry about.

Titan, Deck 2, Main meeting room

Everyone was in the meeting room, including Emmeline. She wasn't surprised when she was invited to join the meeting. She'd been working around the clock with Cyr and her team. A week had passed since the attack, but she felt they'd barely scratched the surface.

Argon and Byron sat opposite to her while Clio and Micah were nowhere to be seen. Admiral Donavan sat at the far end with captains from other ships. Dr. Finch entered the meeting room and took a seat beside Dr. Kent. The exobiologist was a stalky man in his late forties with a graying hairline that was disappearing rapidly toward a patch of sparse hair at the back of his head. He had been studying the remains of the Orias. Beside him sat Aceline, studying her notes.

Emmeline saw Mykel and smiled. Argon couldn't stop talking about him, and she knew why. Argon was a big fan of the captain and his ship, Prometheus. Despite the war, Argon and his friends had been to the marvelous ship and spent hours looking around. After its long voyage, the crew and ship welcomed tourist.

But Emmeline noticed something more. Anastasia and the captain sat close together, talking in whispers. She wondered what they were talking about. Whatever it was, she felt an unprecedented warmth from both of them. She was one of the newest members of Titan, but as soon as people heard that the Prometheus was returning, there were whispers about both the commanders. It appeared they had a history, a long and passionate one.

Emmeline wasn't interested in other people's personal lives, but her feelings towards Commander Waters were different. Unlike her, the Commander was born on Titan, and lived most of her life on the space station. Emmeline remembered the day she had arrived on the station. She had never been so far away from home and felt almost like an alien. Anastasia helped her make it her home. She was like her second mother. Listening, nodding, understanding, yet she kept a firm hand. Despite the war, the gloominess around them Emmeline felt a warmth looking at the woman she admired, and then she turned towards the man she adored. Argon looked confused for a moment, but then just smiled.

A bell rang.

"Good. Everyone's here," said Anastasia as the meeting began. "Let's begin. What about the perimeter shields?"

"Our first installation was successful. The generator is online. We've assembled a team of officers and ten cargo ships to help us. Once all the generators are installed, we should have the shields in no time," reported Adrian.

"That's good."

"May I suggest that we also activate the receptors?" asked Cyr.

Emmeline was surprised. She hadn't heard about the receptors.

"Excellent idea," said Anastasia.

"What are the receptors?" asked Mykel.

"The perimeter has receptors that can be activated from Titan. In case of power loss, the receptors could be used to transmit power from here."

"That means Titan can transfer power to the perimeter directly?" asked Mykel.

"Yes," replied Cyr.

"Do it," said Anastasia.

"That's unnecessary," said Jacob.

Emmeline wanted to roll her eyes, but she controlled herself.

"We want to be prepared," said Anastasia. "Admiral, speaking of being prepared, ten ships have returned. Can we have them stationed near the perimeter?"

"Those ships are to remain at the Challenger colony near Earth."

"Why?" said Mykel.

"We're waiting for the Imperial Command's orders."

"Have we suggested them to station those ship at the perimeter?" asked Anastasia.

"Not yet."

"Why the delay?"

"I think they might feel it's unnecessary at the moment."

Emmeline felt annoyed, and she noticed the distress around the room.

Mykel was about to say something when Anastasia gently touched his arm. "Maybe we should bring it up during our meeting with the Imperial Command," she said.

The admiral didn't look impressed.

"What about the debris? Lieutenant Storm, did you find a data module?" said Anastasia, pressing on.

Cyr bowed her head. "No. We cannot make heads nor tails of the alien ship's internal design. To make matters worse, the parts are fused together, and it's difficult to tear them apart."

"So, we have nothing?"

"Nothing yet."

"Don't give up." Anastasia turned to the doctors. "First of all, Dr. Finch, thank you very much for coming all the way from Earth."

"My pleasure."

"You understand that staying on Titan could be dangerous?"

"I understand. But I do not believe we would have made much progress if I had stayed back on Earth."

"Good to know. Proceed."

The doctor got to his feet, and the large screen behind Anastasia came to life. "Now, as I'm sure everyone here knows, we found some dead aliens," he said. "To be precise, a head, a leg, two arms, and a bone. They belong to different Orias. Using what we found, and my years of study on exobiology, I have made a rough reconstruction of what the Orias might look like."

Everyone exchanged glances. Emmeline felt blood rushing to her face.

"Behold the enemy."

The image on the screen changed, and a few people gasped. Emmeline felt her skin crawl. She involuntarily glanced at Argon, who looked concerned. To her, the lights appeared dimmer, and the savage image on the screen was terrifying.

The creature was about six or seven feet tall with a tough black exoskeleton. Its hexagonal whitish and blue-hued eyes sat deep in an elongated head with a wide jaw. It had a short, thick neck, two arms, and sturdy legs.

"We know very little about this species," said Dr. Finch. The image on the screen changed, showing DNA strands. "You see, like every living being in the universe, including you and me, they have a DNA pattern. We have twenty-three chromosome pairs with three billion DNA base pairs. Now you understand why you are so complicated."

No one laughed, but Emmeline appreciated the doctor's attempt at humor.

"These aliens have forty-six chromosomes pairs, and I have discovered over six billion DNA base pairs. Unfortunately, we do not have a database that contains similar DNA patterns for further study. Just like no two humans are genetically identical, no two DNA patterns for the Orias are identical." The doctor became silent and looked as if he was carefully gathering his words. "I detected something in their DNA sequence that I have never seen in any studies I have done in my lifetime. I could not find any earlier records of similar findings, and I double-checked my work." He paused.

Everyone sensed his discomfort.

"Doctor?" prompted Anastasia.

"Sorry. I have discovered an underlying hidden DNA sequence in the samples."

"Hidden?" asked Adrian.

"Yes. They have two DNA sequences. One which is easily detectable, and another which is hidden as if submerged. It's only a trace."

"What do you mean?" Anastasia asked.

"It appears as if someone has written over their original DNA."

Gasps were heard throughout the room. Emmeline narrowed her eyes. That wasn't possible. No, it couldn't be.

"Are you telling me they were transformed?" concluded Mykel.

"Something like that," said Dr. Finch, nodding. "I don't think the Orias were born. They were created by eradicating another species." The image on the screen changed again. "This is what the Orias look like. Ugly, fat, bipedal animals with two hind limbs, a large head, and a wide jaw. Using my expertise, I pulled out the bits and pieces of suppressed genomes. This is what this species actually looks like. Please keep in mind I have used a bit of my imagination."

Beside the Orias, a picture of a bipedal creature that looked very much like a human appeared. It had an exceptionally short neck, big angular eyes, and a bulky head.

"Oh my God," said Emmeline.

"Are you telling us that someone or something deleted their original DNA and made them into monsters?" said Cyr.

"Yes."

Murmurs filled the meeting room.

"Silence," commanded Anastasia. "Okay. So, each Orias might be from a different species?"

Dr. Finch nodded. "Yes. Or the same. I pulled out this genome from the first leg we discovered in the debris. A second one from the head. Those two Orias originated from same species."

"What about the second leg you found?" asked Cyr.

"I haven't gotten to that yet." Dr. Finch turned to Anastasia. "Commander, we need to be careful. Whoever is sending those ships has the power to alter genomes and might have the power to alter an entire species."

"You mean play God?" asked Argon angrily.

Emmeline felt goosebumps on her skin.

The room became completely silence.

"I have a question," said Evan.

Dr. Finch gave him his full attention.

"Is it something like when the witch changed the prince into a frog?" he asked.

"Lieutenant," warned Anastasia.

But no one could help it. Everyone, Anastasia included, burst into a roar of laughter. Emmeline was happy to see everyone loosen up for a second.

"It's a valid question!" argued Evan.

The humor died out quickly.

Dr. Finch cleared this throat. "Well, Lieutenant, luckily for the prince, he could change back into a human. These guys are not so fortunate."

"You mean this is permanent?" asked Jacob.

"Yes."

Everyone was tongue-tied.

Aceline said, "Could you share your theories about their behavior? They look like animals, but their behavior suggested higher intelligence. Do you think they would be telepathic?"

Everyone turned to Dr. Finch, who smiled. "A very intriguing question. And, fortunately, one I can answer in a few days. I've been studying the attack pattern of the Orias. They distracted our fighters, and the wheel was targeting the perimeter. I agree, doctor. Despite what they look like, their behavior indicates some sort of higher intelligence."

"I'm sure there's a hierarchy," Aceline commented. "Someone or something was giving them orders. In our planet's history, instinct drives most animals, not necessarily strategy."

"If they are telepathic and don't know how to communicate verbally, that could explain why they didn't respond to our hails," said Adrian.

Heads nodded around the table.

"I must examine the brain, but yes, that is possible," answered Dr. Finch.

"That's why diplomatic ways may not work until we get a hold of their leader," said Mykel.

"Adrian, you were conducting continuous scans during the battle. Did you detect any unusual readings or frequencies?" Anastasia asked.

Adrian shook his head. "Not to my knowledge. But I still have the data from the scans. I can go through it again."

"Do it."

"What are you thinking, Commander?" asked Mykel.

"I'm thinking that if we can identify the frequency, they were using to communicate with each other, we can use it to take them down."

"Or communicate with them," said Jacob.

Emmeline wasn't sure communication would work. She studied the surprised look on Anastasia's face.

"Time will tell. Next—" Anastasia started.

Dr. Finch held up a hand to stop her. "I'm not done yet. A week ago, Emmeline reported that she found traces of reptilian DNA in the debris."

Everyone looked at Emmeline, and immediately, she felt intimidated.

"Yes," said Anastasia. "So?"

Dr. Finch's face paled. "In the same debris where Emmeline detected the reptilian DNA, I found a bone. It is a vertebra, part of the spine. I think during the battle, the Orias body was crushed to pieces. We may or may not find the rest of it. Just like the other samples, the vertebra shows signs of genetic altering, and I've found another hidden genome pattern."

"And?" said Dr. Kent.

Dr. Finch gulped. "The vertebra belongs to a human."

Fear grasped Emmeline.

"W-What?" Adrian cried out. "That's impossible!"

"But how could that be? I'm sure none of us were . . . taken," said Argon.

"Are you sure, Dr. Finch?" asked Anastasia in a low voice.

"I'm afraid it's the truth," he replied solemnly. "The vertebra belongs to a human."

"This is preposterous!" said Jacob. "Rubbish I say!"

The room fell silent. Emmeline could feel her palms sweating. She massaged them together in hopes it would relax her.

"But how and when?" asked Dr. Kent.

"To the best of my knowledge, six ships were lost in deep space. Two were destroyed in an ion storm, but four ships vanished without a trace," Anastasia answered.

"How far back was this?" asked Dr. Finch.

"The ships left the solar system about thirty years ago."

"Wasn't there a search?" asked Argon.

"Two ships were sent out to investigate, but they returned empty-handed."

"Are you suggesting they were abducted by these Orias?" asked Jacob.

"I don't know," replied Anastasia. "I'm just saying we've lost people in deep space."

"Is it possible that this bone might belong to one of the crew members on those lost ships?" asked Argon.

"There's only one way to find out," said Anastasia as she turned to look at the doctor.

There was an unsettling silence. Emmeline bit her nails. She stopped when she saw Dr. Kent glaring at her. She immediately straightened up, trying to look strong.

"You all know what's at stake here," Anastasia said. "This is a species that has for no apparent reason declared war on us. To make matters worse, we have discovered that they can eradicate other species. We have no choice. This is our home, and we need to protect it at all costs. Dr. Finch, your priority is to find out whatever you can from the brain. I want to know how they communicate. Then your job is to find a match for that vertebra. If it belongs to any of the crew members who were lost, we can assume that the Orias captured our ship. You can find all the information about those ships in Titan's database. Do you need help?"

"I'd like to work with someone who has knowledge and expertise in working with fossils and DNA."

Anastasia smiled.

"I'd love to help," offered Aceline.

"Thank you."

"Lieutenant Weeds and Olson," continued Anastasia. "I want the shields up and running. Then find out if there were any hidden frequencies or any kind of communications between the alien ships. You can use the help of the Crystal Lab."

The officers nodded.

"Dr. Kent, what about the cloud?"

"Emmeline was right," Dr. Kent said. "It's a doorway, probably to another galaxy, but we have no control over it. However, we could shut it down."

"What do you mean, shut it down?"

"Imagine that they're using a generator on the other side of that doorway. We can overload it."

Everyone looked at each other.

"I'm afraid to ask," said Anastasia. "How?"

"The Phoenix."

"You mean the death ray," Evan said.

Dr. Kent smirked.

Emmeline rolled her eyes, crossed her arms, and glared at Evan.

"Death ray?" asked Dr. Finch. "What is a death ray?"

"An experiment designed by Dr. Kent and Emmeline to create a high-yield particle beam. It could take out an Orias wheel in seconds, and I think we could also use it for scientific purposes. One of Titan's missions is to protect Earth from dangerous unknown spatial anomalies, and such a particle beam could be very useful," explained Anastasia.

"Okay. Then what's stopping you?" asked Dr. Finch.

Everyone looked at each other.

"The last time Emmeline brought it online, it blew up every transformer in engineering and started a massive fire," said Cyr.

"Then it hit the environmental systems, and for the first time in ten years, artificial gravity went offline," added Adrian.

"And Titan's bridge computers overloaded and blew," said Anastasia.

"And the Crystal Lab was very, very close to exploding," said Argon.

Emmeline gritted her teeth. It wasn't fair. It was an experiment, and experiments sometimes went wrong, but that didn't mean it was right to give up. What the hell was wrong with these people?

"So, it's dangerous," said Dr. Finch.

"It needs a powerful energy source, which we don't have. When we linked it to Titan, it drained most of its power. I believe if we learn to stabilize and control the energy required by the particle beam, it should be safe to use," explained Dr. Kent.

"It looks good on the drawing board, Chris. Leave it there," scoffed Jacob.

"I've put in another proposal," said Dr. Kent.

"They will not say yes. Stop wasting your time."

"One day, it will work," muttered Dr. Kent.

Everyone fell silent.

Then Jacob spoke. "Captain Lockhart and I have been recalled by the Imp—"

"Why?" interjected Anastasia.

"To discuss how to handle this war."

"I don't think either of you should leave Titan," she said, looking at Mykel. "I thought we were going to talk to the Imperial Command together."

Mykel rolled his eyes. "The admiral spoke on our behalf."

"What?" asked Anastasia. "But we'd decided to work on this together." She looked at Jacob.

"I know. I found out just before the meeting." Mykel eyed the admiral too.

A sense of anger rose within Emmeline, and she saw Argon scowling.

"And you agreed to leave?" asked Dr. Kent.

There was a tense silence. "We have to do what the Imperial Command says," Jacob replied.

"We don't know if we're being watched. We don't know when these things will attack again. It could be tomorrow or the day after. We must be ready. You're needed here. If the perimeter falls, there might be no Earth or Imperial Command to protect. Do you really have to leave? Can't you speak to them from here?" Anastasia demanded.

"Valid point. I can try. But Prometheus has to go."

"Why?" she asked, again looking at Mykel, who remained silent.

"It's been through an ion storm, and its hull has sustained damage that can only be repaired at the Challenger colony. In addition, the ship has been in deep space for four years, and its engines need refurbishments," explained the admiral.

"I know, but . . ."

"Commander, I think our ships can handle this, and the earlier we do the repairs, the better," said Jacob.

"I think I should speak to the Imperial Command," Anastasia said.

"I think I just said I have, and there is nothing more to discuss." Jacob replied coldly, "They are well aware of our situation. The improvements you have made to the perimeter and the steps you are taking. They trust us to handle the situation. I spoke with some commanders in the fleet, they feel confident that we can tackle the Orias."

Mykel and Anastasia exchanged worried looks. Emmeline touched her neck and felt a sense of dread.

"Admiral, next time, I would like to be included in such

meetings, especially if it involves the future of Titan and the twenty thousand people who live on this colony," Anastasia got on her feet, "I will have a word with them myself. Meeting adjourned."

Emmeline left the meeting room with millions of questions running through her mind. Her heart was pounding, and she felt disheartened. What could they do? What if these creatures attacked again? How would they survive? What if they destroyed Titan? She felt they were defenseless and wished she had never joined the meeting.

It wasn't just Emmeline who felt that way. Adrian's stomach twisted, and sweat dripped down his neck. He waited for the elevator with Evan. Finally, he said, "I don't believe this."

"I know. It's an uneasy feeling knowing that there's someone on the other side of that cloud that could turn you into a monster," said Evan.

His words gave Adrian no comfort. Space was a dangerous place, but he'd always thought he would die in an explosion or suffocate to death. To be reborn as an ugly creature with no mind of its own was a nightmare.

The doors to the elevator opened, and they stepped in. "I know. I feel like I'm going to puke," Adrian said.

"I'd prefer to be a frog than a monster," Evan thought out loud.

Adrian looked at him. "I'd prefer to remain human."

TITAN DECK 1, ANASTASIA'S OFFICE

Anastasia walked up and down in her office, trying to control her rage. She understood that the Admiral outranked her, but she couldn't understand the logic behind his actions. Since he had arrived, he walked around the station as if it was his. She sensed a rise of tension around her people. She could see traders sulking, colonist in distress and many of them demanding to return to Earth. Of course, she couldn't stop them, but it would affect Titan's day-to-day management. But it was surprising that the Imperial Command was denying them the chance to return to Earth until things settle. Her chat with Admiral Vince was futile, and she couldn't reach any of the tribunals. She felt it was illogical not to allow safe passage to Earth non-military personnel. She shut her eyes. *Oh, I feel like…* She dismissed the thought. She rolled her eyes, thinking about Admiral Vince's response.

"Trust Jacob's instincts. We have got a thorough report, and we are satisfied with it."

"Trust facts!" yelled Anastasia. The buzzer sounded, and she calmed herself. "Come in."

She turned to find the concerned face of Mykel. "Hi," he said in a low voice and made himself comfortable on the couch along with the window. She smiled and joined him. He held his head and said, "That was not good."

"No."

"What can we do?"

She took in a long breath, "Nothing. I tried talking to the Imperial Command. They are not listening to me."

"I did the same. They feel that they know everything. I think they are greatly mistaken. I just finished a conversation with the captain of the Marion."

She was keen to hear what others thought.

"He seems comfortable with the ways things are."

"But?"

"I have a feeling that there is more going on here than what is being said."

A gloominess dawned on her, she grabbed his hand, "Don't tell me…"

"Oh, they can't take the Prometheus away from me, not yet. One thing I know for sure… anything happens, my crew is with me."

His words comforted her. He leaned forward, "But Titan…"

Anastasia swallowed and bowed.

"I can't let him hurt you like that…"

"I can handle…"

"Not when you are alone,"

She gasped.

"Yes. I know. You left him. You should have told me," he said, peering into her eyes.

Tears gathered in her eyes. "You were away. You always leave. When can I ever tell you anything?"

"You know I am always there for you. You should have reached out. All you needed to do was call me."

She shut her eyes, looking away from him. Every emotion, every feeling that she had buried for years was threatening to come out. She stood up and was about to walk away when he grabbed her hand. "Not now, Mykel. This is not the time."

He looked her in the eye, "Time will never be on our side. Do you understand? We have to save what we have."

"I know," she replied, her eyes meeting his, "I am trying to save what I have."

"Sorry. I didn't mean to make you uncomfortable. I only want to warn you… Admiral is dangerous."

She looked at him for answers.

"He is just not after Titan. There is something going on… and we are not aware of it."

She wanted to say thank you. Instead; she stepped forward and embraced him. In his arms, she felt the comfort that she longed for.

"I missed you too

Already things seem better.

They parted.

"We need to make a backup plan," she said.

"Do you think we should evacuate the station?"

Anastasia's eyes widened. Every fiber of her body resisted the idea, but what she felt was irrelevant. "If the situation worsens, we might have to."

He nodded in agreement, "We better be ready. What

about your crew?"

She looked him in the eye, "Loyal and stubborn."

TITAN, DECK 4, ARGON'S QUARTERS

Argon sat on a chair in his sister's room while his mother worked tirelessly on the computer in the living room. They had eaten their dinner in silence, and then he read his little sister a story. Selina was now sound asleep, but he wouldn't dare close his eyes. The strategies they were using to defend themselves were good, he knew that. He thought about Emmeline, if something were to happen to him, who would take care of her. Her father was on Earth and couldn't travel to Titan until things settled. Maybe he should tell her to take the Raven and go to Earth. But would she go? No. She was dedicated to her work and Titan needed her. Her work could save lives, save Titan. He walked up to his little sister and sat on the bed's edge. He watched her closely. He had pressed his mother to leave Titan. She wouldn't. He then urged her to send Selina to dad, at least she would be safe. They agreed, and he had put in a request, but he knew it would be denied. The Imperial Command wasn't allowing people to leave, just yet. He couldn't understand why? He thought about the future. Two months ago, he knew exactly what he was going to do with his life? But suddenly, it appeared he was no longer in control.

He trusted himself, his friends, everyone on Titan, but not the man who seemed to hold all the reins. What he witnessed in the meeting room today disturbed him? He wondered secretly if there was a war looming on Titan itself and when it happens, where would he stand?

TITAN, DECK 4, EMMELINE'S QUARTERS

Emmeline didn't want to think about the meeting. The Orias. The DNA and that horrible man. So, for several hours she distracted herself by running algorithms to decipher the plaque.

"Algorithm 365 complete. Unable to complete deciphering," the computer said in a monotonous tone.

Emmeline dozed on the chair, slightly aware of its voice. Suddenly realizing that she needed to go to bed, she slowly got to her feet.

"Running algorithm 365," said the computer.

Emmeline yawned as she got under the sheets and dozed off. She didn't know how much time passed, but she thought she heard the computer again. Assuming it was still trying to decipher the plaque, she decided not to pay it any attention.

Decoding the tablet had not been an easy task. At first, it had been a rock plaque. Then, when Aceline had helped her decode it, it had transformed into a smooth black tablet. As if on standby, a picture of a glowing sun with a face appeared. As soon as she'd tapped it, she'd seen a diagram with unknown symbols.

Despite her busy schedule, she had tried everything. Finally, again pairing up with Aceline, she'd designed algorithms, and the computer had been running them. She heard the voice again. It was a beep now, rather than a monotonous tone. She covered her ears.

"Beep. Beep. Beep. Deciphering complete. Beep. Deciphering complete. Beep."

Emmeline rushed to the computer. She couldn't believe it. It was done. She wondered which algorithm had worked. She observed the diagram and then began reading.

It was unbelievable. At first the computer had identified a key to unlock the plaque. It had found a 70% match in the historical language database for the lighter symbols. Linear A was an ancient Minoan language made up of symbols representing sounds, objects, or abstract ideas. The Minoan symbols were used between 1800 to 1450 BC and found on several clay tablets.

The computer first isolated and identified three letters: 'S', 'C' and 'E'. It ran algorithm and converted the symbols into one English word. SPACE. Once it had the key, it applied it to the rest of the diagram and decoded an unreadable sentence which was overwhelming.

"nepththyslahmuenkiastarteurukgonilibraecrcuisseptuyawhaniamumn aniapeperkwalhnimo"

This was an alien language, and the computer began searching the linguistic database. Her heart was beating fast as she read. The first thing it did was to identify basics of the language, such as noun or pronouns. This was a tedious task, and the computer had run several algorithms and the result astonished her.

"NepththysLahmuEnkiAstarteUrukGoniLibraeCrcuisSeptuYawHani AmumNaniApepErkWalhNimo"

The computer had just capitalized some words. She counted them. "Seventeen," she said to herself. Her jaw dropped. The computer had identified alien names for the stars in the Draco Constellation. She sat back in the chair, not knowing where this was going to lead. Surely, humans had given names to the stars of the constellation centuries ago. But this were words from beyond time, beyond space, written by an intelligent life form. She picked the pad and read further. The computer had done exactly what she would do. It didn't convert the alien star names and applied the decoded sentence to the plaque. And that did it. After the codes were applied to the plaque, a star map had appeared. She recognized the star system immediately. She had seen it before, and there was an area highlighted to the left. She realized what it was and got frustrated. She got up and screamed in anger.

TITAN, DECK 4, DELTA'S QUARTERS

The door to Delta's quarters opened, and Delta looked at Emmeline through squinting eyes. "Don't you sleep?"

Emmeline knew it was 3 am and without a word, she stepped into her quarters.

"Yeah, come in whenever," Delta remarked. The doors shut behind them.

"I've finally deciphered the plaque."

Delta's gloomy face suddenly became attentive.

Emmeline handed her the pad and paced up and down the room.

"This is good! This is awesome! Oh, wow. It's a star map . . . of this system. We have coordinates! We have coordinates!" Delta shouted.

"No. It's not good!" Emmeline told her. "There's nothing there! Delta, it's a waste of time!"

"But this is telling us that there's a planet. You must be —
"

Emmeline cut her off. "Delta, for a year, I've been scanning and studying that region of space. A planet would have been detected ages ago. There's nothing there!"

"Maybe you missed it."

Emmeline put her hands on her waist. "Oh, you think?"

"Sorry. You need to calm down."

"No!" Emmeline shouted and wiped her tears. "I was wrong, Delta. I was wrong. The plaque is just a ruse. It's all a stupid myth! You were right. Dad was right!"

Delta's face fell.

Emmeline felt as if a small part of her died. Maybe the planet had existed years ago, but today, there was no sign of it.

"I'm so sorry," Delta whispered.

Tears filled Emmeline's eyes. "Maybe it's for the best."

TITAN, DECK 4, EMMELINE'S QUARTERS

Emmeline couldn't sleep. Sitting in her quarters alone, Emmeline watched the stars in silence. She realized that in the last two months; she hadn't had the chance to enjoy the view from her window. Of course, everyone else had this view as well, but to her, it was significant. It helped her calm down. Perhaps it was due to the stars. Perhaps it was the gases of Titan, which appeared to be moving in an unrecognizable pattern.

A part of her was happy that the plaque led to nothing. It was a distraction anyway. But it was not unwelcomed. With all the horrible things going around here, she preferred solving clues instead of thinking of politics and Titan's fate. She heard a knock on the door. "Who is it?" she called.

"It's Delta. Open up."

With a heavy heart, she got up and pushed the button. The doors opened, and Delta stepped inside.

"Come in anytime," Emmeline said sarcastically.

Delta turned to face her. "I've been looking at this star chart."

Emmeline hung her head. "It's no use."

"Maybe the area described in this map has changed over time."

"I thought about that. Even if that region of space has changed in the last two centuries, the planet wouldn't have drifted that far, and we would have detected it. It could have been destroyed before mankind began studying the stars," replied Emmeline.

"Maybe we're looking at this the wrong way."

Emmeline arched her eyebrows.

"What if it's not just about the science?" asked Delta.

"What are you talking about?"

"Two months ago, this plaque was a rock," Delta explained. "A disgusting gray rock with several dots and some stupid lines. After you found the first clue, a musical tune, it transformed into a sleek black plaque with another riddle on it. The computer translated that riddle, which revealed a star map. Emmeline, something tells me we can't resolve this by using conventional scientific methods. We need to check out these coordinates. Let's go and see what's out there. Maybe it's something even Titan's most powerful telescopes can't detect."

"Are you crazy? It's beyond the perimeter. No one . . ."

"I think we can pull it off."

"But no one leaves without permission from the Imperial Command, and it would take weeks, if not months, to get it," Emmeline said. "And during an interstellar war, they'll forbid it without a second thought!"

"Emmeline, we don't know what will happen tomorrow. If you want to get to the bottom of this, we can't play it safe."

Emmeline bit her lip. "What if there's nothing . . .?"

"Then you'll have your answer, and the plaque can go to a museum."

TITAN, DECK 5, TRAINING HALL

Emmeline finished her jog and found Argon waiting for her. She took a minute to catch her breath. She'd finished half of her training, and now she was hooked. Yesterday, she'd finally hit the target on its outer edges. She was getting good at using the disruptor. Her confidence was growing that she finally felt she was getting somewhere.

Today, it was time to learn some hand-to-hand combat. For the last week, Argon had been teaching her some defense moves. She couldn't believe it, but she was rather enjoying it.

"What's on your mind?" Argon asked.

She looked up. "Nothing. Nothing."

He eyed her. "Emmeline? I know you. What's on your mind?"

"I need to make a decision," Emmeline said. "I might be wrong. I might be right. I don't know."

"Well, do it, and you'll know. Now, are you ready?"

She nodded and kicked Argon; he quickly blocked it with his hand. He threw a punch, which she dodged. He threw another one, and she blocked it with her hands. She twirled and kicked him again. He blocked her just inches away from his face. She smiled. He smirked, grabbed her ankle, twisted it, and threw her on the thick mat.

"Ah!" she cried.

"Move it! Get up! Get up!"

Emmeline pushed the pain aside, got to her feet, and got in position. "You're going to regret that."

"Am I?"

She squinted, moved swiftly, threw a punch, and then stomped on his feet.

Argon cried out in pain.

TITAN, CRYSTAL LAB

After training, Emmeline knew she had pushed too hard, and now her arms and legs ached. She stretched and decided to focus on work. All day long, she kept telling herself it was a stupid idea, but she couldn't get it out of her mind. She considered other options, but they all seemed undoable. No one believed her, and if she said she wanted to go to find this mythical device, alarms would be raised. She could come under heavy scrutiny and then all her chances to find the device would be lost. If she wanted to know the truth about the plaque, she had to go to those coordinates.

Adrian had asked her to look at the data from the scans of the battle. Like him, she found nothing unusual. The Orias weren't using a frequency they could detect. Maybe it was in their ships. She wished that they had an intact Orias ship. The thought sent shivers down her spine. She never wanted to face an Orias in her life. She gulped and then tried to focus on the cloud data. Dr. Kent had finally liked something she had done and asked her to do some computer stimulations. But she could hardly concentrate. Finally, she gave up and went to see Delta.

TITAN, DECK 9, ARMORY

Argon felt his pulse rise and his heartbeat quicken. Lieutenant Edward Ward was working on the outer casket of the torpedo. A standard torpedo looked somewhat like a missile with a sharp nose. Titan's torpedoes could not only be programmed but also were heavier and bigger, as they were built to destroy comets and interstellar objects. Captain Lockhart's idea to reprogram them to detect increase in energy in Orias ship before they fired and to target the tails was excellent, but it needed patience and time. The torpedoes had to be reprogrammed manually.

Edward reached over to the middle panel and put in the codes. The weapon made a whooshing noise. "Okay. The warhead has been deactivated," he said.

Cyr stood in front of a big screen, working with Adrian to identify the highest level of energy emitted by the ships.

Argon looked at Edward, who nodded and pushed a few buttons on his side, unlocking the outer shell. Now they could see the internal section of the weapon. Edward slowly reached for the flat panel and raised it. If everything went well, they could have the weapons ready in a couple of days.

TITAN, DECK 1, BRIDGE

The bridge of the Titan was silent, and the lights dimmed. During the night shift, three crew members worked silently in the corner. The wide screen was zoomed in on the crew members and ships working on the perimeter.

Adrian had woken up at 0500 hours and returned to the bridge. He was eager to get the perimeter ready. He turned when he felt the presence of someone behind him. He folded his arms and looked at Emmeline and Delta. Bells rang in his head. They never came to the bridge when Anastasia wasn't around.

"Good morning, Adrian," said Delta, breaking the silence.

"Good morning. I'm kind of busy."

Emmeline shot Delta a glance before speaking. "I need your help," she stated.

Adrian shook his head immediately. "I'm busy. We've installed half of the generators, and I have to monitor the robots doing the safety checks."

"How much more time do you think you'll need?" Delta asked.

Small talk. That's never happened before, Adrian thought. "It's hard and slow," he replied. "Maybe another forty-eight to seventy-two hours. What do you want?"

"I wanted to know if there was any debris left beyond the perimeter," Emmeline said.

Adrian looked at Emmeline. "Well, we couldn't gather everything, but I think we got quite enough. Most of its junk anyway." As he spoke, his eyes shifted to Delta, who was walking around his console.

"Oh. I see. Did your scans show anything particular?" Emmeline asked.

A continuous beeping noise distracted Adrian.

"Sir, one of the robots stopped responding to our instructions," another crew member alerted him.

"Excuse me." Adrian walked across the bridge to help.

He glanced behind him, seeing the women standing quietly, unmoving beside his console. Something was off, and he knew it. He turned his attention to the issue at hand. As he looked for the problem, the robot began to respond. "It must be a glitch," he said and returned to his seat. "Look, Emmeline, I'm busy."

"That's okay. Maybe we can do it later. Thanks."

Adrian watched them leave the bridge. They wanted something; he could feel it. He turned to his console and realized it was unlocked.

TITAN, DECK 10, DOCKING BAY

Adrian couldn't rest, and nor could he understand why he felt that way. For no apparent reason, he found himself in the docking bay, standing near Astra. He knew Delta was leaving for another job. That wasn't unusual. Delta staying in one place for too long would have altered the laws of physics. But then again, the girls' presence on the bridge bothered him. Delta was preparing for launch.

"Is Emmeline going with you?" Adrian asked when he got near enough for her to hear him.

"No. She has plenty to do here. Why?"

"Just a question. Where are you heading?" he asked.

Delta smirked. "Since when are you interested?"

"I've always been interested," he answered and then gulped.

Delta smiled widely. She stepped closer to him. "Adrian, what is it?"

"Do you remember when you used me to gain access to the environmental controls?" he said. "You said you were feeling hot and wanted to adjust the temperature. Instead, you altered the gravity settings during a history tutorial."

"The history teacher was boring. I wanted to see if she could fly," Delta replied, stepping closer again. "What is it you really want?"

Adrian cleared his throat. "Four years ago, Professor

Jackson's lecture was being broadcast from Earth to all the colonies. He was using the holo projector technology. You used my access codes and changed his face into a horse."

Delta laughed. "Oh, that was fun!"

"For you. It scared the hell out of me."

Delta placed her hand on his shoulder and looked him in the eye. "Do you think I'd still do that?"

"Yes. Psychological studies have shown basic human personality traits never change. Especially the ones that are rewarding and classified as fun or humorous."

"Oh, dearie."

"Delta, you're always up to something."

Delta touched his face. "And you're always watching out for me, aren't you?"

Adrian was dumbfounded.

"Adrian, you're so nice," Delta said sweetly. "I hope you know that."

"I do. I think that's the problem," he said, not believing he could be so vocal.

Delta smirked. "I'll see you soon." Then she turned and boarded the ship.

Adrian watched Astra take off and cursed himself for not being more assertive.

TITAN, DECK 2, CRYSTAL LAB

The hours didn't seem to pass, even when he had work. Around midday he acted.

Adrian felt a bit uncomfortable, but he stepped into the Crystal Lab, anyway. Everyone looked at him as if he were an alien. That was to be expected; he didn't often visit the Crystal Lab. He marched ahead and found Emmeline working on a console. A wave of relief rushed over him.

She turned and gave him a warm smile. "Hello. What can I do for you?"

"I'm sorry I couldn't help you out."

Emmeline nodded. "It's okay. We're all busy, and it's

not urgent."

Adrian's eyes wandered toward the console where Emmeline was analyzing the debris. "Anything?" he asked.

"Not yet."

The door to Dr. Kent's office opened, and Dr. Kent stepped out. He paused in the middle of the lab, glaring at Adrian. "Is everything okay?"

"Yes. I'm just here to see Emmeline."

Dr. Kent nodded and left the lab in a hurry.

"If you don't mind, I really need to finish this," Emmeline said apologetically.

"No problem," Adrian replied. "See you later."

PERIMETER

"Are you sure they didn't detect us?" asked Emmeline for the third time.

Delta frowned. "They didn't."

Astra flew along the perimeter, 200,000 kilometers away from Titan.

"Where is it?" Emmeline asked.

"Hold on," Delta said, as Astra flew ahead and swayed along the border. A couple of minutes passed in tense silence before Delta reduced speed. "There."

Emmeline leaned forward. The break in the perimeter wasn't clear, but it could be seen. One of the huge pillars holding the perimeter together had broken off from one side and was hanging from the other. The gap was just big enough for Astra to fly through. Emmeline felt very uncomfortable. It was like she was leaving her home, leaving everything behind. "No one bothered to fix it?"

"They probably don't know about this one," replied Delta. "They found a few last year and fixed them."

Emmeline gulped.

Delta positioned the ship to face the perimeter. "I'd prefer it if you kept this between us."

Emmeline nodded.

"Masking Astra's shields."

"How are we doing this?"

"Easy. The one thing no one knows about Astra is that she can mask her signature," Delta explained. "I installed the technology a couple of years ago. In this case, when we go through the shields of the perimeter, the computer should think we're the robots working on the perimeter. That's why I needed the shield modulation frequency from Adrian's console."

"That was clever," said Emmeline.

Delta shook her head. "I don't think so. Adrian can see right through me. I would have preferred someone else. I think he suspects something, but the holo projector should do its job. If he thinks you're not with me, he shouldn't have a cause for concern."

Emmeline's face turned grim. "I hope so."

"What about Titan's scanners?" Delta asked.

"I programmed my holo projection to mask Astra's signature," replied Emmeline. "The computer should ignore Astra's movements. If someone looks, we'll just look like a stray asteroid. But no one can break my codes. Not on Titan."

"Smart," Delta said. "Ready?"

Emmeline's heart skipped a beat. "Yes."

Astra slowly flew through the shields and nearer to the gap. Delta eased the ship into the opening. Emmeline was amazed as she stared up at the mesh of hundreds of hefty metal rods.

Delta's fingers ran quickly across the console. "Adjusting heading."

Emmeline looked ahead and spotted something they hadn't been able to see from the other side. One of the inner pillars had suffered the same fate as the outer one and was hanging right in the middle of their flight path. Emmeline began a scan of the pillar. "Its structural integrity is very weak. This one could fall at any time."

"It's going to be close," Delta said.

Astra decelerated. Delta adjusted their course, and the

ship dipped below the huge pillar. An alarm went off. Emmeline jumped.

"Proximity alert. Proximity alert."

"Don't worry," said Delta.

Emmeline moved forward. "It's too close . . ."

"They're holding," Delta replied calmly. Aware that there was another pillar right in front of them, Delta slowly turned Astra. Another alarm went off, and then there was a loud dragging noise. The girls looked at each other.

"What happened?" asked Emmeline.

"We can do this," Delta replied without answering.

The dragging noise turned into a groan.

"Oh no." Emmeline looked at her screen. "Delta . . ."

"Just a few more seconds."

Astra squeezed through the two pillars and glided ahead.

"Check the pillar," Delta ordered.

Emmeline's fingers ran across the keyboard. "I think it's okay."

Delta nodded curtly. "That was close. I hope it holds when we return."

The rest of the ride was smooth. Soon, Astra emerged on the other side of the perimeter. Both women stared at the space ahead, then at each other.

"This is it," Delta said.

Emmeline gulped. She'd never been beyond the perimeter. She felt like she was abandoning everything she knew. Her heart was beating fast. She didn't know if it was excitement or fear. She turned to Delta and said, "Let's do this and return home as soon as possible."

TITAN, DECK 1, BRIDGE

Even after seeing Emmeline, Adrian felt there was something wrong on Titan. He actually visited every section, including engineering to check. He knew it was illogical, but he couldn't let go.

When Adrian seemed gloomy later, Evan teased him, saying that he was just missing Delta. But Adrian knew that today, that was not the case. It was the fact that he knew her too well. He'd gone out of his way and read the details of Delta's job. She was supposed to head toward the Vesta colony, pick up a passenger, then travel to Earth. He'd also checked her flight plan. Everything looked normal. The last time he'd checked, Titan's sensors had detected that Astra was heading for the colony.

Adrian again wondered what he was doing and why he was so worried about a woman who didn't care about him. She'd left, and she would always leave. He should let her go. But something about tonight bothered him. Something was off, and he was worried Delta could be in danger. But from what?

TITAN, DECK 4, ARGON'S QUARTERS

Argon sat in the dark in his quarters, enjoying the silence. Selina was asleep, and his mom was resting in her room. He tried to focus on work, but he couldn't. Along with Micah, Clio, and Bryon, he had spent most of his day running battle stimulations. It had been an exciting experience. He had hardly seen Emmeline all day and was looking forward to spending time with her. But he'd was disappointed. Annoyingly, and unusually, she didn't want to spend time with him or play hover ball.

The door to Argon's quarters opened, and his sister walked in, marched over to the window, and stared at the cosmos.

He stood up. "Selina?"

She didn't reply, remaining motionless. If he didn't know better, he would have thought she was sleepwalking.

Argon came to kneel beside her. "Selina?"

She remained speechless.

"Darling, what is it?"

Suddenly, her features constricted as if angry, and she turned toward him. "I hate you!"

Argon was shocked. "What? Why?"

"You're going to leave all of us! You're just going to leave!" Selina screamed and ran out of the room.

Argon stood in shock. Selina never behaved this way. Maybe something was wrong with her. He followed her, wondering what he could do to set her mind at ease. To his surprise, she was sound asleep in her bed. He stood there, trying to determine what was a dream and what was reality.

Titan, Deck 1, Bridge

Adrian stretched his back. He couldn't find any communications or frequencies from the battle, but he wasn't ready to give up just yet.

Argon came to stand beside him. "Hey."

"Can't sleep?" said Adrian.

"No," replied Argon, looking at the viewscreen.

"Is Freedom repaired?" Adrian asked.

"Yep. Ready to go."

"What about Raven?" said Adrian teasingly.

Argon rolled his eyes. "The repairs were nearly complete. Then the Orias . . ."

"I know."

"Anyway, I was just wondering, have you seen Emmeline?"

Bells rang in Adrian's head. "Yes. In the lab."

"When?"

"In the morning. Why? You haven't seen her?"

"Oh, I saw her. In the lab."

Adrian relaxed. "Good."

"Yeah," Argon said, his voice unsure.

Adrian knew he was going to regret it, but he asked anyway. "What's wrong?"

"It's just a feeling. Something's off."

"What do you mean?"

"First, it was Emmeline. She didn't feel like herself."

Adrian raised an eyebrow.

"Then it was Selina."

Adrian listened as Argon described the incident. "I think she should have a medical checkup," he suggested when Argon was done. "Maybe she was sleepwalking."

Argon looked worried. "Why would I leave Titan? My family or her?"

"Argon, don't worry," Adrian said. "She's just a kid. Kids say things."

Argon managed a smile. "I'll speak to my mother."

"You should."

Argon left, and Adrian sat wordlessly. He had been trying to ignore his instincts, but he couldn't any longer. He had a distinct feeling that Argon shared his concerns. Something wasn't right.

Chapter 7: The Rogue Planet

Astra

The entire day was uneventful, and Delta was bored. Astra was on autopilot, and Emmeline was busy working. It made sense for her to finish her work so that when she returned to Titan, she could upload it to Titan's computers. Although creating a holo projection of herself had been a good idea, it had limited programming capacity.

Emmeline was happy they'd gotten out undetected, but now the challenge was to find the device and get back in. A loud beep startled her, and Delta quickly checked the sensors. For a second, Emmeline thought that the patrol ships had tracked them down.

"We're here," said Delta.

Fear took over Emmeline. She'd wanted to find this device for a long time, but now that she was here, she wasn't so sure.

Astra came to a halt, and Emmeline felt silence engulf her as the engines died out. They'd left their home behind, and now she understood how vacant space felt. With no other life around, they were alone, surrounded by white specks. It was barren. Lifeless. Daunting.

Emmeline began looking for the planet. It wasn't in visual range, but she assumed it must be nearby. Her fingers danced on the console, moving faster and faster. "Oh, really?"

she muttered and checked again. She sighed and sat back on her chair, looking at the stars.

"Well?" Delta asked.

"Nothing. See for yourself."

Without a word, Delta started checking. After a few minutes, she shook her head. "Damn."

"It was worth a try."

They sat silently together, watching the stars. Astra floated in dead space, and the sun's yellow glow fell over the cargo ship.

Delta leaned forward and admired the view. "It is beautiful."

"Let's go back," Emmeline suggested unhappily. It was no use.

"I thought we had something . . ."

"Let's go . . ." Emmeline's voice trailed away. Without missing a beat, she turned to the console and fired Astra's engines.

"What are you doing?" Delta asked.

Emmeline didn't reply.

"W-what are you doing?" Delta repeated.

"Trust me, will you?"

Astra turned gradually to face the sun and then stopped. Emmeline left the cockpit. She returned with the plaque and placed it on the dashboard. "When the plaque came to life, the first thing it showed was the sun. Then the star chart appeared. Let's hope this works."

They waited. Nothing happened.

Delta eyed her.

Emmeline sighed. "I guess . . ."

Suddenly, the plaque came to life. A glittering yellow light emerged from it. It left the plaque and spread over the dashboard, then began to scatter throughout the compartment.

"Emmeline," Delta said, getting up from her chair and moving away. "What's happening?"

"I d-don't know," Emmeline replied as she moved away too.

The yellow light became brighter and soon engulfed the cabin. The plaque rose as if lifted by an invisible hand. It floated effortlessly and started rotating, at first slowly, then picking up speed. It spun faster and faster.

"Did your grandpa tell you about this?" Delta asked.

"No! No!" Emmeline yelled.

"Should we do something?"

Astra rocked.

The plaque was still spinning, and a bright flash blinded them. Emmeline scrunched her eyes shut. She thought she would feel warm, but she didn't. Suddenly, it turned dark. When she opened her eyes, she saw that a beam from the plaque broke through Astra's shields. It was like a short burst of light in space, disappearing into the distance. Then there was a big burst of light, and a bright spherical opening appeared. At its center, gases moved in an anticlockwise direction. The plaque fell back on the dashboard and became silent.

"What the hell is that?" asked Delta as Emmeline rushed back to her seat.

"I don't know," Emmeline answered. She began scanning.

"Is it a gateway?"

"Or a portal," said Emmeline. "There's heavy interference. I'm not getting anything."

"It's amazing." Delta peered through the front window.

Emmeline looked at her. "It shouldn't exist."

"But it does! The plaque is the key."

Soon, the clouds in the gateway cleared, and a tunnel appeared.

"What's in there?" Delta asked impatiently.

"I don't know." Emmeline checked the readings. "This is unbelievable."

Delta powered up Astra.

"What are you doing?" Emmeline asked.

"We have to go in there."

Emmeline's face filled with horror. "Are you crazy? We

don't know where it will lead!"

"What do the scans say?"

She turned back to the console. "The gateway is stable now. But it could be a bumpy ride. Beyond the clouds . . ." She paused as the numbers began appearing on her screen. "Oh my God."

"What?"

"Oh, my God! I think we found it! There's a planet beyond that gate. I don't believe this. It's incredible!"

"Awesome!"

The console beeped again. "Whoa. Wait. My scans show a lot of seismic activity on the planet," Emmeline said.

"Earthquakes?" demanded Delta. "I hate earthquakes!"

Emmeline didn't answer and continued looking at the data. "The planet is really unstable. I don't detect any other planets. This could be a rogue planet."

"What's a rogue planet?" asked Delta.

"A rogue planet, also called a free-floating or orphan planet, is a planetary mass that orbits the galactic center directly. Unlike Earth and other planets in our solar system, these planets are not bound by gravity to a sun."

"Wow. Can we call it Delta?" Delta suggested, smiling.

Emmeline's face brightened. "Sure, it's a beautiful name. Let's find out more about it." The cockpit became silent once more, and Emmeline continued working. "I detect a faint reading of an energy source."

"Could it be the device?" asked Delta.

Emmeline looked at her. "I don't know."

"We have to go in and find out."

"I'm not sure we should."

"Emmeline, the plaque led us to these coordinates. It opened the gateway, and now we've found the planet. We have to go in."

"What if it collapses and we can't get back?"

Delta looked at her. "Emmeline. We found a way in; we'll find a way out. Collect as much data as you can."

Emmeline nodded. "Well, this doorway appeared from

nowhere. Who knows? The data might appear and disappear, just like the gateway."

Delta grinned. "You're very optimistic, aren't you?"

Emmeline managed a bleak smile. She wasn't sure. In her day job, she analyzed spatial objects that didn't appear out of thin air.

Delta brought Astra to face the gateway. "Here we go," she said.

Titan, Deck 1, Bridge

Adrian returned from lunch and enjoyed his coffee in his chair. He didn't know why he was worried about Delta; he was being silly. She was fine, and so was Emmeline.

He moved back and forth on his seat, watching the army of robots work on the perimeter. He enjoyed the soft aroma and relaxed. Then the console beeped. He leaned forward. He was getting a reading he didn't understand. He glanced at Evan, who was busy working. The console beeped again. He didn't like what he was looking at. Titan's sensors had detected something they couldn't identify. Adrian's heart leaped to his throat. He placed the coffee cup on the floor and unlocked his console. He prayed it wasn't the Orias. They weren't ready. The perimeter wasn't secured. His fears melted away when he went through the data.

"Oh? This is odd," he said involuntarily.

"What?" asked Evan.

"Titan has detected an energy signature at the outer edges of our solar system."

"Is it the Orias?"

"No," Adrian replied with relief. "This is different. Hold on."

For several minutes, he worked as Evan stood beside him, looking over his shoulder. "Oh my God. This can't be possible!"

"What is it?" Evan demanded.

"Look for yourself," Adrian said, transferring the image

to the viewscreen.

The screen showed a bright light beyond Neptune.

"What the hell is that?"

"I don't know."

"Is it the cloud?"

Adrian shook his head. "No. Titan's computers have been programmed to identify the Orias cloud. This is something different."

"How far away is it?" asked Evan.

"About 300,000 kilometers from Neptune."

"Can you zoom in?"

"Titan's sensors are at their maximum capacity." Adrian pushed a button and contacted the Crystal Lab. "Emmeline, this is Lieutenant Olson. Titan just detected an unusual energy signature beyond Neptune. I'm sending you the coordinates. Could you please have a look at it?"

"Sure."

Adrian turned to Evan. "It came out of nowhere."

"Just like the Orias."

THE ROGUE PLANET

Astra gradually entered the gateway. Emmeline and Delta looked at the dazzling spherical radiance enclosing them from all sides. A bright light surrounded the ship, and Emmeline shut her eyes. Astra jolted. Emmeline forced her eyes open to look at her console. The sensors were going crazy. Alarms blared. The cockpit was filled with so many sounds that it almost drove her to delirium. Astra shuddered, and they were pushed forward.

Abruptly, everything became silent. It amazed Emmeline. Astra was in a tunnel leading to uncharted space. It appeared as if the walls of the tunnel were made of billions of stars. They could see several galaxies and nebulas. They watched with amazement as a large comet passed over them. "Wow," Emmeline muttered.

Suddenly, they were pushed off their chairs as if Astra

had hit something hard. The peaceful picture surrounding them vanished. Astra accelerated, trembling, and shaking, and was thrown out of the tunnel.

Delta quickly took control of the ship and brought it to a complete stop. She and Emmeline looked at each other, both breathless.

"Are you okay?" Emmeline asked.

"Yes. You?"

Emmeline nodded and turned to the console. "Well, the gateway is still open, and it's stable. I'll keep a sensor lock on it just in case it closes. We'll know."

The planet sat right in front of them.

"Anything else we need to know about this area of space?" Delta asked, checking all systems.

"Astra can only do short-distance scans," Emmeline replied. "I don't detect any other solar systems, asteroids, interstellar objects, or ships."

"How's the weather on the planet?"

Emmeline examined her screen. "This is unbelievable. I don't know what to say."

"Just say it," Delta said sharply. "Nothing surprises me anymore."

"The earthquakes have stopped, and the weather is settling down. The planet is about half the size of Earth with two big continents, and the rest of it is water. Sensors show the planet has an oxygen-nitrogen atmosphere. The oxygen levels aren't that high, but the air is breathable."

"Okay! It's a smaller Earth."

"This is weird."

"Tell me something I don't know," muttered Delta.

"The energy source is in the mountains in the northern hemisphere," Emmeline continued. "There are two active volcanoes near the mountains."

"Oh, this just keeps getting better and better. We have magical gateways, earthquakes, and now volcanoes. Anything else you want to add to the list?"

Emmeline just smiled.

"Where do we land?"

"You have to get me closer before I can be sure."

Delta powered Astra ahead.

TITAN, DECK 2, CRYSTAL LAB

Adrian rushed toward the Crystal Lab. It had been over an hour, and people on the bridge were getting restless. Jacob wanted to take Freedom to investigate the phenomenon. Anastasia didn't want to endanger any ships and was asking the admiral to wait.

The doors to the lab opened, and Adrian found Emmeline on her console. "Did you get it done?" he asked.

She turned to him, looking puzzled.

"The energy source beyond Neptune. I sent you the coordinates!"

"I checked. There is nothing," Emmeline replied.

Adrian was astonished. "What the hell are you talking about?"

"I don't know what you mean."

"That's not possible. If we detected it, you should be able to detect it!" Adrian gritted his teeth.

Emmeline looked blankly at him.

At that moment, Dr. Kent stepped out of his office. "What's happening here?"

Adrian updated him.

"It isn't there," Emmeline argued.

Dr. Kent glared at her. "Move aside."

Emmeline hesitated but stepped away from the console.

"It should have taken you no more than fifteen minutes to figure out what . . ." Dr. Kent paused. "What the devil is this? What were you doing? Have you lost your mind? You were scanning the wrong region!"

"I was doing what I was told."

"You ignored a request from the bridge," Dr. Kent scolded her as he recalibrated the sensors. "There you have it. What the hell is wrong with you? This was a simple task."

Adrian suddenly realized something. He reached for his pocket and removed a scanner.

"Emmeline. I don't think you're well. Go to the medical bay," suggested Dr. Kent.

Adrian finished his scans and stared at the innocent-looking girl. "It's not her," he muttered, dejected.

"What do you mean?" asked Dr. Kent.

"It's a holo projection of Emmeline."

"W-What?" Dr. Kent reeled back in surprise. He put his hand on Emmeline's shoulder, and it passed through the image. He looked up and saw the small holo projectors on the ceiling. "Oh, my God. Then where is Emmeline? What happened to her?" Dr. Kent reached for the console. "Emmeline Augury, report to your post."

They waited.

"Emmeline, answer me!" Dr. Kent tried again.

There was no reply.

"Computer, locate Cadet Emmeline Augury."

"Cadet Emmeline Augury is not on Titan," answered the computer.

All the blood drained from Adrian's face.

THE ROGUE PLANET

As soon as they entered the planet's atmosphere, it felt as though they had entered a battlefield. The ship shook vigorously, and the surface of Astra began turning red. Emmeline wondered if the planet was somehow resisting them.

Delta pushed the engines hard but was finding it challenging to maintain control. A jolt almost threw both off their seats. Suddenly, the scene changed, and they found themselves surrounded by black clouds. They relaxed as Astra slowly descended toward the planet's surface.

"Wow," Delta remarked as they passed through the clouds and the view became clearer. As far as they could see, the terrain was covered with massive mountains. There was some vegetation, but they couldn't see any forests or tall trees. Most of the ground was covered with rocks and soil. Soon, the black clouds disappeared altogether, and the sun began shining.

Emmeline wondered how it was possible. She looked at the screen. When she had scanned the planet from miles away, this region had been under attack by dust storms and earthquakes. Now there were no earthquakes or dust storms whatsoever. The atmosphere was like Earth's but thinner. She looked out her window. It was quiet, peaceful, and welcoming. She checked if there were any rivers; her scans revealed no sources of water. But Astra couldn't scan the entire planet.

"Okay, where?" Delta asked.

"North, two hundred kilometers ahead."

Delta nodded.

Emmeline scanned for signs of life. There were none. She bit her lip. Perhaps Astra's scanners weren't strong enough to detect them. Who did this planet belong to? Maybe life existed deep in the mountains. She had no way of knowing. She wished she had access to Titan's far more advanced scanner.

Soon, Astra neared one of the largest mountain ranges. The computer beeped, indicating they had reached their destination. Emmeline looked at the cold gray mountains. They were much higher in the west than in the east. "The signal is coming from inside that mountain," Emmeline said.

"We can't land here," Delta told her. "The deep valleys and pointy mountaintops make it impossible."

Emmeline was already trying to come up with a solution. Astra flew above the mountains as Emmeline did her calculations. "Okay. About eight kilometers from here, there's a flat plateau wide and stable enough to hold Astra. Land there. The signal is coming from a creek. We'll have to hike and take this path to enter the mountain," she explained, showing the map to Delta.

"It's inside the mountain?" Delta asked incredulously.

"That's what the scans say."

Dust flew in all directions as Astra hovered over the plateau. A trained pilot like Delta had no trouble setting the ship down. She joined Emmeline in preparing the backpacks. "How much time do you think we'll need?"

"I suppose a few hours at least. I'm worried about the portal. What if someone detects it?" Emmeline said.

"I'm worried about that too. It will be best if we get to this cave as soon as possible and then get out of here."

"I agree."

The hangar door opened, and they stepped out. The air was warm and dry. Now there wasn't a cloud in sight. The sun shone high in the sky. Emmeline pulled out her scanner.

"Anything?" asked Delta.

"No earthquakes. Curious. The oxygen levels have risen since I last checked. There's no sign of any kind of life."

"This planet is weird."

"Tell me something I don't know," Emmeline said with a hint of a laugh.

Titan, Deck 1, Bridge

Anastasia felt the weight of her responsibilities heighten. She tried to be sure of her feelings toward her crew and her duty as their commander. Was she to wait for the girls to return or drag them back home? Neither option was appealing.

At first, no one had been sure if it was Delta and Emmeline, but then they'd found an ion trail left by the ship's engine. It was definitely an Earth ship, and Emmeline's holo projections had come online about five minutes after Astra had left. The girls had somehow managed to get through the perimeter, but no one knew why.

Once he'd decided, there was very little Anastasia could do to stop Jacob. She knew Freedom could catch up with Astra within a day. The situation was getting out of control.

Helplessly, she watched the gates close after the Freedom left. She didn't know what would happen to Delta and Emmeline. She just wanted them back home, but she had a feeling that the admiral wouldn't be easy to handle. The only thing that comforted her was that Argon was on Freedom. She knew he would do everything within his power to bring them back.

"Anything?" she asked Dr. Kent, who was working on the science station. It surprised her that he had asked none of his other students for help. He seemed tense and worried. She didn't know if he was worried about the girls or what they'd found.

"Not yet." He answered.

THE ROGUE PLANET

Emmeline had never missed Titan so much. After hours of walking, she felt as if the muscles in her legs were shredding to pieces. The sun shone above her head, and the breeze was cool. Although she could see and feel everything, she was having a hard time believing any of it was real. The hike down was treacherous, but once they were in the creek, the terrain was mostly flat and covered with a thick layer of rocks. The track snaked between the mountains that appeared to reach for the sky. Emmeline scanned and found that the mountain was over 1.5 million years old.

"Okay, here we are," Delta said, puffing and looking up. About ten meters up was an opening in the mountain.

Emmeline nodded. "Good. Delta, I wanted to ask. Did you get a buyer for that bike of yours?"

Delta smirked. "Not yet."

Emmeline turned to her. "I want the red one."

"Ha! I knew it! Sure, you can have one. I left them in the storage locker on Titan. Take it whenever you want to."

"Thanks. It was fun to ride. I really enjoyed it," Emmeline said. "And I want the friends-and-family discount."

"Hey! Come on!"

Titan, Deck 1, Bridge

Hours passed painfully, and the silence was suffocating. Anastasia put down the pad and thought about the consequences. Emmeline and Delta had broken the law by leaving the solar system without authorization. They weren't the first ones. Many had tried and failed and had been punished for it. Only four men and two women had succeeded in sneaking through the perimeter. They'd wanted to be free explorers and plot their own way through space. But when their requests to leave the system had been denied, they'd broken free and vanished into space, never to return. *Man was not born to follow the rules; he was born to push the boundaries,* Anastasia thought.

But Emmeline and Delta's situation was different. They had pushed the boundaries. Anastasia didn't know why. But she knew they would return. Titan was their home. Emmeline had a family on Earth. *Why the hell didn't they just ask me?* she wondered.

The doors opened, and Dr. Kent entered hastily.

"You found something?" Anastasia asked.

"A doorway."

"I figured."

Dr. Kent shook his head. "You don't understand. It was a doorway built or created by beings more powerful than us."

"Aliens?"

"Yes."

"Hold on. Are you telling me that there's a secret wormhole right under our noses, and we didn't know about it?"

"No. This is not a wormhole," Dr. Kent said. "It's a portal or a gateway, whatever you want to call it. It was probably created centuries ago. The door might lead to another solar system. We don't know!"

Anastasia leaned forward. "What?"

"I can't explain it. We don't possess the technology to explain it, and the distance doesn't make it easy."

"How did it open?"

"That's a question only Emmeline and Delta can answer," Dr. Kent said. "They probably opened it. We need to make every effort to keep that portal open. Who knows where it could lead?"

Anastasia picked up the pad and went through the data. "Looks stable enough. Any planets?"

"I can't say."

"Well, I'm sure Emmeline can keep it open."

"That's where I want your help."

Anastasia raised her eyebrows.

"The admiral," Dr. Kent clarified.

She placed the pad back on the table and held her head in her hands.

"He is a dear friend, but he suffers from tunnel vision," commented Dr. Kent.

"I don't understand him," Anastasia replied. "He's an explorer. How is this any different?"

"Anastasia, whatever he does, he does it with the rules in mind. Rules are integrated into his neurons. Anyone breaking them makes him really, really unhappy. The girls broke the rules, so in his book, they're criminals. What he doesn't realize is that if they hadn't, we would never have found that doorway. We have to deal with the admiral, and we should work together."

"Oh, so now you're on her side?" asked Anastasia.

Dr. Kent looked hurt. "There are things I have had to do. I am not proud of that, but I have to keep the lab running. That won't be possible without the support of the Imperial Command," He paused, and Anastasia felt his pain. He was human, after all. "You should know by now; I would do anything to keep the Crystal Lab and my overenthusiastic students."

Anastasia smiled. "The incident a year ago . . ."

He shook his head. "I get her. Whatever she does, she does it for science and to fulfill her curiosity. God knows she's the most curious creature on this station. But she listens to me."

He paused, then refocused. "Just imagine. Imagine what we can achieve. We need to talk to the admiral. What is his plan?"

"He intends to enter the doorway and get . . ."

"No! He should not!"

Anastasia glared at him.

"Commander, anything we do could trigger its collapse or destruction," Dr. Kent said urgently. "We must be careful. The admiral should wait for them to return."

"Or we could send a probe," Anastasia suggested.

"Now, that's a good idea."

THE ROGUE PLANET

Emmeline was the first to climb. She pushed herself up, holding onto the small rocks poking out of the mountain for leverage. She was faster than she thought, or perhaps she was just happy that they were close. She reached the opening and looked into the dark, narrow cave. She pushed herself up and stood silently. Liquid dripped from the walls of the mountain. Emmeline took a few minutes to scan the interior of the cave as Delta caught up with her.

"Please tell me there's no more hiking," Delta said breathlessly.

"The terrain ahead is flat," Emmeline responded. "Are you okay?"

"Yeah," Delta said, stretching her back. "Will this cave hold?"

"For now, yes." Emmeline turned on her flashlight. Transparent liquid dripped down from the roof of the cave.

"Is that . . .?" Delta started.

"Water," Emmeline confirmed.

They walked through the dark tunnel. It was cold, and the wind howled through the cracks and roared through the dark passageway. Minding her step, Emmeline tried to remain as calm as possible. Despite the drop in temperature, she was sweating. She moved her flashlight back and forth, examining the massive rocks that surrounded them. For the next few meters, the cave turned triangular, and they had to bend down to get through. Emmeline gave a sigh of relief when she appeared on the other side of the tunnel. But her relief was short-lived.

"What now?" muttered Delta.

They turned their flashlights into the void just inches away from their feet. It was so deep and dark that the light disappeared within just a few meters. Emmeline looked up and realized that they were standing in a dome inside the mountain.

"Is this possible?" asked Delta.

Emmeline was already scanning the interior. "The rock is natural, but did you notice that?" She pointed to a large piece of rock. "It was sliced to create this."

"Wow. Someone or something made this."

Emmeline angled her flashlight at a narrow rock bridge. It was no more than forty centimeters wide and was the same color as the mountain.

Emmeline held her flashlight in one hand and put her scanner in her pocket. She lifted her left foot, rested it on the bridge, and waited. She took her next step, then another. When she was halfway across, she gave Delta an approving look. She crossed the bridge and entered another narrow passageway. Delta was right behind her. They had to squeeze through, trying to dodge the sharp ends of the rocks poking out of the mountain. Once they were out, Emmeline felt enormous relief.

"You have got to be kidding me," muttered Delta.

Emmeline bowed her head. The passageway opened into another structure, but rocks blocked the entrance.

Delta held up her scanner. "We can't blast through it," she said. "But we could move a few of those stones." She pointed toward the top of the cave.

Using all their might, they moved two stones, creating a large enough opening to crawl through. Emmeline peered inside. Besides a small light in the middle, the interior was completely dark. She heard a soft tapping noise.

Emmeline crawled through the opening, and once she

had emerged on the other side, she carefully walked over the stones.

Once she was clear, she scanned the entire cave. The walls were made of wet black stone. Water leaked through the roof. In the back of her mind, she was already thinking about their journey back to Astra and wondering if there was a way to shorten it. "It's safe," she announced.

Except for the small yellow light, their flashlights were the only source of illumination. They gradually made their way toward the light. At the far end of the cave was an oval-shaped stone-carved structure. It was about four feet tall and two feet wide. Inside the oval structure was the source of the dim light.

"Incredible," Delta said, touching the soft surface of the stone.

TITAN, DECK 1, BRIDGE

Anastasia stood with Dr. Kent, watching Jacob on the screen. Anastasia could tell he was angry. His face was stern, and she was sure she could see a vein bulging on his forehead.

"Commander, I understand, but we have to set an example," he said.

"It's not about setting an example," replied Dr. Kent. "It's about humanity's future. Fine! She broke a few rules. Of course, disciplinary action should be taken. But not before considering all the facts. If you put away the only person who's qualified to work on the portal, what the hell is Titan for?"

"Dr. Kent, I think you've said enough!" Jacob argued, his voice rising.

"I haven't even started. I strongly suggest you wait, or the science committee is going to hear about this. Patience is the key, Admiral."

"I know you know people in high places. That changes nothing," threatened Jacob.

"I know you are in command of Freedom, but as the head scientist on Titan, I have to tell you, you would risk everyone's life on Freedom, including Emmeline and Delta's if you enter the portal without studying it. The best course of action would be to send a probe."

"What will that accomplish?"

"It will give us more information," Anastasia interjected.

"We are at war," said Jacob. "I can't just wait around. What if the Orias show up?"

"It would be just a couple of hours, and we can communicate with the girls." Dr. Kent said.

"I'm sure Emmeline has a reasonable explanation," said Anastasia.

"I don't agree! We are entering the portal and bringing them home. Law will be enforced!" shouted the admiral. The screen turned black.

"Ahh!" Dr. Kent shouted.

Anastasia bowed her head. "You did your best."

"Commander, we should stop the admiral. He's not thinking straight, and I have a very bad feeling about this." Dr. Kent walked up and down the bridge.

His reaction stunned Anastasia. Dr. Kent had never shown so much concern. For the last ten years, she'd thought he never thought of anyone but himself.

"What can we do?" Dr. Kent asked.

"I don't want to send another ship, but I want the girl's home safely and the portal investigated," Anastasia replied.

"Well, Commander, we want the same things," Dr. Kent said. "The science committee is going to hear about this. Are you with me?"

Anastasia thought it was best to play the power game. She nodded.

"Is there any way we can contact Emmeline?" Dr. Kent asked.

Anastasia looked at Evan.

"No. She's out of range," he replied. "Perhaps when Freedom gets to the portal, we can talk to her."

THE ROGUE PLANET

Emmeline's heartbeat faster as she got down on her knees to look at the light. Suddenly, it became brighter, almost as if it sensed her. At the heart of the bright light, she saw a solid yellow object.

"How do we get it?" Delta asked.

Emmeline had already begun scanning. "There's no force field around this stone structure," she replied as her hand moved over the stone. Then she focused on the base of the structure. "I don't detect any traps or mechanisms." After a few minutes, she turned her scanner toward the bright light. "This is interesting. My scanner doesn't detect the object at all."

"What? But it's there! It is the source, right?"

Emmeline put the scanner away and outstretched her hand. The object glowed brightly. Her heart was pounding. As her hand got closer, to her surprise, she felt cold. She slowly reached for it, but her hand went right through the object. "Ah!" Emmeline cried out, withdrawing her hand.

"Oh, damn. It's not real!" Delta called out.

"It's a reflection," Emmeline concluded.

"If that's a reflection, where's the real one?" Delta asked.

Emmeline observed the small stone oval box from the inside. She looked up and saw no conduits or any kind of technology.

"Anything you can remember from the plaque?" Delta prompted her.

Emmeline tried to force herself to visualize the plaque. When she was unsuccessful, she got her pad out of the backpack and looked through the images of the plaque. A beeping noise echoed in the cave. Emmeline turned to Delta, who was looking at her communications device. "What is it?" Emmeline asked.

"It's Astra," Delta replied. "It has detected a ship approximately four hours away from the portal."

The blood drained from Emmeline's face.

"Oh, this is not good," said Delta.

"Oh my God," Emmeline murmured, feeling as if the entire cave was moving.

"What are we going to do?" Delta asked.

Emmeline held her head. "I don't know. I don't know. Maybe we can escape."

"And go where? Titan is our home."

"Oh, I'm so sorry. I don't know. I'm sorry I got you into this!" Emmeline said sadly.

"No. You didn't."

"Okay. Okay. They know we snuck out. Maybe we can apologize."

Delta looked at her.

"We have to do something! Can we just say we were curious?" Emmeline suggested.

Delta bowed her head. "That won't do, and you know it."

"What if we find the device, take it back, and explain to them what it can do?"

"That's a good idea. Do you know what it can do?" Delta asked incredulously.

"Look, so far, the myth seems to be true. It can be a source of unlimited power. If we get the piece, we have proof that this device exists. That could be our bargaining chip."

Silence engulfed the cave. Emmeline wondered if this could work. Delta's communicator buzzed again. They exchanged worried glances. She looked at the device. Astra was transmitting the details of the ship.

Delta's face paled. "It's the admiral."

Emmeline banged her head. "Oh no. Why the hell does it have to be him? We're ruined! Damn! I'm so close. This isn't fair! It's right there!" she yelled, marching around in circles. "We have to do something! We have to get to Commander Waters and Argon."

"Astra, come in. Astra, come in. This is Admiral Donavan. Respond," Jacob's voice rang through the communications device.

Emmeline banged her head again.

"As you said, we need a bargaining chip and a pretty good one." Delta said, turning toward the yellow light.

Emmeline's face turned stony. "I'm not handing over the device to anyone! No! Not to that damn arrogant admiral. Not to Dr. Kent! No! I'm not giving it to them. The plaque belongs to my family. It belongs to me!"

"I'm not saying that," Delta drawled. "I'm saying we use it to our advantage and get ourselves out of this mess. Emmeline, at this point, it can save us. We can put in an appeal with our seniors. Then we can contact the science committee. But be ready to face some consequences. The admiral is a stubborn man. Do you think your father would help?"

The communicator buzzed again, and Delta silenced it.

Emmeline felt hope. "Yes. Yes. I know he'd be mad, but yes. He would help."

"Okay. This is the plan. Once we get the device, we return to our space but tell the admiral we will only speak with Commander Waters. The admiral will threaten us, but as citizens of Titan, we have that right. We can directly appeal to be taken to Commander Waters. We will explain our situation. Give her the data and if no other choice, the piece. We're not running. We're going to stand our ground and work this out. Do you agree?"

Emmeline nodded. "Let's hope we can find it first."

As Delta anxiously walked around the cave, Emmeline looked through her pad and her notes about the mythical device.

"Did you find anything?" Delta asked her a few moments later.

"I'm so stupid," Emmeline muttered.

"You missed something?"

Emmeline dropped her head. "I should have seen this before!"

"Seen what?"

"When I was running algorithms, it deciphered the star map."

"Yeah."

"But I never told the computer to stop. The computer kept running more algorithms and decoded an image embedded in the star map. I had programed it to save whatever patterns it found and then keep analyzing."

"What image?"

The picture on the pad changed. The stars disappeared, and a diagram of the mythical device appeared. They could tell that there were seven parts of the device, as there was a bit of a gap between each. Six pieces looked like petals around a central round piece.

"Seven parts? Are you telling me there are six more pieces out there?" Delta said in disbelief.

"I didn't know," Emmeline said. "I just found out!"

"Okay. Where are those pieces?"

"I have no idea. I just saw this!"

"Could that be a part of the device?" Delta said, pointing to the glowing object.

"Yes. Yes. It is. The first part. Look it matches the image."

Delta's face turned white. "Where do we find the rest of them?"

"I don't know," said Emmeline. "But we have to start somewhere."

"This is not good. Could this piece have any powers?"

"I don't know! We have to get it before we can make any assumptions."

Emmeline's heart sunk. Without the complete device, there might be no way to prove that the mythical device had unlimited power. Time was precious, and she felt they were getting nowhere.

Emmeline marched around the oval structure, looking high and low, then sulked. "Nothing. Absolutely nothing. It's all stone. There's no technology, and if there is, we can't detect it." Then her eyes drifted away from Delta as if she had been transported somewhere else.

"I've seen that look before," remarked Delta.

Emmeline walked past her and reached out to touch the

wall. It was cold and wet. But that wasn't what had attracted her to it. She hadn't noticed it before because of the darkness. But there, carved into the stone, was a mark. A symbol she had seen before. There were seventeen small dots on the wall. Their shape and size were just like the markings that had appeared on the back of the plaque when she'd first found it. She smiled and turned.

"What?" Delta asked.

Emmeline picked up the pad and scrolled through the files. "Hold on," she said. "Ah! Found it."

The musical tune echoed through the cave.

The glow intensified. The girls moved away from the stone structure. Brightness engulfed the stone, then started spreading. The light spread throughout the entire cave and glittered. It was so bright that they had to shut their eyes.

Emmeline momentarily opened her eyes and was surprised. What she saw terrified and amazed her at the same time. Beautiful sparkling golden lights surrounded them. She looked to her side. Delta's eyes were closed. She tried to tell her to open them, but she couldn't speak. She tried again, but she had no voice. Delta didn't move. Emmeline tried to call her. But she remained still, as if frozen in time.

Emmeline looked around and touched a string of glitter. It melted away. She wondered if she could walk and took a step forward. A large bubble appeared in front of her, then another. A group of bubbles, about twenty centimeters in radius, floated in the golden mist.

Emmeline stepped closer to them and noticed images inside the bubbles. She turned to Delta to show her, but she still did not move. Emmeline focused on one bubble. In it, she could see an asteroid field. It was enormous. She wondered what it meant. She turned to the next and could see an Earth-like planet. Then a third bubble floated in front of her. Carcasses lay on the ground, and a black dragon-like creature flew above an immense structure. It looked like a historic castle. She gasped. Suddenly, the bubble filled with blackness. She peered in. A pair of red eyes appeared and glared at her. She felt as if those eyes saw through her and knew exactly what she was doing. She gasped and stumbled backward.

The next thing she knew, she was on the ground. She quickly got to her feet and found Delta, who looked confused.

"Did you see that?" Emmeline asked shakily.

"Yes. The flash. It was too bright."

"No." Emmeline shook her head. "The bubbles."

Delta eyed her. "Bubbles. What bubbles?"

Emmeline's mind struggled to comprehend what had happened, but they had limited time. She had no choice but to focus on the problem at hand. She walked toward the stone box. The glow had disappeared. She got on her knees and peered inside the oval structure. She saw a hole in the ground where the piece had stood. She reached for her flashlight and illuminated the interior. A smile of satisfaction spread across her face as she saw the golden piece. It was about five centimeters long and curved. She slowly reached down, thinking of the risks she had taken, the things she'd had to go through to get here, and congratulated herself on a well-deserved victory. Even though she may not have found the entire mythical device, she still had a way of explaining all this. The piece, to her amazement, was cool and lightweight, and there were no markings on it.

Delta came over to have a look. "It's beautiful."

FREEDOM

Jacob had never thought he would be glad to see this anomaly, but he was. He was fascinated and curious. The eyes of every crew member on the bridge were glued to the viewscreen. The moment of awe seemed to last forever. When they had detected the portal, they'd never thought it would be so enchanting.

For a second, they all forgot what they had come here for. It was the admiral who broke the silence. "Any sign of Astra?"

The pilot, Eugene, suddenly realized his duties. "Yes,

sir. Astra is on the planet on the other side of the portal."

"Are there any other planetoids?" Argon asked.

Jacob controlled himself. He knew why Argon was here; it would come to nothing. Punishment was due for those who broke the law, and these girls were no different. No one would be left unpunished, not on his watch.

"None," Eugene replied after a moment.

"Open a channel," Jacob said.

Argon turned to him, and their eyes met. Jacob could feel his hatred. In fact, he could feel even his crew's disapproval of his actions. But he was a man of his word, and he represented the Imperial Command. The law had to be followed. "Freedom to Astra, do you read me?" he said.

Everyone waited. There was no response.

"Emmeline and Delta, this is Admiral Donavan. Do you read me?"

Still silence.

"Is their ship intact?" asked Jacob.

"Yes, sir," Eugene told him.

"Are they receiving our hails?"

"Yes, sir."

"Can I try?" asked Argon.

Jacob's face turned stony. "Go ahead."

Argon tried a couple of times, but still, there was no reply.

"Sir," said the communications officer. "Titan is hailing us."

Jacob scowled.

"To be specific, Dr. Kent is hailing us."

Jacob rolled his eyes and accepted the call. "Yes, Dr. Kent?"

The viewscreen split in two. On one side, they could see the doorway. On the other side, Dr. Kent's face appeared. "Have you sent the probe yet?" he asked.

"You know I'm the admiral, right?" Jacob retorted.

Everyone on the bridge tried to hide their amusement.

"Yes. I am aware of that. Admiral, have you sent the

probe yet?"

"No. I'm trying to contact Astra."

"Well, while you're waiting, why don't you send it?" Dr. Kent suggested impatiently.

"Admiral," said Anastasia with a warm smile. "Could you please send the probe? It would help us figure out our next move."

"Sure," Jacob replied. He nodded toward the tactical officer, Lieutenant Tessa Clark.

A couple of minutes passed, and Tessa announced, "The probe is ready, sir."

"Fire away."

A small flash of light left Freedom and approached the portal. The crew watched as it disappeared into the circular abyss.

"Okay. The probe is transmitting. Telemetry coming through," Eugene announced.

"Transmit it to Titan," Jacob ordered. Everyone was quiet for a moment. "Hail Astra again."

"No reply, sir."

Jacob did not like to be ignored. Who did these girls think they were?

Anastasia appeared on the screen.

"Yes, Commander?" said Jacob.

"We've never seen anything like this before," she said. "As the probe passed through the portal, there was a disturbance on the planet's surface. Dr. Kent informed me that he detected seismic activity in the southern hemisphere of the planet."

"So, if an object passes through the portal, it affects the entire planet. Why?" asked Jacob.

"We don't know. What we know is that this portal opens into another galaxy. We'll need time to figure out which one," Anastasia replied.

Half an hour passed without incident.

Suddenly, an alarm went off on Titan's bridge. "What happened?" Anastasia asked.

Adrian's voice rang out.

Anastasia turned her attention back to Freedom. "Admiral, the probe has stopped transmitting."

Jacob turned to the tactical station.

"The commander is right. The probe has not only stopped transmitting. It's vanished," reported Tessa.

"What?" Jacob asked. "How can that be?"

"The probe was designed to go through the portal and orbit the planet. But as soon as it entered the southern hemisphere, it vanished. I can't detect it any longer," Tessa said. "Admiral, I suggest caution. There might be an alien ship, or an entity hidden from our sensors."

"Hmm."

"Sir, if there is an alien ship out there, we might be seen as an unwelcome guest, maybe hostile. We shouldn't make an enemy of them," Tessa added.

"I agree," said Anastasia. "The Orias are enough."

Jacob scoffed.

They waited again. Jacob walked up and down on the bridge. He glared at the portal again. It remained open and stable. "Has the probe appeared?"

"Negative."

"Interesting. It appears that something really doesn't want us to know more about this region of space," Dr. Kent remarked.

"This is a waste of time," Jacob said. "I think mine is the only plan we're left with. We should go and get them."

"No!" Dr. Kent protested before anyone else could. "We don't know how that will affect the planet or Astra."

"I've had enough of this."

"Sir, I think—" Anastasia began.

Jacob cut her off. "Silence! We're here to get them out. That is what I'm going to do! Now take us in!"

Argon took a step forward. The admiral gave him a warning look.

THE ROGUE PLANET

Somehow, the trek back to Astra seemed faster. They had been jogging for the last couple of kilometers. Emmeline's clothes were drenched with sweat, and she was breathless. But they had little time. Astra was so close. They'd be heading home soon. Emmeline reached for the rock over her head and climbed after Delta. Suddenly, the mountain trembled. Emmeline grabbed the rock tightly. Cracks began to form in the mountain.

"Emmeline move!" shouted Delta.

Emmeline looked to her right. She could see rocks crumbling and rolling to the ground. The flat terrain was disappearing fast. She grabbed the next rock and climbed hurriedly. Delta helped her. Both women stood on the edge of the mountain. The sky became dark, and thunder clapped. The mountains made loud groaning noises. In a matter of minutes, the entire terrain changed. The ground beneath them shook. They lost their balance and fell. When Emmeline looked up, she saw a huge cloud of dust in the distance. The tip of a mountain fell off and tumbled downward.

"Emmeline, run!" Delta shouted.

FREEDOM

Freedom's crew members were stunned. They felt as if they had been miraculously transported to another universe. The enchanting white light captivated them. The ship shook, and alarms blared, but neither discouraged them from looking at the vast set of galaxies. Even the admiral was in awe.

"Sir, we have a problem," reported Tessa. "As soon as we entered the gateway, the seismic activity on the planet doubled. It's now mostly in the south pole, but I'm afraid if we go through the gate, it might destroy the entire planet."

"Are you sure? We're halfway through the portal," said Jacob. "Once we get to our people, we'll want to observe this phenomenon."

Tessa took a few minutes to complete the scan. "Sir, I believe I am right. The closer we move to the planet; it appears to affect the planet. We don't have the equipment nor the right crew to monitor such a phenomenon. Titan does."

Jacob shrugged his shoulders and looked disappointed. He was right; he was always right. "Fine. Fine. Back off! We'll wait for them, then!"

"Reversing engines," announced Eugene.

"Any signs of the probe?" Argon inquired.

"It hasn't reappeared," Eugene replied.

"Any other life signs?" inquired the admiral.

"I detect two life signs on the planet, human. No other life signs detected." Tessa reported.

Freedom shook and shuddered, and the engines roared. Freedom swung inside the portal. The engines screamed as all power was drained from them.

"Eugene?" Jacob asked.

"Sir, the engines aren't responding."

"What?" shouted Argon, coming to stand next to him.

"Full power! Reverse now!" ordered Jacob.

Freedom trembled as the engines pushed backward.

"Sir, the earthquakes have engulfed the southern pole," Tessa said urgently.

"Pilot!"

"Sir, I'm giving it all she's got. This is it. We can't do anything more!"

Freedom shuddered more violently. Jacob gripped his chair.

"Admiral, the structural integrity of the ship is collapsing. Shields are down to fifty percent. There are hull fractures on Decks 2 and 3. If we don't stop, Freedom will collapse inside the portal. We have to go through. We have no choice!" said Tessa.

Argon turned to the admiral, then spun on his heel without a word. His face red, he raged out of the bridge. *Damn him*, Jacob thought ruefully.

THE ROGUE PLANET

Emmeline never knew she could run so fast. Like a ghost, the dust cloud emerging from the collapsing mountains was following them. Thunder clapped overhead, and the ground vibrated under her feet. Emmeline looked behind her as she ran up the small hill. The dust cloud wasn't far away. She couldn't see anything beyond it. They were nearly there. As soon as she reached the top of the hill, she was delighted to see Astra still intact.

Delta paused for a moment, breathing hard, and turned. "Come on!"

Emmeline had to stop for a moment. She felt like her legs were tearing apart. "Go! Go! I'll catch—"

At that moment, there was loud, resonating noise, and the mountain below trembled. Emmeline lost her balance and fell forward. She immediately got to her feet and was about to run, but then she stopped. She felt as if a large animal was moving beneath her. She looked up. Delta stood near Astra, facing her.

Thunder echoed, and a crack appeared in front of Emmeline and began to widen.

"Delta!" Emmeline screamed.

Realizing what was happening, Delta ran toward her. The mountain broke, and its first victim was Astra. The ship tilted, then groaned as it fell into the abyss. The cracks in the mountain appeared faster and wider. Delta looked at Emmeline.

"No!" Emmeline cried, and she threw herself ahead, trying to grab Delta's outstretched hand. Her fingers touched Delta's, and she tried to grab her wrist, but it slipped from her grip. Emmeline fell on the rock's edge. Delta screamed, waving her hands helplessly as she disappeared in a cloud of dust.

CHAPTER 8: JUSTICE IS ARBITRARY

FREEDOM, BRIDGE

Freedom jolted.

"Sir, I've sent a distress signal," said Tessa as Freedom appeared on the other side of the portal.

"Astra. It's gone! It's gone!" shouted Eugene.

"Are you sure?" Jacob asked.

"It was on sensors just a minute ago. I've lost it!"

"Look for life signs! Tell me they're alive!" Jacob sat on the edge of his seat.

"Sir, there's an unauthorized launch of one of our shuttles," said Tessa.

Jacob rolled his eyes. "Let me guess."

"It's Argon."

Jacob bowed his head. The small white craft flew at high speed toward the planet.

"Sir, should I ask him to return?" Tessa asked.

Jacob faced her. "Do you think he will return?" He turned to the viewscreen. "The shuttle is faster. It can land on the surface and save any survivors. What about the portal?"

"It appears to be stable for now."

"The earthquakes?"

"The planet is still on the verge of collapsing."

Jacob frowned. "How long?"

"I can't say," Tessa replied.

Jacob looked at the planet and felt terrible. There was very little he could do now. "Open a channel to Argon."

"Channel open, sir."

"Argon, let us know if we can be of assistance."

"Sure," Argon replied coldly. Then he ended the transmission.

"Sir. I'm detecting only one life sign on the planet," said Eugene. "Human in the northern hemisphere."

"No one else?" Jacob asked.

Eugene turned. "No, sir."

"Do you have the coordinates?"

"Yes, sir."

"Send them to Argon."

Silence fell for a moment.

"What's causing the earthquakes?" Jacob asked.

"Unknown," replied Tessa.

"This is all wrong and weird!" yelled the admiral.

"Sir, Argon has landed on the surface," Eugene confirmed.

"Sir, I'm detecting something. Two hundred kilometers port side," yelled Tessa.

"What?" asked Jacob. "Get ready to . . ."

"Sir, it's the probe," said Tessa excitedly. "I thought it was destroyed,"

"It survived," Jacob replied. "Grab it quickly. I'd like to know where it went."

"Sir," said Eugene. "Argon reports that he has found Emmeline. She's unconscious. He's returning to the ship."

"What about Delta?"

Eugene shook his head.

"Not even a body?"

"No, sir."

Jacob bowed his head, but it wasn't his fault. The girls should have listened to him. "Do we have enough power to go back?"

"We have enough."

"Sir, we have the probe and shuttle," said Tessa.

"Let's go!" Jacob told Eugene. "Let Chris solve this mystery," he muttered.

Freedom turned and flew back toward the portal. As soon as it entered, the planet blew to pieces. Freedom jolted. The engine roared. Alarms went off. "Sir," Eugene called.

Jacob's heart sank. "Oh no. Don't tell me."

"The portal is collapsing!"

"Increase speed!"

Freedom surged into the portal. "Sir," Eugene said. "The portal will close in ten seconds, nine, eight . . ."

"Engines to maximum. Reroute power from anywhere you can!" Jacob ordered.

"Seven, six . . ."

The admiral opened a ship-wide channel. "Brace for impact!"

As soon as the words left his mouth, the white light around Freedom began closing in. The ship trembled. The roar of the engines echoed throughout the bridge. Lights dimmed.

"Come on!" Jacob shouted, banging his fist. The stars ahead were disappearing. All he could see was a small opening, and it was closing in rapidly.

"Five, four. Sir, we won't make it!" shouted Eugene.

"We have to make it! Punch your way through if you have to!"

The portal collapsed behind Freedom; the shock wave threw the ship out. The helm blew, launching Eugene off his seat. The ship spun out of control. Alarms screamed on the bridge.

"Engines are down. Engines are down!" shouted Tessa.

In front of Jacob's eyes, the stars were spinning. "Take helm control," he ordered her. "Stabilize the ship!"

Tessa jumped into action. Freedom thrusters came online, and soon, the ship came to a complete halt. Jacob got to his feet and checked on Eugene. His face was severely burned, and he was unconscious, but he was still alive. He looked at Tessa.

"The portal is gone, sir," she reported.

TITAN, DECK 10, DOCKING BAY

"You don't need to be here," Evan told Adrian.

The crew of Freedom disembarked. But unlike last time, when they'd emerged as victors today, their heads were low and their faces long.

"Something tells me I should be here," replied Adrian. He waited. One by one, everyone left the ship. He folded his arms and bit his lip. It was true: he'd lost her. But he didn't want to believe it. He wanted to see her. He wanted to feel her hair and listen to her voice at least one last time. For the last twenty-four hours, he'd kept wishing that Astra would show up on sensors, that somehow, she had survived. But his wish had not been granted.

The admiral appeared at the door. Rage stirred inside Adrian, but before he could say anything, Dr. Kent came out of nowhere.

"Are you happy now?" Dr. Kent shouted at the top of his lungs.

The entire docking bay came to a standstill.

"Doctor . . ."

"You arrogant son of a bitch! Could you for once in your bloody life listen to someone?"

Anastasia came and stood between Dr. Kent and Admiral Donavan. "Gentlemen, please."

"This is unacceptable. What you did was wrong!" Dr. Kent yelled. "Because of you, an innocent girl is dead. You and your stupid rules! We could have saved her." Dr. Kent's voice trailed off.

Argon and Emmeline appeared at the door. Looking at Emmeline, Adrian felt worse than ever. She looked as if life had left her. Her face was pale, her lips dry, and her eyes sunken in despair. The death of Delta had taken her soul. Argon held her, and she walked like a person who had been sick for years. Adrian didn't have the heart to ask her about Delta, but he wanted to. Everyone fell silent as Argon helped Emmeline out of the docking bay. The doors closed behind them.

"We're all angry. The best thing to do is stay calm," said Anastasia.

Dr. Kent looked at Jacob as if planning to eat him alive. "I have always obeyed the rules set by the Imperial Command, and I have respected your judgment despite our disagreements. I trusted you. I was blind. I thought you could see what I saw. I didn't realize I was making robots, not scientists, and I punished my students for thinking out of the box because the Imperial Command wants everything fucking neat. I punished Emmeline just for being curious. But today . . . I realized something. You are a monster! You have no humanity left in you! You took away a life, and destroyed our chances of studying the portal. You think so highly of yourself; you are the real criminal!"

"Chris, my friend I…"

"I am not your friend. Not anymore. We are done and I will not forget this." Dr. Kent stormed out.

Jacob looked at Anastasia. "Is there anything you want to add?"

Adrian wanted to punch him, but he controlled himself.

"Just this," she said coldly. "You had more friends twenty-four hours ago. Emphasis on the word *had*."

TITAN, DECK 3, MEDICAL BAY 1

Anastasia wasn't in the mood, but Dr. Finch wanted to tell her something very important. She entered Medical Bay 1 and felt her stomach churn as she eyed the six corpses of the Orias. A part of her wished they would just vanish so she could handle the situation with Emmeline. She had to save her; she hadn't been able to save Delta, and that would haunt her for the rest of her life. She tried not to be emotional, but she had no idea how she was going to tell a mother she had lost her only child.

"Thank you for coming, Commander," said Aceline, studying her face. "Are you all right?"

"Yes. Thank you. Tell me what you found."

The medical lab was a small section of the medical bay, which was an extensive medical facility for the colonists and crew of Titan. There were three medical bays in total, but this one was the biggest. The lab was separated from the hospital by a gray wall with a large window and was equipped with the latest medical equipment.

Dr. Finch beckoned Anastasia toward the console. On it was the face of a young man with thick blond hair, blue eyes, and a chubby face.

"Who is this?" Anastasia asked.

"Ensign Tyler Lore. The vertebra Emmeline found in the debris belonged to him."

Anastasia's heart melted. Tyler was as old as Delta. Another young life lost. Part of her didn't want to know any more.

"He served aboard Nightingale, an Earth ship that disappeared without a trace thirty years ago."

The computer showed pictures and profiles of the rest of the crew. Anastasia wondered what had happened to them.

"The Nightingale's last known coordinates were in Sector 256 of Tetra System that was surveyed by Prometheus two years ago. They found no traces of the ship or the crew," reported Dr. Finch. He turned to the corpses that lay on the observation beds.

"Are any of them . . .?" asked Anastasia, trying to put her mind at ease.

"Human? No, but one thing is curious," he said, walking toward the two corpses at the far end of the hall. "These two are from the same species, and so are the limb and the head that we found. The Orias are intriguing. Warm-blooded. We could say mammals like you and me. Their blood is green, and they're very smelly. They're vertebrates, and they have circulatory, muscular, digestive, and neurological systems. Their circulatory and neurological systems take up most of their energy, and interestingly, they have very slow digestive systems, meaning that they don't have to eat very often."

"What do they eat?" Anastasia asked.

"Anything living."

"You mean they're carnivorous?"

"Yep."

"Okay. What else?"

"They have three lungs and require an oxygen-nitrogen environment to survive, but they can survive in thinner air. The third lung can store oxygen. While you and I would die in a couple of minutes without oxygen, these fellows can survive for over an hour at least." Dr. Finch walked toward one of the corpses he had just autopsied. The insides of the alien's body were gray.

Anastasia tried not to puke. "Let's talk about communication. How do you think they might communicate?"

"By roaring."

"What?"

"Yes. Animals communicate using signals, visual and auditory. From what I can understand, the Orias communicate with each other using sound-based signals."

"So, they're not telepathic?"

"No. They're less likely to be telepathic themselves, but I think they're *controlled* telepathically."

"Controlled?" Anastasia asked.

"After examining their brain's anatomy and physiology, it seems unlikely that they can strategize, but from what we've seen, they do."

"So, something or someone is controlling them."

"Yes. There has to be a controller of some sort on the Orias ship, or they are controlled by a very powerful telepathic being."

"Okay. Anything else?"

"The age," Aceline remarked.

Anastasia smiled at her.

"It seems the Orias do not age," Dr. Finch said.

Anastasia looked from one doctor to the other. "That's impossible."

"Not for the Orias. Let's take a look at the tissue samples." He moved in front of a screen. "I've taken samples from each specimen for comparison."

"These look identical," Anastasia said.

"They are, and they show no signs of cellular degeneration."

She turned to glare at him.

He continued. "Let's say a boy of ten years, a middle-aged woman, and an old man are turned into Orias. They'll have no cellular degeneration as long as they live. It's like the aging gene is switched off."

"They're immortal?" Anastasia asked.

"Let's just say that they don't degenerate, but as you can see, they can be killed," Dr. Finch explained. "It's like their original bodily mechanisms just freeze."

"But this information is invaluable for us," Aceline added with a smile.

"How?"

"We can calculate at what time their original bodily mechanisms froze and determine how long they have been Orias."

Dr. Finch smiled. "We've already found a pattern." He led Anastasia to the first body on the left. "His bodily functions stopped approximately two hundred years ago." Dr. Finch walked to the next one. "This one became an Orias about ninety years ago." He came to stand at the next table. "He has been an Orias for about fifty years, and these three Orias, including those we've just found a few body parts from, have been a part of the Orias for the last twenty years."

"Oh my God," Anastasia whispered.

"It means these could be the last species they might have eradicated before they showed up in our solar system."

Anastasia felt a wave of unease wash over her. She stared at the bodies, hoping no one on Titan would turn into that.

TITAN, DECK 1, ANASTASIA'S OFFICE

Everyone waited silently as Jacob went through the

reports submitted by Dr. Finch and Aceline. Anastasia glanced at Adrian. He was still pale, but he looked better than yesterday. Evan was, as usual, at his side. Anastasia looked at Dr. Kent. For the first time in the last decade, he looked gloomy and distracted.

He tried not to look at Jacob, but the admiral appeared unmoved. He carried on with the same air of authority, as if nothing had happened. It was very different for her; she couldn't sleep a wink. And she had found both Argon and Adrian at the Midnight Orchid in the middle of the night. She joined them, and she offered her condolences to Adrian. She felt torn. In ten years of her career, she had never lost a crew member. She recalled the horror she felt, and how she had to conceal her feelings when she told Delta's mother about her daughters' death.

The admiral finished reading the report and sat back. "So, they're like dinosaurs. Very strong, can survive on limited food and oxygen, do not degenerate or age, and are slaves."

"Well, dinosaurs were bigger, but you get the idea," replied Anastasia. "Any luck finding their communications frequency?"

"No, not yet," said Adrian.

Anastasia turned to Cyr.

"After Dr. Finch submitted the report, we began going through the debris again to find a mind-control mechanism. We haven't found it yet."

"Keep looking. What about the data module?"

"We're still looking."

Anastasia smiled. Patience was the key, and she understood that everyone was under pressure. "Thanks, Dr. Finch and Dr. Keston. We really appreciate your input."

Dr. Finch nodded. "Now I plan to dissect the brain. Hopefully, we can find something else that could be useful."

"Do it," said Anastasia, thinking that it would be good to keep everyone busy.

TITAN, DECK 1, ANASTASIA'S OFFICE

Two days later, things had settled down a bit. Anastasia called Dr. Kent and Admiral Donavan into her office to discuss the situation regarding Emmeline.

"We need to talk about this."

"No. We need to sue him," said Dr. Kent, pointing to the admiral.

Despite her feelings, she said, "Gentlemen. I know a lot of things have happened in the past few days. It has taken its toll on all of us."

"No. That's not it . . ."

Anastasia didn't let Dr. Kent continue. "Dr. Kent, you're forgetting a very important fact. The portal didn't open by itself. There's a high probability that Emmeline opened it. Has it occurred to you that if she can open it once, she could do it again?"

The doctor leaned back in his chair. "I know. I'm just angry."

Anastasia smiled. She felt the same, but she didn't have the luxury to express her anger. Her disappointment. Her pain. "That's understandable. We've never lost someone so close to us. Admiral, it would have been really good if you'd worked with us on this. I understand your position and your authority, but everyone, including your tactical officer, warned you about entering that portal. When the probe disappeared, you shouldn't have risked your ship and your crew. Delta and Emmeline were alive and well."

"Look . . ."

"In the near future, I would appreciate it if you would let the experts help you in such matters," Anastasia said firmly.

"My job was to bring them back," Jacob argued. "To uphold the law!"

"No one told you to take that job," Dr. Kent pointed out. "They would have returned, anyway."

"Several people have gone past the perimeter and never returned."

"But Titan is their home. Delta was born here, and Emmeline is dedicated to her work. They have friends and families. They would have returned," said Anastasia. She took a deep breath. "Admiral and Dr. Kent, I understand that at the moment, the situation isn't ideal, but you're all I've got. You're all Titan has, and we have about twenty thousand innocent souls on this space station. The Orias will come, and we might be our people's only defense. I have no choice but to ask you to work together."

Both men's faces turned stony.

"And Dr. Kent, I've asked Argon to lock down Emmeline's research for now. No one is to get access to it without my authorization. We need time, and so does Emmeline. She had to be taken to the medical bay."

"Why? What happened?" asked Dr. Kent.

"She's in shock, and the doctor says she's not mentally stable. She doesn't sleep, eat, or talk. It's understandable. Her best friend, someone who was like her sister, is dead."

Dr. Kent's face turned grim.

"I've gone through her data in an attempt to understand what she was doing," Anastasia said.

"You mean the mythical device?" Dr. Kent asked.

The room fell silent.

"W-What? What is that?" asked Jacob.

"You know about it?" said Anastasia.

"Yes, I do," Dr. Kent replied. "It's folklore."

"I don't think so," Anastasia stated.

"What are we talking about?" asked Jacob.

Anastasia told the admiral what she knew about the mythical device.

"And you let her do this?" Jacob demanded of Dr. Kent.

"I don't control her. If she wants to chase myths in her time off, it's up to her!"

Jacob turned to Anastasia.

"I didn't intervene because she's a researcher; she was researching. From what I can gather from her notes, the device is real. She found it."

Dr. Kent raised his eyebrows.

"What do we do with this device?" asked Jacob.

"You're not getting your hands on it," argued Dr. Kent.

"Gentlemen, let's focus on the problem at hand, Emmeline's future," said Anastasia. "There will be a preliminary hearing by the tribunal."

"Will she be court-martialed?" asked Dr. Kent.

"That depends on Emmeline's story and how we present it," Anastasia told him. "We know Delta's death was an accident. But the fact remains that she and Delta crossed the perimeter without authorization. They found a hidden portal and landed on an alien planet. The Imperial Command has strict rules and procedures. They broke the law. What were they doing? Why didn't they tell anyone? What was so important that they thought it was best to sneak out? Why the secrecy? Whether or not we like it, Emmeline will have to face the music and answer these questions."

"Let's not forget the Orias," said Jacob.

Dr. Kent held his head in his hands.

"I agree," said Anastasia. "Whatever happens, defeating the Orias takes precedence."

"Commander, once Emmeline is better, I know she'll be under scrutiny and probably serve a sentence. Can she still work at the Crystal Lab?" asked Dr. Kent.

Anastasia smiled. "I'll see what I can do."

"Let me know if you need anything from me."

"I don't believe you," said Jacob. "After everything she's done. Broken the law, defied you. You still want her to work with you?"

Dr. Kent eyed him. "Yes, especially after everything she's done."

Haides Castle

"I've felt it again," said a voice in the dark void. "Twice, after a very long time. The sensation is thrilling."

It was more like a shadow than a physical being. A black

smoke whirled through the barren hall. It formed the entrance to a gigantic ancient fortress. Its walls were made of huge pointed towers bent inwards. The ground was as black as charcoal, uneven and arid. The sky above offered one of the best views in the galaxy. An enormous creature bellowed as it flew over the dark structure.

The black smoke moved through the hall, left the structure, and came to a standstill at the edge of the mountain. As far as one could see, there were millions of dark clouds gathered around the gloomy mountain ranges that surrounded the fortress.

A forest encircled the mountain on which the castle had stood since long before the dawn of time. The trees were dark and crooked, forming an unbreakable web around the fortress, making it almost impossible to reach.

The black smoke spiraled. There was no wind, just dead silence. Then, in the distance, a dull roar echoed. The smoke retreated and vanished into the castle.

Miles away from the castle, from within the forest, a red mist emerged. It rose above the trees and whirled up toward the edge of the mountain. Moving through the large entrance, it disappeared into the fortress.

Sturdy walls surrounded the red mist, and again, it felt sorrow for the figures buried within them, their carcasses separated by large columns and their faces frozen in time. The mist came to a stop in the middle of the stony passageway. On both sides were rectangular pools full of purple liquid. There were no ripples, no sounds. The passageway ended, leading to a spacious platform, upon which was a hefty chair. Behind the chair was a glimmering circular band. Unknown scribbles sparkled on its surface. Inside the circular band was a blend of bluish-whitish smoke, which moved in an anticlockwise direction. The dome-shaped ceiling displayed various star maps.

The red smoke took a humanoid form. Now, just a few paces from the throne, there stood an ageless bald man with simple features. In human years, he looked to be in his forties.

He was well built and had a calm and collected look about him. His bright blue eyes showed his patience. He wore a long white overcoat, which touched the floor. He bent a knee.

"My queen. You called?"

"Aithon. I do not understand why you take this form."

"I have the right."

"Yes. You do," she replied. "And you shall have it. Have you sensed it too?"

Aithon stood up straight. "Yes, my queen."

"We have finally found it."

Aithon remained silent.

"Explain your silence."

"It's puzzling because it was not one of our ships," Aithon said lowly.

"I see."

A slight tremor shook the castle. Aithon looked through the windows of the large hall. A fleet of Orias ships flew over the castle.

"Ahh. Our ships have returned after conquering another realm."

Aithon bowed.

"After all this time you have served under me, you still do not approve," the queen noted.

"My queen. I am entitled to my own thoughts."

"Yes."

"Your father . . ."

"My father was a fool!" screamed the queen. Her voice was so loud that it traveled to distant parts of the kingdom. Thunder crashed in the sky. The dark clouds circled the castle like a bad omen. The flying beasts hovered over the fortress.

"My apologies," Aithon said, getting back on his knees.

"Do not remind me of my father. Because of him, I have to search the galaxies for what is my birthright."

"Yes, my queen."

"They burned this planet and buried its civilization and stripped away its beauty. I will restore it, no matter what the cost."

Aithon said nothing. The wind calmed down. The clouds disappeared, and so did the flying beasts.

"Tell me why I am sensing it if we have not found it,"

"Because someone else has discovered it," Aithon told her reluctantly.

The wind blew again.

"How?"

"I don't know."

"Where?"

Aithon hesitated.

"Where?" the queen repeated.

"It is a realm far away. The species is humanoid yet advanced."

"And we have not conquered it yet?"

"Our scout ship returned with some interesting information. I sent a small fleet, but . . ."

"They failed?"

Aithon became silent. "Yes. The fleet failed, but the three scout ships returned with valu—"

"Returned? And you spared them!" the queen roared. "You should have thrown them in the valley of fire! Why haven't you sent a bigger fleet?"

Aithon had learned it was best not to respond to the queen immediately.

"Why wasn't I told?"

"It was a survey mission."

The black smoke whirled again. It was apparent the queen didn't approve.

"What do we know about this realm?" the queen asked.

"It is small and insignificant," Aithon replied. "They live in their own world and are explorers and have limited ships."

"Then they are no match for us. We should eliminate them."

Aithon remain silent.

"Do these limited beings have it?"

"Yes, one of the pieces," Aithon said.

"That means they have discovered the first piece while

we have been searching the galaxy and have failed! My father forced me into millions of years of slavery. I have waited long enough. What is mine should be returned to me! I should send you to oblivion!"

The gale returned and rushed through the castle.

"My queen," said Aithon gently. "You ordered me to look for the pieces. I have done so. Even if they have discovered it, they do not know how to wield its power. They are not destined to use it. You are. They are created differently."

The gale disappeared. "You are right," the queen conceded. "Their ignorance could benefit us."

"The best thing would be to get it before they learn more."

"Bring it to me."

"Yes, my queen." Aithon stood upright. He bowed again and walked away.

"On the other hand," said the queen.

Aithon stopped and turned.

TITAN, DECK 2, CONFERENCE ROOM

Anastasia was disturbed. It wasn't going as she thought it would. In the last week, Titan had turned into a political circus and a center for criticism. She had presented all the evidence to the tribunal. She had interviewed Emmeline, and understood the situation. But it seemed like the Imperial Command was not listening, and they began scrutinizing Titan. An investigation had begun looking into the officers who worked at the station, including herself. She had a feeling that this was a war she wasn't going to win and wasn't looking forward to the preliminary hearing.

She found herself in a large dark hall, facing three rectangular screens. It was all wrong. What had begun as a venture to seek a simple solution for the naive actions of two young women had turned into a tense situation. She was sure that the admiral was playing both parties, and she felt her trust in his abilities fading. In the last two weeks, she could see a growing divide between the crews of the ships and Titan's crew. She had heard from various sources that the admiral had been grooming the ships' captains to take his side. Not that they liked him, but they feared the consequences if they didn't follow his orders.

Anastasia felt that the Imperial Command was using the incident to distract themselves and everyone from the truth. The truth about war and the danger from the Orias. It was apparent that because they had won the first war; they thought they could handle anything. It was arrogant and wrong. It was interesting was that the Imperial Command was not only questioning Emmeline's motives, but also everyone involved. Titan's crews' loyalties were being tested. This was disturbing. This week all the senior officers underwent a review, including her. Anastasia felt her integrity as a commander was being questioned.

Judge number one was Dr. Victor Hall, an elderly fellow whose face was creased with wrinkles. He was representing the science committee in this hearing. Anastasia could see his hands shaking as he read his notes.

Judge number two was Lady Vermont. She represented the people of Earth. She was a sharp-looking woman who appeared to be in her thirties but, surprisingly, was one of the oldest humans alive. Some called her a celebrity; others called her a freak. Why? She was a result from an experiment of humanity's longtime dream of becoming immortal. Turning off the aging genome. They'd found a way all right, but it had turned the subjects into maniacs who'd committed genocides and, one by one, had to be terminated. But somehow, Lady Vermont had survived. As a child, she'd differed from others. Quieter, smarter, and most of all, normal. The symptoms of craziness had never appeared in her, although she'd been constantly monitored for over fifty years. While scientists had questioned her survival and never left her alone, she'd put her time to good use. She'd studied law, worked harder than anyone, and now she was a member of the formidable tribunal. Someone who had power in the Imperial Command, and from what she had heard, Lady Vermont knew how to use it.

Anastasia knew she still underwent scans, but the Imperial Command now considered her an asset, not a threat. The fact remained that she wasn't normal. And immortality or long life had another heavy price: the subjects were sterile. While Lady Vermont's life had made others envious, she did not impress Anastasia. She felt the woman was hiding something. Or maybe she just didn't like politicians.

Judge number three was Admiral Keith Vince. He was a stern-looking man whose only mission appeared to be to intimidate other people. Anastasia assumed he was around her age, but he was bald with hardly any visible eyebrows. His skin was pale, and he didn't have any facial hair. His appearance added to his intimidation because he almost looked like an artificial being.

"This is a highly unusual situation, Commander," stated Lady Vermont.

"Of course," said Anastasia. "One of our young scientists was looking for a source of energy. She found it, but in the process, someone was killed. You must consider that this could be one of the finest findings of this century. I don't understand. Instead of focusing on what was found and investigating the portal, we're sitting here and focusing on punishing the only person who actually believed and had the guts to go after it."

"And there were consequences," stated Lady Vermont.

"There are always consequences in science and war," Anastasia argued. "She's a bit naïve and immature. Yes, restraint is required, but logic suggests that we might need people like her at this time."

"What time?"

"We are at war," Anastasia declared. "The Orias might attack at any time."

"This hearing has nothing to do with that."

Anastasia looked at their faces. "It has everything to do with it. The Imperial Command is underestimating the Orias."

"From what we've seen, our fleet did an exemplary job,"

said Admiral Vince. "It fought the Orias and protected the perimeter. You have all the help you need. You've erected shields around the perimeter and developed advanced weaponry. You have an entire squadron on standby, not to mention six of Earth's biggest ships. And then there's Titan."

"We barely survived the last battle. We need to be ready," Anastasia said.

"Is that why you were reluctant to send Prometheus to return to Earth, even for repairs?"

"Yes, because . . ."

"But you have no authority. Prometheus will follow orders and report to the Imperial Command," said Admiral Vince.

"Well, we are trying to fix it here . . ."

"Commander, I think you're overreacting. Nothing can penetrate the perimeter," he added.

Anastasia was dumbfounded. The tribunal made a few notes.

"If you are blaming this girl for breaking the law, you should also reconsider the Admiral decision to enter the gateway. He was asked repeatedly not to enter the portal, but he did. That lead to the earthquakes, destruction of the planet and Delta death."

"That would have never happened if the girls had followed procedures and reported to you," answered Admiral Vince.

She thought was best not to argue.

"You may now step down, Commander," said Admiral Vince.

Anastasia got to her feet, turned, and walked to sit beside Argon. Officers who were directly linked with the incident occupied one side of the hall. Emmeline sat alone on the other side, facing all her friends. There were a few silent spectators, including Mykel, whose face showed growing concern. Anastasia didn't know if it was for her, Titan, or Emmeline. Next, Dr. Kent was called to the stand.

"I have reviewed your statement, Doctor," said Dr. Hall.

Dr. Kent nodded.

"You have a high regard for the young lady."

"She is hardworking, dependable, and one of my brightest students."

"And yet she has endangered lives twice."

Dr. Kent lowered his head and glanced at Emmeline. "She can be a bit . . ."

"Reckless?" said Lady Vermont.

The doctor said nothing.

"The record show that two years ago, she conducted an experiment that involved radioactive material. A project that you now call the Phoenix. She got the material without your authorization and used it without training, endangering everyone's lives on Titan," said Dr. Hall.

Anastasia and Argon looked at each other.

"It resulted in damaging several systems on the space station and nearly destroyed the lab."

Again Dr. Kent said nothing.

"But you took complete responsibility," Dr. Hall added.

"Yes, and that's why I took extra caution," explained Dr. Kent. "Since then, I've been very strict with her. I put additional systems in place so it wouldn't happen again. I checked all of her activities and experiments. I took away her privileges to order equipment and materials. Everything needed to go through either me or Anastasia, and that worked. I have to mention that the idea of the Phoenix sparked due to her little experiment."

"If you hadn't taken responsibility, what would have happened?" asked Lady Vermont.

Dr. Kent bowed. There was a long pause.

"Dr.?"

"She would have been disqualified," he replied, glancing at Emmeline, "It would have tainted her record and she could never become an astrophysicist."

Now Anastasia understood why Dr. Kent was so careful about everything Emmeline did or submitted to the science committee. He was protecting her. A sense of guilt engulfed her. She always blamed him and thought he was punishing her.

"But this search for this mythical device was a personal endeavor," Dr. Hall continued.

Dr. Kent remained silent.

"Rather than doing scientific research, she was out chasing myths," added Admiral Vince.

"Which turned out to be true," Dr. Kent grumbled.

"What does this thing do?"

"You'll have to ask her."

To that, the tribunal had no response.

"Dr. Kent, you may now step down," said Admiral Vince.

Anastasia bit her lip. The tribunal seemed to check their statements and the extent of their support for Emmeline. That wasn't unusual. If the Titan crew backed Emmeline, the issue would be taken to the high court, which would involve the science community and a broader audience. It could work for or against Emmeline.

After hours of scrutiny, the judges turned to the group.

"Looking at the entire picture, each one of you is indirectly responsible for what has occurred. This is indeed a tragedy," said Lady Vermont in a firm tone. "Never have I come across such a situation. Commander Waters and Dr. Kent, you are her seniors. You were aware of what she was doing, and yet you didn't act. Instead, you indulged her." Her eyes shifted to Adrian. "You knew there was a high possibility that Delta Dune and Emmeline Augury had left the system and broken the law, but you told no one. In the tribunal's view, all of you have lost your good judgment because of the bonds you have created with each other."

Everyone looked at each other in astonishment and confusion.

Next, Emmeline was called to the stand. A shiver passed

through her body, and she avoided looking at any of her friends. She hadn't spoken to anyone, not even her father. Due to the circumstances, the Imperial Command allowed him to come to the station. Arthur had not come to visit her, but Argon informed her that she had his support. The room was dark and cold, and she felt three pairs of eyes boring into her soul.

"Could you explain what happened?" Lady Vermont asked her.

Emmeline nodded. She spoke in a low, unenthusiastic tone as she explained her actions over the past couple of months.

"That's quite a story," said Dr. Hall when she was done.

Emmeline said nothing.

"Can you explain these phenomena?" asked Lady Vermont.

"No. I can't explain the gateway or how someone or something was able to hide an entire planet. We need to study it further," Emmeline replied.

"Where is this . . . piece now?"

"I gave it to Argon Keston."

The judges nodded.

"Your record is outstanding. Despite your mistakes, your research is excellent, but I cannot ignore the fact that you have broken the two biggest laws of our society," said Lady Vermont.

"The consequences are not only going to affect you," Dr. Hall said. "They're going to affect everyone."

"What do you mean?" asked Emmeline, glancing at her friends. "It's not their fault."

"It has been proposed that this situation has not been handled well. Perhaps room for new people should be made," said Admiral Vince.

Emmeline couldn't breathe. Her gaze moved from one face to another. There was murmuring in the hall, but she ignored it. "They have to suffer because of what I did?"

"Young lady, there are always consequences. This is a

preliminary hearing. Nothing is determined," explained Lady Vermont.

"Can you elaborate?"

The tribunal members looked at each other.

"We were planning to outline these later, but now is a better time. These are the recommendations of this tribunal to the Imperial Command," stated Admiral Vince. "Lieutenant Olson should be dismissed and transferred to Challenger colony. Of course, he may appeal. Commander Waters and Dr. Kent's records will show misconduct. The Crystal Lab will be handed over to the science—"

"What?" roared Dr. Kent.

"Remain silent!" Lady Vermont's voice echoed throughout the room. "These are just the *recommendations*. Let the admiral finish."

Emmeline lowered her head.

"A science committee will monitor all projects and experiments at Crystal Lab. There will be changes in the chain of command. Commander Waters will report directly to Admiral Donavan. The fleet, including the Prometheus will serve under the admiral. Of course, there will be further discussion about this."

Emmeline felt as if the room just became darker. When the admiral finished, Lady Vermont turned to Emmeline. "We went through your logs for the last month. There's something else you should have reported."

Emmeline felt everyone's eyes on her. She didn't understand. "I . . ."

"In your logs, you state that you may have found the remains of Alexander Hendrix."

Emmeline's jaw dropped, and gasps sounded in the meeting room. Emmeline had never dreamed that knowledge would be used against her. She didn't know if it had any bearing on what had happened. Her eyes turned to her friends. Everyone was staring at her.

Admiral Vince looked coldly at her. "He was a wanted man, a man who robbed us of the truth about Nemesis. You had DNA proof that he'd died, and yet you did not report his death or the location of his body. That is a criminal act."

"I-I . . ." Emmeline now recalled the message from the clinical lab. Yes, the bone Delta had extracted from the body underneath the rocks had belonged to Alexander Hendrix. She recalled the small container she'd found with the rocky plaque, but she'd been so excited about finding the plaque that she'd completely ignored it.

"I'm not done yet. Did you find any data on him? Any module or anything that would show what he was up to?" asked Admiral Vince.

Emmeline pressed her lips together and shook her head.

"Child," said Lady Vermont in a long tone. "Answer very carefully."

Emmeline didn't like the way she called her a child. But she forced herself to focus. "Isotopes. Amino acids."

"Yes. What about the isotopes?"

"What's she talking about?" asked Argon.

Anastasia shook her head.

"Hush! Do not interrupt," said Lady Vermont.

Emmeline explained that she had found some data in Alexander 's logs and compared the findings with the plaque, revealing that the plaque and Nemesis were linked. Silence fell over the meeting room. All eyes were on her.

Dr. Kent covered his face with his hands. "Oh, shit," he muttered.

Tears gathered in Argon's eyes, and Anastasia looked as if the life had been sucked out of her. Emmeline now realized why Delta had been so adamant about her discussing her findings.

Lady Vermont's face turned red. "You found an alien object on Earth that was linked to one of the most catastrophic incidents in the history of mankind, and you didn't think to tell us!"

"Please believe me. Please. I didn't know what to do with it."

"You should have reported it to Dr. Kent! You should

have told Commander Waters! You have direct access to the science committee. You should have reported this finding!"

Emmeline buried her head in her hands and sobbed.

The meeting room became still.

"Child," said Lady Vermont in an acidic tone.

Emmeline regained control and looked up.

"I would have spared you for your indulgence and your curiosity. Sometimes, children make mistakes. But I represent the law. Do you understand? You left the system without authorization. I cannot overlook the fact that you and Delta were on this planet, and as a result of an accident, she died. Your actions put lives at risk on Freedom." Lady Vermont paused, considering her words. "I was almost ready to look past that, but your failure to share important information about Nemesis and the fact that you found your long-lost ancestor can't be ignored. Do you understand how these facts come together?"

For a moment, Emmeline forgot where she was. Her heart was pounding, her face was covered with sweat, and her palms were damp. She looked at Argon, who sat still. "Yes," Emmeline replied in a small voice.

"These facts will be presented during your court-martial. You have a right to legal representation or a plea. We are not unfair, but we will not tolerate ignorance."

"I want to submit a plea," Emmeline said without thinking.

Lady Vermont shook her head. "Child, this is not the final hearing. Get a legal representative. He or she will guide you. I also suggest, discuss this with your superiors," she explained.

"I want to submit a plea," Emmeline repeated, still looking at her hands.

"Choose your words very carefully, child."

"Emmeline," said Anastasia, leaning forward. "Don't . . ."

"I've just realized something," Emmeline said, ignoring her commander. "I'm a criminal. I don't deserve your forgiveness, but I want to plea for my friends."

"Emmeline," muttered both Argon and Dr. Kent.

Lady Vermont remained calm. "Before you continue, do you know and understand the consequences of such an action?"

"Of course, she doesn't know. She's not thinking straight!" shouted Argon.

"Order in the court!" shouted Admiral Vince. "Cadet Argon Keston, if you do not behave, I will throw you out of this courtroom. The accused has the right to speak."

"I started this," Emmeline continued. "They had absolutely nothing to do with it. I was the one who read those diaries and found the maps. All they did was support me. They shouldn't be punished for believing in me."

"History of crime shows that although the accused is mostly responsible for the crime, the ones who ignore and support them should also carry the burden," replied Lady Vermont. "If you take on this burden, the allegations against the Titan's crew could be dropped. I cannot make any promises. But it will increase your sentence. You do not have to make this decision today. You do not have to make a decision yet."

"I have to make this decision," Emmeline argued.

Within a moment, everyone was on their feet, all speaking at the same time.

The sound of the gavel echoed in the meeting room. "Silence!" shouted Lady Vermont. "I will have order in the court."

The voices died out, and everyone sat down.

Emmeline looked at her friends and saw their concern and horror. "It's not their burden to bear."

The other judges were about to speak when Lady Vermont raised her hand. "Do you know what you are saying?"

Emmeline lifted her head. "Right now, I might be looking at spending the rest of my life in prison. If I take absolute responsibility, I may be condemned to death by madness. The tribunal introduced the law over a hundred years ago . . ."

"Yes, it did. For madmen, for psychopaths, for criminals who have no conscience! Terrorists who massacred innocent people. They are sent to the Specter colony and their sentence is to relive their crimes and horrors, day after day. Their lives are prolonged by medicine so they can suffer like their victims. It is barbaric, dangerous, and controversial, but it has worked. The idea was to make an example to discourage criminal activity. But do you know that in the last century, this court has only served ten people that sentence? It does not wish to include a child on that list!"

"That is not your burden to bear," Emmeline cried out.

Lady Vermont leaned close to the screen, and her eyes bore into Emmeline's. "But it is. This court is adjourned!"

Chapter 9: Alternatives

Titan, Deck 2, Meeting Room

The preliminary hearing ended, and Emmeline was escorted back to her cell. The members of Titan gathered in the meeting room. Anastasia was still in shock. She couldn't believe what had happened. Emmeline had condemned herself to save them, to save her. Why would she do this? She owed them nothing. Could it happen? Would Emmeline suffer just because her seniors were a bit lenient with her? Would she, her commander, just stand by and let a twenty-year-old suffer? Just because she was curious. Just because she couldn't weigh the consequences of her action. She was young, inexperienced. This was insane.

"I don't believe this. They can't take my lab!" shouted Dr. Kent above everyone else. "How the hell did this happen?"

"What the hell is wrong with Emmeline?" Argon complained.

"She feels guilty," said Jacob.

"Why?" spat Adrian. "You should be feeling that!"

"Adrian," warned Evan.

Anastasia watched her world turn mad; her people lose control. There was chaos, distrust, and anger. Micah, Byron, and Clio stood silently behind Argon. Cyr stood with Anastasia, and Evan stood with Adrian. Dr. Finch, Aceline, and Mykel stood quietly in a corner.

"What are we going to do? This is madness!" said Evan.

"I think we need to do something," insisted Argon.

"Quiet!" Anastasia shouted. "Everyone, calm down,"

"Comm—" Argon began.

"The last time I checked, I am still in command, and you will listen to me!" Everyone fell silent, and Anastasia saw a hint of surprise on the admiral's face. *Yeah, I am still their commander*, she thought. "Thank you. I know this is hard."

"This feels wrong," said Adrian. Murmurs of agreement sounded around the room.

"Commander, may I say something?" said Argon. "What gave them the idea that we did so well in the first battle? We barely survived it."

"It's not what," replied Dr. Kent. "It's who." He turned toward Jacob.

The meeting room became silent, and all eyes turned toward the admiral.

"Admiral Vince is right. Anastasia is overreacting. You all are! I just set things right. I had to."

"They sent ten Orias ships. Eighty men and women are dead, and four Earth ships are destroyed," said Mykel. "What if they send fifty more? Do you think we have enough resources to handle that?"

"Admiral, they were scanning the perimeter," said Anastasia. "That means they were looking for loopholes. Who knows? They might have transmitted that information to their headquarters. No, we're not overreacting."

"You are under my command. You follow my lead. My orders. Understand?" Jacob yelled.

"We serve no one but Titan and its people," argued Micah.

"Oh my God," said Dr. Kent after a moment of silence. "It was your idea to replace Commander Waters and me!"

Anastasia felt anger rise in the room. But she'd already known. For the last week, she'd often seen Jacob talking to people, and she was sure he was the one who had been misleading the Imperial Command. She didn't think he was lying to them, but he wasn't telling them the truth either.

"Yes. It was my idea. If Titan was under my command, nothing like this would have happened. I should be in command," Jacob declared.

"Oh, really?" shouted Dr. Kent.

Jacob nodded. "You are delusional. I'm trying to save you. I fought for you. I saved you. I am saving you! You're nothing without me! Don't you agree, Captain Lockhart?"

Anastasia couldn't believe her ears. All eyes turned to the captain.

"Depends on what and who you're fighting for," replied Mykel.

The meeting room turned cold.

Jacob's face reddened, and the two men glared at each other.

Anastasia stepped between them. "Admiral, I understand. Titan is not your home, and you may not have the same attachments as we do. Please give me some privacy with my people? I'd really appreciate it."

"You're kicking me out?"

"I'm their commander. This is a very delicate matter, and right now, I need to speak with them. Privately."

The admiral shot a disapproving glare at Mykel and walked out.

"Who the hell does he think he is?" said Adrian.

"The most powerful man on this station," replied Mykel.

"It feels like they're trying to tear us apart," said Adrian.

"They are!" Argon shouted.

"Please. Stop. Everyone." Anastasia raised her hands. "We will not lose our heads. We will not argue. We will not do anything rash. IS THAT UNDERSTOOD?" She waited.

Everyone except the captain and the doctors stood at attention. "Yes, ma'am!"

She felt a bit better already. "Good. Dr. Kent, develop a plan to save your lab. We need it. You boasted about having some influence in the science committee?"

"I do."

"I recommend that you use it. Make it fast. Something tells me the admiral is already working against us. Lieutenant Olson, I want you to compile a thorough report of everything we've done for the last couple of months. You're not going anywhere!"

"Yes, ma'am."

"Argon, find a good representative for Emmeline and then . . ." She paused. "First of all, who can talk some sense into her?"

Everyone looked at each other.

"Arthur," said Dr. Kent.

It was a good idea; Emmeline was deeply attached to her father. "Of course. Argon, urge Arthur to talk to her. Stupid girl." Anastasia took a deep breath and controlled herself. "Okay. Let's not forget the Orias."

"The perimeter is secured," said Evan. "I think . . ."

"Now. Ships?"

"Still short," Evan said.

"Prometheus?"

"I can't disobey a direct order from the Imperial Command," said Mykel. "I have to go."

It felt as if gravity had suddenly become stronger in the meeting room, and the temperature rose. "We understand," said Anastasia. "It's nice to know you have our backs."

Mykel smiled.

Dr. Kent folded his arms. "I don't like it. She's the most powerful ship. We need you."

"Don't worry. I'll get back ASAP," assured Mykel.

"Now, who can study the piece?" Anastasia asked.

Everyone's faces turned blank. They looked at each other. She turned to Dr. Kent, who blinked several times.

"I wouldn't know where to begin."

Anastasia bit her lip. "Maybe we can look at that later. Argon, until then, it stays in your possession. Do not give it to anyone without my authorization. Do you understand?"

"Yes, ma'am."

"What about the probe from Freedom?"

"Nothing. It's gibberish," Dr. Kent said, throwing his hands in the air.

"What do you mean?" Anastasia asked.

"We've got the data but can hardly make any sense of it. And I am sorry. I can't focus! If the circumstances were different, I would ask Emmeline to look into it. But that may not be possible now."

Anastasia hung her head. "Cyr, work with the doctor and see what you can find. Any luck with the debris?"

"I'm glad to say yes!" replied Cyr. "We've found what appears to be a data module. We're now working to integrate it with our systems."

"Good. Just be careful. It's alien technology. Make sure it's safe before initializing any data transfer."

Cyr nodded.

Anastasia turned her attention back to the group. "We have some challenges ahead, but we need to stick together. Please, please don't do anything rash. Everyone, I urge you to try not to piss off the admiral."

They nodded, trying to control their amusement.

Soon, everyone began to leave, and Argon approached Anastasia. "Whether or not we keep our heads together, Emmeline's life is ruined."

Her heart sank.

"She'll be sentenced to life," Argon continued.

Anastasia nodded solemnly. "If only she'd told us about Nemesis and Alexander. We could have controlled the damage."

"I don't think she realized it was important. It wasn't intentional."

"I believe you. What we need is to make sure the jury believes her." Anastasia hoped her words gave him some comfort, though his face remained thoughtful and pale. "I know what you're going through," she told him. "Please, just be patient."

He nodded and left.

Anastasia remained behind for a few minutes to

compose herself. Two months ago, she'd wanted to leave Titan, but now she wanted to fight for it. The idea of being dismissed or demoted by the Imperial Command for overlooking the actions of a naive girl seemed ridiculous. She turned and realized that Mykel was still there.

"How are you doing?"

"I'm doing great. How about you?" Anastasia replied sarcastically.

He smiled. "Nice try. I know you better than that."

He stepped closer. She wished he wouldn't. He held her hand and said, "I know you hate it when I leave."

Anastasia was surprised. It had never occurred to her; he knew.

"I know you need support right now," Mykel continued. "I don't know if you need me . . ."

"I need you," she replied. "In command of one of the most powerful ships."

"You'll understand, then. I have to go."

She felt like crying, but instead, she smiled. "You always leave."

"And I always come back."

Anastasia checked her memory. He was right. For the last decade, he'd made every attempt to stay in touch with her. She was married and tried to remain as formal as possible. She felt he had returned to her. Since the day Prometheus won the battle against the Orias, he had never left her side. He was back in her life. Was she ready to return to his? "Mykel, now isn't the time."

He smiled. "It never is. Anyway, mark my words, if the admiral keeps troubling you or Titan, I'm going to punch him."

Anastasia rolled her eyes. "No, you won't. You're too sensible for that."

"I think the Imperial Command is being naïve."

"Tell me, Mykel, when was the last time they lost control of something?"

His eyes met hers.

"They're scared," Anastasia said. "They're afraid

because they couldn't control or predict this. For a long time, they've been sitting on that planet, writing procedures and processes of how everything should be. This mythical device and the portal came as a shock to them. Then there is Emmeline. They figure, they can't control her and they don't like that. And then there are people like the admiral. He is feeding the Imperial Command with wrong information and making the situation worse by pinning down the only person who could actually crack the puzzle."

"He has turned this investigation into a personal agenda against Emmeline to gain control over Titan," said Mykel.

"I believe you. I think I saw it coming. He thinks he can resolve everything if he's in command of this station. He thinks he can set an example by condemning Emmeline."

"Huh!"

The doors to the meeting room opened, and Aceline stepped in. "Oh, am I disturbing?"

"Not at all," said Mykel.

"I have something I really need to discuss," Aceline said. "Captain, it's about the planet you call Proserpina."

"Yes, what about it?"

"In your reports, you said that you think the species there died of natural causes."

"Yes. We think an asteroid hit the planet and eradicated all life. That's not uncommon."

"Are you sure?" Aceline asked.

Mykel nodded. "I'm pretty sure it was an asteroid."

Aceline looked worried.

"What is it?" asked Anastasia.

"The captain took some rock samples from the surface. We separated the samples, which we thought were from the asteroid. Captain, the samples of the meteorites are made of the same components as Nemesis, except one isotope is different. The isotope in the meteorites is O-16. In Nemesis, we detected O-17."

Anastasia felt as if Titan shook a little.

"What? Are you sure?" asked Mykel.

"We cross-checked the data seven times!"

"Are you telling me there are more of them out there?" asked Mykel.

"I don't know," Aceline replied. "We analyzed Aluminum-26, which can be used to detect the age of the meteoroid. According to our readings, that asteroid hit the planet almost hundred and fifty years ago."

"What are you saying?" said Anastasia.

"The odds of two identical comets hitting two planets at the same time is next to impossible."

"Unless someone or something planned it," suggested Mykel.

"Hmm. If it were an invasion, wouldn't they want the planet intact? Why destroy it?" asked Anastasia.

"That's a good question. Our scans show that Proserpina was flourishing. Thirty percent of it was water. A humanoid species occupied all five continents. The population was close to three billion. There were hundreds of different species of plants and animals, just like on Earth. We found several infrastructures, automobiles, industries, and military establishments. We think they were on the verge of discovering space travel. It would have been an excellent resource for the invaders, then why destroy it?" said Mykel.

No one had an answer to that question.

"Captain, we need to go back to that planet and do a thorough search," Anastasia said. "A century ago, if our fighters hadn't broken Nemesis into pieces, that would have been Earth's fate. We need to know who's sending these comets and why."

Mykel turned to look at her. "What do you think the Imperial Command is going to say about this?"

TITAN, DECK 10, BRIG

Emmeline sat in the dark brig. She remembered reading novels about criminals who were confined for a long time. Some of them went crazy, and some didn't change, while others changed for the better. She wondered which she would be. Would she be able to accept that she'd made a mistake, get over it, and die in peace? She thought about all her friends and how her choices had made their lives so difficult. It wasn't fair that they had to suffer for something she'd done.

Emmeline's heart skipped a beat, not for fear of death but for fear of the man who stood in front of her. She bowed her head. He hadn't come to see her since she'd been sent away. She knew either Argon or Anastasia must have urged him to talk to her.

Arthur remained silent as the guard stepped out and gave them their privacy.

"Father . . ."

"I told you not to do anything stupid."

Emmeline looked up. Dressed in white, in the dim light, Arthur looked like an angel. She thought it was best not to speak and to accept her fate. If she argued or explained herself, it would just make things worse. But she felt she should say goodbye. She pushed herself to face him. "Dad, I'm . . ."

"Why didn't you fight?"

Her eyes lowered. "I-I couldn't . . ."

"Yes. You could have. You should have! You didn't even explain yourself properly! You should have stood your ground. You should have fought for your life!"

"There's nothing to fight for."

"There is always something to fight for."

She turned away from him. "Nothing I do will bring Delta back."

"True," said Arthur. "That is a mistake you must live with. Do not make another one."

"That's why I should go away." As soon as she said those words, Emmeline felt as if a slab of rock had fallen on her. The silence was overwhelming. She turned to make sure her father was still there.

He stood still like a statue, lifeless. "Why are you doing this?"

"I have to make this right!" Emmeline said. "I have to

make this right!"

"You can't," Arthur told her.

Emmeline shook her head. "But I have to protect my friends. I can't let them suffer because of my mistake. I let Delta down. I won't do that to the others!"

"This doesn't have to be your fate."

"It is my fate, Dad. Just like you said, I ruined everything! Just like Grandpa!"

The expression on Arthur's face didn't change. "You're right. It is your fate. I've accepted that. I don't like it, but I accept it. You were always different, even when you were a child. Chasing butterflies into the unknown. Entering dark caves just to fulfill your curiosity. I'm sorry I didn't believe you."

Emmeline's face fell.

"It was your destiny to find the device that no one thought existed. You found it. But you lost one battle; you did not lose the war. Everything is worth fighting for."

She blinked several times. She didn't understand what he wanted. "Dad . . ."

"Tell me one thing, if you got a chance, will you take it? Will you fight?"

"Ahh…"

"Please…for the sake of your mother. For the sake of the people who love you, tell me you will take the chance. You will fight. You will not surrender."

Emmeline took a step back. She tried to push herself to think, "Dad…I don't know."

"Soon a choice will fall on your shoulders. Things will change. They're going to change fast. Remember, I'll do anything for you and I'll always love you, no matter where you are." His words rang like a bell in Emmeline's head as he walked away.

"Dad! Dad! What do you mean?" she called out.

But like a monk who had taken an oath of silence, he stepped out, and the heavy door closed behind him.

Titan, Deck 3, Midnight Orchid

Argon tried to enjoy his whiskey, but it was hard. He tried not to get frustrated about the situation, but he felt he was the only one who was trying to save her or set things right. But he had a distinct feeling Emmeline didn't want to be saved. She wasn't thinking straight. He knew everyone would do their best, but in the end, it was up to him and Arthur; they had the most to lose. Everyone else could move on, but he didn't know if he could. He didn't know if he should.

He looked at the pad again and read the update about the preliminary hearing. Things were changing fast. He felt a shadow over him and turned to find Clio, Byron, and Micah glaring at him.

"What are you doing here?" Clio asked.

Argon looked around. There was a large crowd spread across the hall. "Just like everyone, I came in for a drink."

Byron sat down beside him and signaled the bartender. Micah and Cleo sat on his left.

"Sorry about what's happening," Byron said.

Argon held his head. All this time, he had been trying to avoid talking about this. But it seemed there was no avoiding it. "It's all ruined."

"No, it's not," said Byron. "Patience. We'll sort this out."

Argon sat back in his chair. "You haven't heard?"

Everyone shook their heads.

"Two hours after our gathering in the meeting room, the Imperial Command passed on a few orders. The first one was to remove Emmeline from Titan."

Everyone's face turned grave.

"They're coming to take her away tomorrow," Argon said.

"I'm so sorry," said Clio. "Is there anything we can do?"

"I don't know."

"Any other orders?" asked Byron.

"Take a wild guess."

"They want the piece," said Micah.

Argon nodded. "And everything she's discovered over the last two years. The maps, the algorithms, Alexander 's secret rainbow letter, the plaque, all the data about Nemesis and the rock sample she found on Earth . . ."

"They're going to take everything from her," muttered Byron.

"Bloody politicians," said Micah.

"No. Bloody admiral," cursed Argon. "I could see the look in his eyes when he found out about the piece. He's going after it. He is hungry for power, and that piece could give it to him."

"Well, we can get a legal representative and get her out," Byron said.

"Yes," Clio agreed.

"Once she leaves Titan, we don't know what will happen to her," Argon replied numbly.

Soft music played in the background as everyone became silent.

"So, what's the plan now?" Micah asked. "What are you going to do?"

"There is no plan," Argon replied. The bartender refilled their glasses. He sipped his drink in silence.

"We know you better than your own shadow. You always have a plan A, B, C," Byron stated.

Argon managed a bleak smile. "What can I do? I'm not an admiral. I'm not a scientist. Even the commander of Titan can't do anything!"

"I can think of plenty of things," Micah said thoughtfully.

"Come on. Anastasia's already managing it. We have to trust the process," said Argon.

All his friends gawked at him.

"Really?" said Micah. "And you want us to believe that?"

"It's the truth,"

For the next hour, they remained at Midnight Orchid, chatting and drinking. After the group left the bar, they moved to sit around a table near a wide window. In the dim light, Argon saw Arthur. He sat at the bar and ordered a drink.

Argon continued to chat with his friends but kept a close eye on Arthur. A few minutes passed. Arthur turned with a drink in his hand, and their eyes met. Arthur gave him a slight nod, then finished his drink and left. Argon felt a bit of relief, but also sadness. Soon, everyone called it a night.

TITAN, DECK 4, EMMELINE'S QUARTERS

It was 0300 hours, and Argon lied when he said he was fine. He had been planning, thinking, and worrying. There was a lot at stake, and he knew it would cause his family pain. But he had to do something. There was very little choice. Selina's words echoed in his head.

"You are going to leave us all…"

How did she know? Did she see the future? Last night he wanted to talk to his sister, but he couldn't. He wasn't that brave. He couldn't see her cry.

He paused in front of Emmeline's door and looked up and down the passageway. When he was sure he was on his own, he punched in the codes and entered the room. He put down his travel bag in a corner and surveyed Emmeline's quarters. He'd never been in her quarters alone and felt uncomfortable entering her bedroom. He opened the closet, kneeled down, and opened Emmeline's secret compartment. He was glad it was still there.

He reached for the backpack and unzipped it. The plaque, the preserved document, the black stone in its glass container, and the piece were still there. He knew, although Anastasia had every right to keep the piece on Titan, in time, they would have to hand it over to the Imperial Command, who could use it as evidence in Emmeline's trial or give it to the Crystal Lab. But he felt that it didn't belong to anyone but Emmeline. The plaque originated in her family, and the piece belongs to her.

He left the bedroom and took a seat in front of the

computer. He smiled and remembered how he'd helped Emmeline set everything up when she'd first been assigned her own quarters. He wondered if she'd changed the access code to the computer. He punched in the code.

"Access granted."

He smiled. Argon spent a few minutes trying to locate all files regarding Emmeline's work. He instructed the computer to download all the files onto a pad. Then he got up, walked into her room, and grabbed the travel bag from her closet. He packed the picture of her family and all the small gifts he'd given her. Everything he knew she'd appreciate. Then he chose a few clothes she could wear.

"Download complete," the computer announced.

He picked up the bags and rushed down to Deck 10. He walked past the small fighters and cargo ships. He glanced behind him. Today, it seemed it was taking him longer than usual to reach Hanger 23. When he got there, he stood silently to look at Raven. The door opened, and he entered the ship. He walked to the cockpit and placed the bags on the floor. He sat in the pilot's chair and stared out. He thought about his family. He knew his mom would understand, but he wasn't so sure about his dad. He was going to miss his little sister. Tears gathered in his eyes, and he sensed a pain in his chest. He was going to miss his friends, Anastasia, his life. He didn't know what was going to happen. He sat back and wondered if he was making the right decision.

Titan, Deck 4, Argon's Quarters

It was close to five in the morning when Argon returned home and snuck into his little sister's room. Selina was asleep on her bed, holding her bunny. He kissed her forehead and watched her sleep for as long as he could. Then he entered his mom's room. He kissed her on the forehead and sat down beside her.

Aceline opened her eyes and smiled. She touched his face. "What is it, my dear?"

He kissed her hand. "Nothing, Mom."

She smiled. "Go to sleep. I'll see you in the morning."

He nodded and watched her fall asleep again.

TITAN, DECK 1, ANASTASIA'S OFFICE

Anastasia watched Prometheus preparing to leave. Part of her didn't want it to leave. It was silly. Her personal feelings didn't matter. Sometimes, she wondered if commanders or captains could have feelings. If the Orias were to attack Titan, she would have loved to see him one last time, even for just a moment.

Prometheus's engines came to life. The massive ship slowly moved away from its docking space and turned in the direction of Earth.

Tears gathered in Anastasia's eyes. With twenty thousand souls aboard Titan, she still felt all alone. She couldn't understand herself. The crew was on her side. Titan was armed to the teeth. Freedom and Marion were here, and they had four more ships that could defend them. There were shields around the perimeter, and Titan's shields were impeccable. She knew she should feel safe, but she didn't.

On top of all this, Anastasia had been ordered to remove Emmeline from Titan. She didn't like that one bit. She'd tried to get around it, but the Imperial Command was adamant. They also wanted her to give them the piece. She was torn as to whether she should fight to keep it or release it to the authorities. What good would it do on Titan if Emmeline was gone?

She felt like she was losing hope. Would she be able to save Emmeline? She'd already let Delta die. She should have controlled the admiral.

Anastasia looked down at the pad. It contained all of Emmeline's notes about the mythical device. Emmeline had been right so far, and Anastasia thought that if this device had power, they could use it to protect themselves from the Orias.

Only if the Imperial Command would give her time, things would be better.

She had been preparing a powerful presentation to steer the science committee away from condemning Emmeline and the Crystal Lab. She had also been studying laws laid by the Imperial Command. She knew her enemy very well, and if she was to face the admiral to save her crew and command, she had to be prepared. Mykel had been right; Jacob wanted to take Titan away from her. She couldn't let him do that.

TITAN, DECK 1, BRIDGE

Adrian couldn't sleep, so he began his shift early and sat on the bridge, watching the computer as it ran a final diagnostic test on the perimeter. The receptors were working perfectly, and Titan was prepared to recharge the shields if necessary.

Prometheus had left an hour ago. He watched it fly away. He'd already made up his mind. He was going to help Emmeline as much as he could. Delta was gone, but he could save her best friend. Then he would resign. Titan didn't hold any more interest to him. He had a sinking feeling that the commander would be replaced. He didn't know if he could work for someone else, and he refused to work under Jacob. The truth was he'd remained on Titan for so long because he was attached to the idea of a woman he could never have. An idea of love that didn't exist. Even if it had existed, he'd never had the courage to find out.

He shut his eyes and remembered the day he had seen Delta on Titan. Since that day, her absence had haunted him. Whenever she'd gone away, he'd spent most of his time brooding. It was no use now. She was gone, and he felt more alone than he'd ever felt in his entire life. Evan had been right; he should have told her.

The computer beeped. Like a robot, Adrian pushed a button, and the computer continued its work. Then another beep. Adrian became alert. It wasn't his console; it was in the science station. He slowly got up and walked over. Putting the weight of his body on the panel, he pressed a few buttons. His eyebrows shot up, and he narrowed his gaze at the screen.

"That can't be right."

TITAN, DECK 9, BRIG

Argon waited patiently for the guards to change duties. He took in a deep breath, disregarding any thoughts that told him this was a bad idea. He knew it was a bad idea, but he had no choice. As planned, one guard exited the brig, and the next guard began his duty. Argon remained hidden as the first guard walked past him, entering the elevator.

The lights in the corridor flickered. A smile spread across Argon's face. With internal security disabled, he had sixty seconds to break in and escape. He ran toward the brig, and the doors slid open.

The security guard slowly stood up. "Argon?"

Argon pointed a disruptor at him. "Don't move. You know I won't miss."

The guard raised his hands. "This is a mistake."

Argon fired. The shot stunned the guard, and he fell to the ground. Argon pressed the codes and opened the door of the brig. "Emmeline?"

Emmeline stepped out of the dark brig. "I knew it! I knew you'd do something stupid!"

"Yes. It's stupid. It's illogical. Don't tell me the math! You can spend the rest of your days in prison, or we can find this mythical device!"

Her face turned thoughtful.

"Make your choice because it will define you."

She remained silent as if weighing her options.

"Emmeline?" Argon pleaded, extending his hand.

She grabbed it. "Once we get to the ship, I can mask our signature using an algorithm I created."

They rushed out of the brig. "Okay. First, we have to get to the hangar deck," Argon said. "Then we take Raven and travel to the Vesta colony in the asteroid belt. Your father has arranged a ship and a pilot who will steer us past the perimeter."

"Argon, we have to figure out where the second piece is."

"One thing at a time," he said as they entered the elevator. "Tell me about this mythical device. Is it very powerful?"

"Yes, once I figure out how to use it."

"Good."

"Why?"

"Because I'm going to use it to blast the Imperial Command."

Emmeline gawked at him. "We're not doing anything like that! Clear?"

He gulped. "Clear." The doors of the elevator opened. They rushed down the hangar deck.

"I never thought we'd have to leave like this," Emmeline said.

"Me neither."

They came to an abrupt stop. Jacob blocked their path. Three guards stood behind him.

"I knew it! I knew you'd do something foolish!"

Argon could feel Emmeline's grip tighten around his hand. "Admiral," he said.

"I don't believe this!" Jacob yelled looking past Argon.

Argon turned and saw Micah, Byron, and Clio right behind them.

"You'd better let them go," Byron said, pointing his disruptor at the admiral.

"You shouldn't be here!" Argon told Byron.

"This is unacceptable! Wrong! I trained you, saved you, and this is how you repay me! Traitors! Don't you know who I am? You are finished. Did you hear me, finished! I will see that you are crucified!" Jacob shouted like a madman.

The group was stunned. Even the guards glanced at each other.

"He has serious impulse control issues," muttered Byron.

Argon glared at him.

TITAN, DECK 4

It moved swiftly through space. *This is so easy*, it thought. For a moment, it paused and admired the gigantic structure. It wondered if it could slip inside. This was going to be delightful. It was afraid of being detected, but what could they possibly do to it? It circled the beautiful black structure. Soon, it flew through a window and appeared in a small gray area. It didn't understand what this place was and thought it was rather confined and peculiar. It floated, ready to leave the area, but then it paused.

A picture on the wall caught its attention. It was of a humanoid creature. Like Aithon. But this one was different. It had a distinct look, with strange attire and peculiar features. At the bottom of the picture were two words: "The Queen."

It liked it. It wanted to know why Aithon liked to take this form. Focusing on itself, it slowly changed. The blackness came together and began taking shape. It started at the bottom and worked upward. Within minutes, it looked exactly like the person in the picture.

The queen felt exhilarated. She ran her left hand over her right. She touched her face and felt a smooth surface. Her skin was warm and tender. She slowly walked ahead and saw her reflection in the wall. She gently touched the shiny object on her head. The gems in her crown sparkled. She ran her hands all over her body and wondered why she hadn't tried this before.

TITAN, DECK 4

With his scanner in his hand, Adrian almost ran down the corridor. He was detecting an unusual reading. At first, it had appeared near the perimeter. Then it had moved toward Titan and entered the station, easily penetrating the shields. He had already alerted the commander.

Two guards followed him closely. He paused and turned to his left. "Oh," he muttered when he saw that he had arrived at Evan's quarters. He pushed the bell and waited. When there was no reply, he pressed the bell again.

Soon, the door opened, and Evan appeared in a loose T-shirt and track pants. "What the hell are you doing here? I'm not on duty until 0800 hours."

"It's in here," Adrian muttered to the guards.

"Whoa! What? What's in here?" Evan asked, looking around.

Something rattled.

"It's in there," Adrian repeated.

"It?"

The doors to the restroom opened, and Evan gasped. "Oh my God!" he said. "She looks exactly . . ."

"Like the singer whose picture hangs in your quarters!" Adrian finished for him.

Evan frowned. "But she's dead."

"I wish you hadn't told me that."

The queen stood in front of them, wearing a shiny black dress. She looked at her hands as if seeing them for the first time. "Fascinating."

"Identify yourself," said one of the guards.

The queen just stared at him.

"Who are you?" asked Adrian.

Her deep blue eyes turned completely black. She flipped her hand, and light sparked through her fingernails. "I am the queen."

"Stand down."

The woman's eyebrows shot up. A flash of light hit the guards, and they disappeared.

"Oh my God!" shouted Evan.

"Get the hell out of here!" Adrian yelled, pushing him. They ran out of the room and down the corridor. "Computer, intruder alert!" shouted Adrian. The alarm sounded throughout the space station.

"Are you thinking what I'm thinking?" Evan asked as they ran.

"I never know what you're thinking!" Adrian shouted glancing over his shoulder.

The queen stepped into the corridor.

"Adrian, I change my mind. I would rather die than turn into a frog!" Evan shouted.

CHAPTER 10: DISAGREEMENTS

TITAN, DECK 10, DOCKING BAY

The alarm startled everyone.

"I thought I disabled it," Argon said to Emmeline. His eyes widened when he saw a huge figure appear behind the admiral. "Watch out!" he shouted.

The group ducked.

Argon and Micah fired together. The Orias was hit, and with a loud screech, it fell to the ground and disappeared.

"The Orias. How did they get inside?" asked Byron.

"Get to your ships," Jacob ordered. Three Orias appeared behind Argon and his friends. "Get down!" he yelled and fired.

Titan jolted.

Anastasia's voice echoed in the corridors. "We are under attack. I repeat: we are under attack! All hands to battle stations! All hands to battle stations!"

Argon and Byron fired. Laser beams hit the Orias, and they turned to dust in seconds. Breathless, Argon looked at Emmeline and then looked past her. "Oh no. Not now," he murmured.

The group stared through the window at the enormous purple cloud beyond the perimeter.

TITAN, DECK 1, BRIDGE

The command center was buzzing with activity.

"Are the ships ready?" Anastasia asked.

"Commander, the crews are scattered around Titan. They're trying their best to get to their ships." Evan replied.

"What about the perimeter shields?"

"They're holding," reported Adrian. "Commander, the cloud is back."

The image on the screen changed. Anastasia gulped as she watched the huge cloud moving at a slow pace.

"If my calculations are correct, in ten minutes, the Orias fleet will be here," reported Adrian.

Anastasia took a deep breath. "All hands. You have eight minutes to get to your ships before the Orias enter our space. I repeat: you have eight minutes!"

"Commander! We've been boarded. I can detect over twenty Orias on Decks 10, 9, and 8," Evan reported.

A wave of dread came over Anastasia, but she had to make the call. "Computer, activate internal security."

"Access code required."

Anastasia jumped to her feet, walked to Evan's console, and placed her palm on the screen.

"Authorization accepted. Activating internal security."

TITAN, DECK 6, INTERNAL SECURITY

On Deck 6, the dark corridors brightened. Light poured through dozens of opaque doors. The humanoid shadows didn't move, but red lights on their foreheads began blinking. The red lights disappeared, and the opaque doors slipped away. Through them marched the first robot, then the next, and soon, all corridors were filled with an army of robots. Six of the robots were painted red, and the others were white. The robots stood in formation behind their commanders.

Anastasia's face appeared on a screen ahead.

"Commander, Otis reporting for duty."

Otis was the leader of the robots.

"Otis, eliminate the Orias," Anastasia said in a cold voice.

"Affirmative."

The hefty doors opened, and the robots darted out at great speed.

TITAN, DECK 10, DOCKING BAY

The admiral rushed toward Freedom, ordering the squad to engage the enemy.

Argon was confused.

Byron faced him. "This is the best chance you'll get. Get out. We'll handle them,"

Clio and Micah nodded.

"No! No!" said Emmeline.

"Go! Just go!" Clio said, rushing down the corridor.

"I think she's right," Micah said, following her.

Argon looked at Emmeline.

Byron placed his hand on Argon's shoulder. "You must leave. I am going to miss you. Watch your back, my friend."

Argon felt as if someone had stabbed his heart, "You too."

Giving him a last glance, Byron followed Micah and Clio.

Argon stood in the corridor, looking at the door.

"Argon, go," said Emmeline.

His heart melted. He wanted to save her. He wanted to save his friends, Titan, everyone. But he had to make a choice. "No. I won't leave you."

She placed her hands on his face. "Titan needs you. You wanted to free me; I'm free. I'll take Raven and disappear."

His eyes filled with tears. She would be alone. What if something happened to her? He needed to be there to protect her. "No . . ."

"Argon! If Titan is destroyed, everyone will die. You

have to protect Titan."

He was speechless.

"Go. Fight this one. Then come and find me. If you can't find me, I will find you," Emmeline said with a small smile.

Argon smiled, and his heart filled with warmth. "I . . ."

"Thank you for not giving up on me."

To Argon's utter surprise, Emmeline stepped forward and kissed him.

TITAN, DECK 1, BRIDGE

"Commander, Freedom and Marion have headed for the perimeter, and fifteen squadron ships are following them," Evan reported. "Four other ships will be ready for launch in the next two minutes."

"There should be sixteen squadron ships. Who's missing?"

"Argon."

"That's not like him," said Anastasia. "Commander Waters to Argon. Report."

There was no answer.

"Commander Waters to Argon. Your squadron is leaving. Report for duty."

Again, there was no response.

"They're leaving without their squadron leader?" asked Evan.

"They're following the admiral's command," replied Lieutenant Hawk from tactical.

Anastasia had no time for this. "Show me the cloud."

The vast purple cloud filled the screen. She twisted her jaw and clenched her teeth tightly. If they wanted to win this one, they needed to change their strategy.

"Commander, internal security has engaged the Orias," Evan said.

"On screen."

"Showing Decks 6 and 7," announced Evan.

Suddenly, the bridge filled with screams. Anastasia sat

back. One Orias was attacking a woman. Then one of the robots fired, and the Orias disintegrated. The robots were taking the creatures down, but there were casualties. Anastasia hoped it wasn't too late. She opened a channel.

"All non-essential personnel report to your quarters. Clear the corridors, observatories, and other public places on the space station. All non-essential personnel report to your quarters now!"

Evan turned to look at her. "It's going to be tough to control the colonists. They're frightened."

That was understandable.

The doors to the bridge opened, and Dr. Kent and Dr. Finch rushed in.

"What the hell is happening?" asked Dr. Kent.

"Doctor, take your station. We'll need you," Anastasia said, but she caught him staring at the vast cloud. "Dr. Kent."

He nodded and rushed toward the station.

"Dr. Finch, you shouldn't be here."

"Where do you suggest I go?"

TITAN, DECK 10, DOCKING BAY

Argon fired, and the alien was thrown back. Emmeline handled the other one. The beam drilled through its limbs. The Orias cried out with a deafening screech. Both Argon and Emmeline covered their ears. They fired again, and it perished.

"Good shot!" Argon called.

"They're hard to miss," Emmeline said.

"They're not as strong as their ships." Argon's communicator went off.

"Argon. Where are you?" asked his mother.

"Mom! I'm heading to my fighter. Stay in the quarters. Stay there with Selina."

"Argon, come home at once!" she demanded.

"Mother, please. Just stay in your quarters."

Titan shook. Then Argon heard a voice he'd hoped he wouldn't have to hear.

"Argon," said Selina.

He paused; his heart broke. He knew he was leaving her forever.

"I understand. I can see. I'll see you on the other side," she said.

"Selina . . ." His voice faded away when a group of aliens appeared in the corridor.

"They just keep coming!" Emmeline shouted.

The aliens advanced toward them. The doors to the elevator opened, and a group of robots stepped into the corridor. "Step away," said the lead robot.

"Move aside," Argon said, shielding Emmeline.

There was an exchange of fire, and the Orias were ambushed quickly. Argon shot down the last one. He looked down at the pile of dead aliens.

The leading robot approached Argon. "Are you all right, sir?"

"Yes. Thank you! Please keep them off this deck."

"Yes, sir."

The small group of robots walked down the corridor.

"How did they get in here?" Argon asked Emmeline.

"I don't know," she replied. "But they seem . . ."

A shock wave hit Titan, and it shook, causing Argon and Emmeline to lose their balance.

"What was that?" Argon asked, helping Emmeline up.

Emmeline accessed the nearest viewscreen. Six Orias wheels were attacking the perimeter at the same time. "Oh my God!" mumbled Emmeline.

The shock waves hit Titan. Alarms screamed. The lights flickered. Argon grabbed the wall to maintain his balance.

"We're too late!" Emmeline cried out.

TITAN, DECK 1, BRIDGE

The crew on the bridge stared at the vast fleet of Orias. Several Orias Wheels flew towards the perimeter. All ships fired at once, their beams merging, creating a large fireball that hit the perimeter. Titan jolted again.

"The perimeter shields are down to twenty percent," Adrian reported sadly.

"Any word from the Prometheus?" she asked Lieutenant Hawk.

"No. I can't raise her. Something seems to be jamming our signals."

"Can we send a distress signal to Earth?"

"No. We can't."

The space station shook again.

"Engineering, we need to keep the perimeter intact. Any suggestions?" Anastasia said.

"I could pull power from the distant generators and use them to power these. If that's not enough, we can transfer power from Titan using the receptors," said Evan.

"Do it!" Anastasia told him. "Open a channel to Freedom."

"Channel open," said Evan.

"Admiral, it may not be safe to open the gates—" Anastasia started.

"I know."

The bridge fell silent. Anastasia rose from her chair.

"Open them anyway," Jacob's voice rang out.

Anastasia's heart sank. "No."

All eyes turned to her, and Jacob's stunned face appeared on the left side of the screen. "What did you say?"

"I said no. The fleet will not survive if I open the gates. I will not condemn four hundred men and women to their deaths."

Silence consumed the bridge.

"What do you suggest we do?" asked the admiral acidly.

"Sit back and wait. They're focusing on one aspect of the perimeter. They will break it, and when they do, we will engage them. Only a few Orias ships will be able to enter our space. It will buy us time, and by then, Prometheus and other ships from Earth can join us."

"You mean fight like a coward."

Anastasia felt her blood boil. She had been waiting to play this card. Unfortunately, she knew it could be the wrong time. "Lieutenant Clark, tell me the odds of survival of Freedom and the fleet."

Jacob's face turned stony.

"Our scan shows over fifty Orias ships," reported Tessa. "There's a big ship at the other end of the battlefield. It stands as if awaiting instructions. If the Earth fleet crosses the gates, death is imminent."

"Lieutenant Hawk," Anastasia said. "Do you agree?"

"Affirmative, Commander. We should change our strategy," said Titan's tactical officer.

"We'll all die one day," said Jacob.

"Yes. We will. But it matters when and for what! Admiral, I cannot let you or the fleet leave," Anastasia said firmly.

"You have no authority over me."

"According to our laws, until and unless we have received direct orders from the Imperial Command, we are not supposed to engage a formidable enemy. We are to stand back. To your knowledge, have you received such orders?"

Titan shook.

"They're attacking us!" Jacob spluttered.

"Admiral, you are wasting our time and resources. We should . . ."

"You don't understand. We have to win this! We have to destroy them. I cannot lose under any circumstances!"

"Our odds of winning once the fleet crosses the gates are next to none. You have received data and several warnings about the consequences of your actions, and yet you insist on proceeding. This shows that your judgment as commander has been impaired. This is not the first time this has happened and the results could be disastrous. In the view of the Imperial Command law, a commander that leads a fleet to imminent danger and death could be considered suicidal. Based on that fact, I declare that you are not psychologically fit to command. Under Section 234 of the Imperial Command Code, I relieve you of your command!"

The floor shook. Anastasia could feel her heart pounding, and she looked at her crew, who were staring at her. The crew of Freedom looked equally shocked.

Chapter 11: Judgment day

Titan Deck 1, Bridge

Silence dominated the bridge.

"What?" Anastasia asked, returning Adrian's stare.

"You asked us not to piss him off," he replied in a low voice.

Jacob's eyes moved to her side. "Are you just going to stand there?"

At that moment, Anastasia realized that Dr. Kent was standing next to her.

"She's right, Jacob. Winning isn't important at this time," replied Dr. Kent.

Jacob's face turned red. "I do not see your authority to relieve me! Eugene, open the gates. I will return and see what I can do about you, Commander!"

"If you return," Anastasia replied coldly.

The screen turned black.

"He's mad!" declared Dr. Kent.

"Lieutenant Weeds, open a channel to the fleet," Anastasia ordered.

"Yes, ma'am."

"Imperial Fleet, this is Commander Waters. Admiral Donavan is no longer in command. Do not leave the system."

"Commander, the gates are opening!" yelled Adrian.

"Close them."

"I can't!"

"Lieutenant Weeds?"

"Commander, Freedom is jamming our signals!" reported Evan.

This was unbelievable. "Get the message through, Lieutenant!"

"Maybe I should yell!" said Evan.

"Lieutenant Weeds, I've isolated a frequency. Use it and relay the message quickly!" yelled Lieutenant Hawk from the tactical station.

Everyone waited in tense silence, watching half of the fleet leave the system.

"Damn!" cried Anastasia.

"No one's responding!" Evan told her. "They're getting the message, but they're not listening."

Anastasia gritted her teeth in anger. On the viewscreen, she saw the squadron ships stopping on the other side of the gates.

Evan faced her. "It's the Titan squadron."

"Tell them to get back here." At least she could save someone. She returned to her chair. The small ships turned around. "Keep the gates open."

"Commander," said Dr. Kent loudly. "I'm getting a reading I don't understand!"

Before she could respond, the view screen zoomed in on an area near the gates. Anastasia noticed the stars vanish in one of the sections. The darkness was close to the squadron ships. The darkness moved fast, and before the small ships could escape, it swallowed them alive. The squadron vanished in seconds.

Shock hit Titan's bridge crew. Anastasia sat with her eyes wide open. Byron, Clio, and Micah were gone. Just like that. A small group of Orias ships raced toward the gates, but everyone was in such a state of shock that they couldn't respond.

"Close the gates! Close the gates!" shouted Dr. Kent, rushing toward Evan, who immediately did as he was told.

No one spoke, each mourning in their own way. Anastasia had thought she was saving them, but there was no saving anybody. Not anymore.

Evan broke the silence. "Ma'am, I've been trying, but I can't raise Prometheus or the Imperial Command."

"Keep trying," she said numbly. "What about the fleet?"

Evan turned. "They're not responding. They have engaged the enemy."

She shut her eyes.

"This is getting out of hand. What should we do?" asked Adrian.

Another shock wave hit the station.

"We can't just sit here!" said Evan.

The admiral might have chosen his own death and the death of every ship under his command, but Anastasia was not him, and Titan was home to over twenty thousand souls. If she died saving them, she could rest in peace. Building up her courage, she said, "Prepare for separation."

Every eye in the command center turned toward her.

"Commander?" asked both Evan and Adrian.

"We have no other choice."

"But the colonists?" asked Lieutenant Hawk.

"I have a plan. Prepare for separation. Lieutenant Weeds, make the announcement," Anastasia insisted.

"Yes, ma'am," Evan replied. "Attention all colonists. Attention all colonists. Titan's separation will commence in ten minutes. All non-military personnel should move to the outer section and enter the pods. I repeat: all non-military personnel should move to the outer section. This is not a drill. This is not a drill. All non-military personnel should evacuate the inner section." The message repeated.

Anastasia opened a channel to the engineering section. "Cyr, tell me we have power and weapons ready."

"We're ready down here."

"Good. Any ideas on how we can stop the Orias from boarding Titan?"

"We could try changing shield modulations," Cyr

suggested.

"Do it," Anastasia told her. "Adrian, what about the perimeter shields?"

"They're holding. Now at seventy percent and stable."

"Let's keep them that way. Cyr send a bust of power to the perimeter."

"Affirmative."

They watched as a ball of white light left Titan and headed towards the perimeter. It smashed against one receptor. They felt a jolt.

"Perimeter shields restored to seventy-five percent," Adrian reported.

"Again." Ordered Anastasia.

TITAN, DECK 1, BRIDGE

Minutes passed painfully, and Anastasia sat on the edge of her seat. She watched helplessly as the handful of ships tried to keep the Orias away from the perimeter. She wished the admiral had listened to her. They were failing miserably. She gasped when she saw Marion burst into a ball of flame. "Oh no," she muttered, getting to her feet.

She felt her heart skip, but there was nothing she could do about it. She slowly sat back down. Freedom and the other five ships were hardly keeping up. Five of the squadron ships were fighting, and the others had disappeared. "How long until Titan is ready?"

"Ma'am, seventy percent of the civilians are in the pods," said Evan. "We have to wait. Otherwise . . ."

"Can't you do anything to speed up the process?"

"No," replied Evans.

Anastasia banged her fist on the chair's handle.

TITAN, DECK 10, DOCKING BAY

"This feels wrong!" Emmeline said, looking outside.

Argon was busy preparing Raven for launch. "Don't worry."

"I can't leave. We should join the fight!"

"No!" Argon placed his hands on her shoulders. "You have to go."

"Argon, the situation has changed. I won't leave . . ."

"Emmeline, go! I can't let the Imperial Command get hold of you!" Argon insisted. "Prepare for launch."

She reluctantly nodded and ran inside the ship.

Argon turned to the console and put the ship on autopilot. He punched in the coordinates. He'd already told his mother and Selina to join the other civilians. Titan wasn't safe anymore.

The engines started. Emmeline began launch procedures. The clamps were released. The ship made a whooshing noise. The hangar door began to open.

"Okay, let's move," Argon said, turning around. Then he froze. He watched in terror as it moved through the air.

A black demonly smoke hovered over the ships in the docking bay. It took a form. In front of him stood a beautiful woman. "You have it," she said.

He glanced at the disruptor on the console.

"Give it to me," she demanded.

Argon grabbed the disruptor. He screamed. A black metallic spear had pierced through his leg. Blood dripped on the floor. Screaming in pain, he looked at the creature in front of him. He grabbed his leg and fell on the console. He heard a whooshing noise. Above him, hanging in the air, was another spear.

"Tell me where it is," the woman demanded.

Argon could no longer feel his leg. He groaned in pain and looked at her with pure rage. "Go to hell!" he shouted. Then he cried out. His head! He felt as if something had grabbed it and was drilling through his skull. It pounded with increasing agony. His temples felt like they were going to explode. "Ah!" he cried. Suddenly, the pain stopped.

"Emmeline," said the creature. "Where is she?"

Panting, Argon's eyes shifted between the spear over his head and the creature in front of him. Before he could decide what to do, he heard footsteps.

The creature looked past Argon and smirked.

"No! Argon!" Emmeline screamed from inside the ship.

"Go to hell!" he muttered and pushed a button.

The doors of Raven closed. He pressed another button, and the hangar decompressed immediately. Raven was thrown out of the docking bay. Once in space, the autopilot kicked in. The AI stabilized the ship, and it surged away from the battlefield. Argon smiled, watching her leave, and said his goodbyes. He turned to look at the creature, knowing his fate was sealed. Its eyes burned red, and he screamed as the spear tore through his heart.

TITAN, DECK 1, BRIDGE

Anastasia tried to maintain her balance, but it was proving difficult. She watched helplessly as people died protecting the perimeter. The perimeter was becoming unstable. Shockwave after shock wave hit Titan.

"Commander! Commander!" shouted Aceline on the commlink.

"Doctor, you should leave with the other colonist."

"I can't get hold of Argon. I feel like something has happened to him. Something's wrong. He's not answering. I'm not leaving without him!"

Anastasia didn't have time for this. "Aceline, this is no time to argue. Take Selina and leave. Now! I'll try to find him. Go!"

Aceline didn't reply. She closed the channel.

The computer announced, "Eighty percent of separation process complete."

Anastasia wished it would hurry. The quicker she could remove the civilians, the sooner she could join the battle.

"Commander," called out Cyr. "We have a problem."

"Tell me something I don't know," she muttered.

"The generator on Deck 10, Section 17, has stopped working."

Anastasia raised her eyebrows. "So, fix it!"

"I can't! It would have to be done manually."

"Call security."

"They have their hands full. Half of the engineering staff are fighting to keep the Orias out. Can I ask Lieutenant Weeds?"

"No!" Anastasia interrupted her. "I'll go."

"Commander!" Adrian protested.

Anastasia glared at him. "Lieutenant Olson, you are in command. Continue the separation process."

"Commander…" said Adrian getting on his feet. His face full of concern.

Anastasia felt proud. "Adrian, I'll be back. Take care of Titan until then…" The truth was, she wanted to do something until the separation process was complete. It was driving her nuts, and she had to locate Argon.

Titan, Deck 10, Docking Bay

The elevator opened on the south side of the docking bay. When they stepped out, Anastasia and five of the security guards were met with smoke and darkness. She coughed, turned to the nearest panel, and vented the gas out. The emergency lights came to life. The corridor was silent, barren. Her heart beat so fast that she feared it would stop. She glanced at the guards, and two of them moved ahead. They hurried through the long corridor and soon found the generator. She punched in the codes, and the door slid open. She saw the problem immediately. There was a coolant leak. "We need to replace this."

While the guards kept a watch, Anastasia put down her repair kit and opened it. The first thing she had to do was disconnect the corrupted coolant pack from the generator. As she began working, she realized it was hard to concentrate with the constant announcements and alarms beeping. Once it was disconnected, she replaced the coolant pack with the fresh bag and began integrating it into the system. She felt like she was in a sauna. Sweat dripped down her face and neck. Once she had secured the pack, she punched a few buttons, and the doors closed. Reaching out for the nearest panel, she called engineering. "Cyr. Try now."

The generator came online immediately.

"Awesome!" Cyr said.

The computer announced, "Ninety-five percent separation process complete."

"Adrian, tell me all the civilians are ready and secure," said Anastasia.

"We're almost there," he replied.

"What about the perimeter?"

"Believe it or not, it's still holding. The shields in one section are weakening, though."

"Cyr, can we transfer more power?"

"I don't think it will help now…"

"How many Earth ships remaining?"

"Three."

Anastasia shut her eyes. "Okay."

The floor beneath her shook vigorously, and the corridor turned dark. She grabbed the wall to maintain her balance. The lights flickered. Another alarm blared loudly. A conduit blew in front of her, and fire raged.

"Commander!" the guard pulled her behind him.

Within minutes, the corridor was full of smoke.

"It's better if we go the other way," said the guard.

Anastasia nodded.

They rushed in the other direction, and she traced Argon's communicator to the docking bay. She came to a sudden halt when she thought she saw something. The alarms, the screams, the blasts, and the jolts all vanished. Taking sharp breaths, she took a few steps forward. Tears rolled down her cheeks. Argon lay on the floor in a pool of blood, a spear thrust through his chest.

"No. No. Not like this," she mumbled.

The hangar doors shut with a loud thud.

"Commander!" someone shouted.

Laser blasts brought her back to her senses. She looked up and saw the guards firing at a black smoke hovering over the hangar deck. The lasers were bouncing off it. A group of Orias materialized.

"The Orias are here!" a guard screamed. The guards opened fire.

But Anastasia's eyes remained fixed on the black smoke. She hastened toward the weapons locker and grabbed a shield. The smoke floated over her and then materialized into a woman.

"Who the hell are you, and what are you doing on Titan?" Anastasia demanded.

"Are you their leader?" asked the creature.

Anastasia stood up straighter. "Yes. I am."

"Interesting." The woman looked at her from top to bottom.

"What the hell do you want from us?"

"I want the device, and I want you to die!"

A spear appeared out of nowhere and surged toward Anastasia. She put the shield up, and knocked it over. She fired her disruptor. The laser went through the creature.

"You cannot kill me. I am the queen."

Anastasia raised her eyebrows.

Another spear appeared. Anastasia moved swiftly, missing it by inches. The spear hit the floor and pierced through it, creating a small hole. She grabbed and pulled it out with all her strength and threw it at the queen who grabbed it in mid-air and smiled.

Anastasia pulled the spear out of Argon's body. The queen turned back into smoke, which rushed through the deck and appeared inches in front of Anastasia. The smoke became the queen once more, and she swung the spear.

Anastasia ducked. She took her chance and kicked the creature. She felt better. There was some space between them.

Their eyes met, and the queen smirked.

A whooshing noise distracted Anastasia. Then she realized the spear had turned into a sword. *It's all a game for her*, she realized.

The swords clashed, and the queen threw her weight with her weapon. Anastasia grunted and blocked it with the shield. She swung her sword, missing her opponent by mere inches. The queen swirled, and her next attack was more powerful. Anastasia blocked the sword inches from her face and kicked her. Both women stopped, breathless, and stared at each other with hatred.

"Give up. You are no match for me!" the queen shouted.

Anastasia kept the shield close to her chest.

The queen laughed. "What do you think you can do with that?"

Anastasia smiled as something dawned on her. "Shield fire!"

The outer rims of the shield became bright. It vibrated in her hand, and a flash of light hit the queen. She was thrown back and landed on the floor.

"That's what it can do!"

"Fifty percent power remaining," the shield said.

Anastasia moved back when the queen turned into a ball of whirling smoke and headed straight for her. Suddenly, she reappeared. Swords clashed in the air again. Anastasia felt the queen's strength. She freed her sword and attacked again. "Get off Titan!" she yelled in anger.

Titan shook, and Anastasia lost her balance and fell to the floor. The shield slipped out of her hand. She looked up; the alien queen rushed toward her. Anastasia rolled and got to her feet. She grabbed the shield and stood up.

The queen smiled, and her eyes glittered. She was creating a ball of white light between her hands. "Get ready to die!" she shouted and threw it at Anastasia.

Anastasia raised the shield. The white beam hit it with full force. "Ah!" she screamed as she felt herself being pushed backward. She could feel her hands weakening. The shield vibrated vigorously. She heard a cracking noise. "No!" she yelled, trying to stay on her feet. Suddenly, the pressure was off. Breathless, Anastasia peered out to look at the queen.

She looked surprised. She stood straight, confusion in her eyes.

The shield buzzed and came back online. "Power transfer complete. Two hundred percent power restored," it announced.

Anastasia raised her eyebrows. "Well, isn't that ironic? Fire!"

The beam hit the queen, and she turned to dust.

Anastasia stood breathless and sweating. She looked behind her; one guard was down, but the Orias were dead. The remaining guards joined her.

"We can take her," one guard said.

Titan shook again.

The computer announced, "All personnel return to your posts. Titan is ready for separation."

The smoke gathered again and turned into the vicious woman once more.

Anastasia moistened her lips. She wanted to kill this thing, but she also wanted her people out of harm's way. Her eyes flickered to Argon. Enough blood had been spilled today.

Powerful turbulence hit Titan. Anastasia lost her balance and fell to the floor. She quickly got up.

The alien queen stood straight. The shock wave didn't seem to bother her. "Where is she headed?" asked the queen.

Anastasia just glared at her.

"Where is she going?"

She knew she wanted to know Emmeline's whereabouts. "Go to hell!" Anastasia spat.

"I will kill every one of you until you bring her to me."

Anastasia was about to respond when Adrian's voice crackled over the communicator. "Commander Waters, come in. Commander Waters, respond."

Without taking her eyes off the queen, Anastasia reached for the switch. "Yes, Lieutenant Olson."

"Commander, a small part of the perimeter has been

breached. The Orias are entering our space. All our fighters are dead! Freedom and two other ships are hardly keeping up. They need us. They need us now!"

A wide smile appeared on the queen's face. "All of you will die today." The queen turned back into smoke, which shot through the hall and left Titan.

For the last time, Anastasia looked at Argon. Then she turned and ran.

TITAN, DECK 1, BRIDGE

Anastasia threw the sword and her shield on the floor of the bridge. "What's our status?"

"Believe it or not, we're ready. Although not all civilians are accounted for," said Adrian.

"What about the Earth ships?"

"Freedom and two other ships are still blocking the Orias from entering our system."

"Commander, I'm detecting another ship!" shouted Lieutenant Hawk.

Anastasia frowned.

"It's Prometheus."

"Looks like they finally heard our hails!" said Evan.

"Open a channel," Anastasia ordered.

Mykel's face appeared on the viewscreen. "Sorry. It appears I'm always late."

"Where have you been?"

"Thirty minutes ago, all transmission from Titan stopped and our attempts to contact you failed. It could only mean one thing. So, we turned around, just to make sure."

Anastasia nodded.

"I've warned the Imperial Command. More ships should be here," Mykel said.

"Thank you, Captain."

The viewscreen showed Prometheus joining the battle.

"Start separation process. Lieutenant Olson, take control

over the helm. Lieutenant Weeds, initiate remote bridge protocol," Anastasia said.

"Yes, Commander. Otis is ready."

The image on the screen changed. A robot stood at attention. "Commander."

"Otis. Are the citizens of Titan secured?"

"Not all citizens are accounted for, but ninety-nine percent of citizens are secured."

Anastasia nodded. It would have to do. "Await further instructions." The screen went blank. "Initiate separation sequence."

A loud whoosh rushed through the space station. Outside, a cloud of smoke erupted, spreading in all directions. If someone didn't know better, they would have thought Titan was on fire. All the corridors that connected the outer and the inner section began to retract.

"Commander, the retraction process has commenced," Adrian said.

"When it's done, ease us out slowly,"

"Yes, ma'am."

"Lieutenant Weeds, take over the outer section."

Soon, the gas disappeared. The inner section slowly moved downward. The outer section began to stand erect. The large passageways that had retracted once more began moving toward the center.

"We're clear of the outer rim," announced Evan.

"Is it stable and ready?"

"Not yet, Commander."

"Ma'am, Titan is ready for initialization," said Adrian.

"Bring all thrusters online and initiate flight mode."

They all felt a tremor. Outside, the lights above Titan came to life. The word "TITAN" glowed underneath them.

"Engines," ordered Anastasia.

"Firing engines."

Again, they felt a tremor. A single red rim of light appeared at the back of Titan. Then another. Then another. Over a dozen rims of red light now fiercely glowed in space.

"Commander, the perimeter is becoming unstable. It can't take it anymore," said Adrian.

"Just a few more moments," she told him. "What about the outer section?"

The viewscreen split in two. The circular outer rim of Titan stood erect. The passageways looked like spokes that had come together. It looked like a giant wheel.

"Ready when you are, Lieutenant Weeds," Anastasia said.

"Initiating outer section thrusters and firing up engines." All eyes turned to the screen. The four engines at the four corners of the wheel came to life. "Engines online," announced Evan. The enormous wheel slowly moved forward. "Destination?" he asked.

"How much time to Earth?"

"At this speed, four days."

Anastasia shook her head. "Not good enough. Full power to thrusters."

Evan turned. "They'll run out of fuel."

"We have to get them out of here," said Adrian.

Anastasia became thoughtful, then turned toward the panel on her left. "Lieutenant Weeds, I'm sending you a set of coordinates. It will take them to the lower orbit of Saturn. Its gases will protect it from any scans, and it should remain hidden and secure until the Imperial Command gets here."

"But what if, after finishing us, they begin looking for the colonists?"

"Trust me. They're looking for someone else."

Everyone looked at each other.

"You have your orders, Lieutenant," Anastasia said firmly.

Evan hesitated for a moment, but then turned. "Full power."

"Contact Otis."

The robot reappeared on the screen.

"You are headed for Saturn," Anastasia told it.

"Yes, Commander."

"Four days past today, you will survey the situation. If it is safe, contact the Imperial Command and head toward Vesta, the nearest colony."

"Yes, Commander."

Anastasia got on her feet. "Remember, Titan's colonists are your first and only priority. Protect them at any cost. Use whatever means necessary to conceal yourself, regardless of what happens to the perimeter, the fleet, or Titan. Do you understand?"

"Understood, Commander."

The bridge crew watched as the wheel rocketed away from the battle. Another shock wave hit Titan. The viewscreen changed, and they saw a large ball of fire. Everyone became silent.

"They have destroyed two more Earth ships! Now it's just Titan, Prometheus, and Freedom."

Anastasia closed her eyes and held her head. But she didn't have the time to mourn.

"Three Orias ships just slipped into our space. They're heading toward the outer section," Adrian announced.

"You know what to do."

"Yes, ma'am!"

Titan swung and picked up speed, and the gap between it and the Orias ships vanished in seconds.

"I've been waiting for this for a long time," muttered Adrian.

"Fire!" shouted Anastasia.

Torpedoes launched with incredible speed. Within seconds, the Orias ships were crushed.

"Yes!" Adrian cheered.

But Anastasia didn't feel like celebrating just yet. "Bring us about."

Titan turned around and fired, neutralizing the four ships that had just slipped into their space. Their upgrades to the torpedoes were working well. A beam hit Titan, and it shook. Sparks flew, and the lights went out for a second. Titan's computer located the three Orias ships and fired again.

A blast blinded the crew momentarily. From the corner of her eye, Anastasia saw Freedom return to her realm, chasing two Orias ships. "Status of the colonists?" she asked.

"At this speed, they should be out of range within five minutes."

"Keep them busy. Do not let any Orias ships get past us. Do you understand?"

"Yes, Commander."

"Lieutenant Hawk, show me the perimeter."

Everyone's hearts sank. Their job was to protect the perimeter, and right now, they were watching as the Orias destroyed it.

Titan shuddered and dipped. Anastasia grabbed her chair. A loud beep sounded.

"Commander, the perimeter is overloading. It can't take it anymore. The shield is at twenty percent," Adrian reported.

A loud blast occurred close to Titan. A shock wave hit them, throwing everyone off their chairs. The lights on the roof blew to pieces, and debris fell to the floor.

"What the hell was that?" Anastasia shouted above the screaming alarm.

"Freedom!" Adrian replied. "It blew and breached our shields!"

Everyone fell silent and looked at the screen. A huge part of the ship floated in space, lifeless.

"Prometheus?" Anastasia asked, her heart jumping to her throat.

The view on the screen changed. Two Orias ships were attacking the ship. Prometheus fired and blew one of the ships to pieces.

"Looks like it's good," Evan remarked.

"Engineering, what's our status?" Anastasia shouted, getting back in her chair.

"I'm trying to keep the perimeter from blowing up. I've been reinforcing it by transferring power to the receptors and rerouting power from other generators," Cyr replied. "I'm sorry. I can't do anything else."

Anastasia sat up straight. "Maybe we can. Adrian, what's the distance between the last Orias ship and the perimeter?"

Adrian examined the panel. "Less than two hundred kilometers."

"Show me their formation."

A diagram appeared on the screen. The Orias had no particular formation and were scattered haphazardly on the other side.

"Cyr. Give me a vantage point," said Anastasia. "Imagine if I want to light a fire. Where would I do it?"

"Working on it." The viewscreen changed to show another diagram. A section was highlighted. "I don't know why, but seventy percent of their ships are at this point," Cyr said.

Slowly, Anastasia got off her chair. "Six weeks ago, you told me we had 120 percent power."

"Yes. So?"

"Transfer thirty percent to the perimeter generators in that section."

"That's too much," Cyr argued. "It will overload and blow up."

"How big?"

"W-What?"

"How big of an explosion?"

"Substantial."

Every eye turned to Anastasia.

"Location of Prometheus?" she asked as Titan jolted once more. The screen showed that Prometheus was chasing two ships that were heading toward one of Saturn's moons. "This is our chance. Do it."

"Ready. I suggest we move back," Cyr said.

"No," said Anastasia. "Execute."

Three blasts left the space station, heading for the perimeter. Titan vibrated. At first, just a bit. Then the vibration grew stronger. Anastasia grabbed the arms of her chair. Alarms blared. The perimeter, studded like glowing stars, changed. At first, it turned slightly red. Then it turned into a red web.

Before the Orias knew what was happening, a section of the perimeter blew and turned into a huge fireball. The blast spread in all directions, destroying everything in its wake.

Anastasia smiled as she saw the Orias ships being wiped out. But soon, the fire approached Titan. "Brace for impact!" she screamed.

Titan shook, tossing everyone from their seats. Fire flooded the outer hull. Its special shielding deflected the fire into space. Titan was designed to soak up energy. When the fire hit the convertors, they quickly began turning it into fuel.

When she looked up, Anastasia saw that the screen was tilted. A moment later, she realized it was Titan. The bridge crew got to their feet and took their stations.

"Let's see what happened," Anastasia said, getting back in her chair.

They looked at broken perimeter. It had served them well for years, and now it was no more. It wasn't totally gone, but there was a gap almost ten kilometers wide.

"Status of the Orias fleet?" Anastasia asked.

Evan checked his panel. "We destroyed most of their ships."

Anastasia wondered if that was enough.

"Commander, our communications are back online. I have contact with the Imperial Command. And we have an incoming message from Prometheus," said Lieutenant Hawk.

Anastasia nodded.

The message came in. "What was that? Are you okay?" asked Mykel.

"We are good, thanks. We overloaded the perimeter."

"What?"

"Yes. We overloaded the generators creating a blast took out most of their ships."

"Wow. Good move! We might just win this one."

But at what cost? Anastasia thought.

"Commander, we just received a message from the

Imperial Command," said Lieutenant Hawk. "A new fleet led by Lady Vermont should be here in ten minutes."

Anastasia nodded; a bit surprised. A tribunal leading the fleet was unusual. She turned to Mykel. "Captain, we . . ." But the transmission was interrupted, and the screen went blank. "What happened?"

"I don't know!" Evan replied.

"That was a mistake," said a deep voice.

Darkness engulfed the bridge. A face appeared on the black screen, and as it brightened, Anastasia and her crew could see the queen herself.

"That was a mistake."

Anastasia felt her pulse rise. She'd never thought she would see her again, especially not so soon. "Was it?" she said, getting to her feet.

"You will perish. You are no match for us. I am superior in every way. My power extends across the seven realms, and I will take what is mine."

Anastasia stayed silent.

"You are menial, insignificant beings! And I will crush you."

Her words were met with silence. A coldness spread across the bridge.

"If I didn't know better, I'd think we were being insulted," said Evan to Adrian.

"I know he was nuts, but at this moment, I like the admiral more. At least he didn't call us menial," replied Adrian.

Anastasia tried not to smile. The women continued to glare at each other. A mix of fear and surprise filled her.

"You are powerless! Insignificant!" she spat, "You will surrender and serve under me. If you resist, I will destroy you and assimilate your species! This is my realm; I will be your queen. You will either serve me or die!"

A sense of shock hit Titan's bridge crew, and they turned to their commander. Anastasia stood flabbergasted, trying to understand what was happening. Should she retaliate? Should she surrender? Or play the game. She smirked and returned to her chair. She thought about all the lives that had been lost and all the ships that had been destroyed. And for what? Power. Beings hungry for power.

"Commander, Prometheus is hailing us," said Lieutenant Hawk.

She nodded. The viewscreen divided into two. Mykel was about to speak, but Anastasia signaled for him to wait. She looked at the panel and made a note of the coordinates from where the queen's signal originated. "You have no idea who we are, have you?" she said to the queen, punching buttons. "You never reached out, talked to us. If you would have asked us… let's say, nicely I would have considered your request."

"I do not make requests… I…"

"I am not finished yet," she said firmly, "You will not set foot in this sector of space. This is no one's realm. It belongs to every living creature in this sector. You have no authority here."

Silence struck the bridge.

The two women glowered, neither looking away.

"I shall kill you myself, and I'll enjoy it," said the queen.

"And I shall give you no such pleasure," replied Anastasia. "Titan, initiate attack pattern twenty-five," she ordered.

The computer took control, and sixteen long-range, high-yield torpedoes flew toward queen's ship. Anastasia had used her time well; she had created defensive automated programs that were executed on voice commands. The torpedoes hit the Orias fleet in an instant, and Anastasia enjoyed the momentary surprise on the queen's face. The screen went blank.

"Five torpedoes hit the main ship," Evan confirmed, "It has sustained heavy damage."

A ball of fire erupted.

"Six Orias ships just exploded."

"Nice work!" muttered Evan.

"Commander… the Prometheus is in trouble." reported

Lieutenant Hawk.

Five Orias ships surrounded Prometheus, and it was struggling. A blast from the Orias ships punctured a hole in its hull.

"Adrian!" Anastasia shouted.

Titan tilted, aimed, and fired, destroying two ships. Then, slowly, it hovered over Prometheus. Its vast shadow fell over the Orias ships. It didn't fire. It just hovered there, waiting.

"Commander?" asked Adrian.

"Wait for it."

The Orias ships stopped dead in space, and their taillights dimmed. Then they suddenly withdrew.

"Fire!"

Titan wiped out the three ships in an instant.

Mykel's face appeared on the screen.

"How are you holding up?"

"We are fine. I don't know how long we can keep this up."

She nodded, "Status of the Orias."

"Over twenty ships are standing on other side of the broken perimeter. They are just standing there, doing nothing."

"Interesting."

The two Earth ships waited.

"Status of the colonists?" asked Anastasia.

"Gone," Adrian reported. "Beyond sensor range."

"And no Orias ships followed them?"

"None."

"Tactical, status of our weapons?" asked Anastasia.

"We have a full complement of over 2,000 torpedoes. We haven't even begun to use the phasers. Let's not forget the attack drones," said Lieutenant Hawk.

"That could be enough," replied Anastasia.

"We don't know," Lieutenant Hawk told her.

"Well, we never got the chance to shoot down a comet, but we can shoot down the Orias," commented Adrian.

"We can hold them off. The fleet will be here soon," Evan said to Anastasia.

But she got to her feet and came to stand near the viewscreen. Her eyes settled on the main ship. "They'll never stop coming until she . . . it is dead." She returned to her chair.

The large group of alien ships began moving toward Titan and Prometheus. Anastasia's commlink buzzed.

"Ready when you are," said Mykel.

"Let's take them down."

AURORA

"Sir, we're at the coordinates," said the pilot of Aurora.

Aurora was a bit smaller than Prometheus. Today, it was leading the small fleet into battle under the banner of Lady Vermont.

"All stop," ordered Captain Allan. The fleet slowly came to a complete stop. Captain Allan, a stout man with an expressive face and green eyes, rose from his chair and walked toward the screen.

Lady Vermont came and stood with him. She felt his eyes and everyone else's on her. No one expected tribunals to leave Earth. She was curious, and Anastasia's words had affected her. She had hoped the commander had been mistaken.

Three hours ago, Earth lost all contact with Titan. That was very unusual indeed. It was as if it had disappeared from their sensors.

Then they'd received a hail from Prometheus, and they'd suspected an Orias attack. A fleet was assembled and sent to the perimeter. They had heard from Titan and Prometheus about half an hour ago. Then nothing. Complete silence.

A huge section of the perimeter was damaged. Sensors showed it was no longer operational. Debris floated everywhere. A few disabled Orias ships drifted in space. A large piece of hull coasted in front of the screen. Four letters sparked everyone's attention: "FREE."

"Where is our fleet?" asked Lady Vermont.

"Gone, ma'am. Destroyed," reported the pilot.

"Where are the Orias?" asked the captain.

"I don't know, sir. They've vanished as well. But I'm detecting some sort of energy signature. It's weak."

"What kind of signature?"

"Nothing I've seen before."

"Where is Titan?" demanded Lady Vermont.

"Ma'am, we lost contact with Titan and Prometheus. I can't find them on my sensors."

Lady Vermont's eyes widened. "What do you mean? A space station that big doesn't just vanish into thin air. Look for them!"

The crew began working. The operations officer checked for signs of Titan. The tactical section looked for weapons signatures. Those at the helm looked through the debris.

"Well?" Lady Vermont demanded after a few moments had passed.

The pilot looked terrified.

"What?"

He said shakily. "There's a lot of debris. But none of it belongs to Titan or Prometheus."

Lady Vermont's face turned stony. "What do you mean?"

"They're gone! They've vanished!"

TO BE CONTINUED

END OF BOOK I

REALM BOOK II
POSEIDON

The wrath of the Orias queen has taken everything from Emmeline Augury. Her home, her family and her love. The only thing left after the battle is pain and revenge.

Powerless and hunted by the Orias and Imperial Command, Emmeline decides not to yield and channels her anger to find the second piece and vows to kill the queen.

But she's facing a being as powerful as the gods themselves. A being that has risen after a millennium and is full of rage, anger and hunger.

Can Emmeline destroy the queen or will the queen triumph? The answers lie in the wake of the Poseidon.

PREORDER POSEIDON

About the Author

H.G. Ahedi holds a PhD in biomedical sciences and is a fictional writer. Reading is one of her favorite hobbies, and she loves watching movies and series while sipping tea. She spends a lot of time writing and when she is bored of her desk; she wants to hop on a plane and travel the world. As that is not always possible, she explores local Sydney beaches, parks, and enjoys a nice cup of coffee.

A Note to Readers

Enjoyed Fall of Titan? Please leave a review and share your thoughts about the book. I would really appreciate it, and thank you in advance!

OTHER BOOKS BY H.G. AHEDI

When Roumoult Cranston drives to Newburgh, a hired assassin awaits him. While trying to unearth this mystery, he discovers a darkness within himself and could be hanged for murder. Black Moon is a mystery thriller with a supernatural twist.

When three men commit suicides without reason, the hunt for answers become a frantic race against time.
If you are interested in gripping crime thrillers, you should read Haunted.

If you love scandals, secrets affairs with explosive consequences then you should read, Calculated Murder

A soldier trying to survive, a scientist trying to save his world and a dark force that will define them both. Transcendence is a historical sci fi novella that will keep you at the edge of your seat

www.ingramcontent.com/pod-product-compliance
Lightning Source LLC
Chambersburg PA
CBHW011915130726
47903CB00016B/3035